the VACATION RENTAL

a novel

KATIE SISE

Little a

This is a work of fiction. Names, characters, organizations, places, events, and incidents are either products of the author's imagination or are used fictitiously. Otherwise, any resemblance to actual persons, living or dead, is purely coincidental.

Published by Little A, New York

www.apub.com

ISBN-13: 9781662507748 (hardcover)
ISBN-13: 9781662507731 (paperback)
ISBN-13: 9781662507724 (digital)

Cover design by Faceout Studio, Amanda Hudson
Cover image: © Chelsea Victoria / Stocksy; © fotograzia / Getty Images

Printed in the United States of America

First edition

Praise for *The Vacation Rental*

"With superb plotting and finely crafted characters, *The Vacation Rental* surprised me at every turn! An insightful thriller about family secrets and long-held grudges, written by a truly talented author."

—Wendy Walker, bestselling author of *What Remains*

Praise for *Open House*

"Part murder mystery, part interpersonal drama, a serviceable whodunit (or did anyone?) with a host of compelling characters . . . this novel has just enough twists to keep its readers along for the ride. Sleuths will delight in piecing together clues and untangling lies alongside the protagonists."

—*Kirkus Reviews*

"A chilling thriller, *Open House* tracks a missing art student who vanished ten years prior and how her disappearance connects with a recent attack during an open house in a small university town. It also showcases the unending loyalty of close girlfriends and sisterhood in life or death."

—*Good Morning America*

Praise for *We Were Mothers*

"Katie Sise's *We Were Mothers* expertly snaps readers to attention with its grandiose opening . . . Timing, inner discourse, and believable fiascos blend together, producing fantastic scenes . . . Her observations and vulnerability carry the read."

—Associated Press

the VACATION RENTAL

ALSO BY KATIE SISE

We Were Mothers

Open House

The Break

For my loves, Brian, Luke, William, Isabel, and Eloise

ONE

Anna. New York City, New York.

Carter slips a hand into the waistband of my skirt. His mouth is warm against my jaw, his hands expertly working a zipper. We're back in my apartment, shrouded in warm air and seclusion, exactly where Carter likes us to be. My place is in downtown New York City on Norfolk Street, a one-bedroom overlooking Houston Street. It's not spacious, but there are windows everywhere, and no plants, only clutter and dark navy walls covered in things I like. Mostly photographs I've taken. This summer I'm planning to escape the city to a countryside vacation rental, and I wonder how I'll feel surrounded by someone else's art.

My eyes settle on my photographs as Carter presses me back against the side of my desk. Maybe adorning your space with your own work is vaguely narcissistic, like posting selfies, but they're my darlings, after all. Black-and-white photos usually, some color, and mostly folks on the street because there's a fine line between images you intrinsically own (like those taken in a public space), and images taken at an event or on private property. Near the kitchen is a black-framed photo of a man dealing tarot cards outside the New York Public Library, and next to it, a keening elderly woman in Bryant Park doing something expected (feeding pigeons) but with tears flecking her wrinkled cheeks and two-carat diamonds sagging on her earlobes. I suppose the diamonds could be fake. You have to get so close to objects and people to figure out how real they are.

In my living room there's a photograph of a twenty-something man with a shaved head in an Italian restaurant, and then there's the photo that got me the cover of *Time*, which led to freelancing at *Vanity Fair* and *Culture*: a man at a women's march holding a sign that reads, **As a Man, I Would Like to Apologize for This.** Next to that is the only photo I didn't take myself—one of my mother, but you can't see her face. The photo was taken from behind her, and you can see that she's holding my twin brother, Sam. He's just a baby, a ball of flesh swaddled in a cotton blanket we shared.

He's dead now. He was always my other half, my twin flame, until the same tragedy we both endured became something I could survive and he couldn't.

Carter's hand trails up my stomach, his tanned fingers crossing my navel. I'm careful not to knock into my laptop. It's locked, because there are photos I don't want Carter seeing, not because they're revealing, but because I haven't edited them yet or trashed the ones that don't belong. And then there are the vacation rental sites dotted with the beautiful homes outside the city, and I really don't need him seeing those.

"Do you want a cigarette?" Carter asks. He likes to prolong sex. There's so much more waiting and talking than I'm used to, and by the time he gets to it, I'm ready for him. He's the opposite at a restaurant. You'd think with all the access from his job—and by the way he dresses and how he moves—that he'd be the kind of man who would order wine and take a swirl and sniff. But instead, he drinks wine like he eats red meat: in hungry, enthusiastic swallows.

"This isn't sex in a movie, Carter," I say.

He cocks a dark eyebrow like he's trying to figure out my meaning.

"I don't *smoke*," I say.

"Oh, that's right," he says casually, and then his laugh turns into something else. His voice is nearly a whisper when he says, "Come closer."

I do. He slips a hand behind my neck, brushes his lips against my collarbone. He doesn't shut the shades, and I imagine all of Houston Street watching us. What if someone from work ever saw us together? I fought hard to get Carter, and it amazes me that he can be so cavalier, so sure that he can hold on to the people and things he thinks are his.

Carter's wearing a navy suit even though it's blazing hot outside. Dark curls, deep blue eyes, olive skin. He was the features director at Italian *Vogue* before coming to *Culture*, and he once told me people in Italy just assumed he was a native until he opened his mouth and couldn't speak Italian. He looks the part: sophisticated in a different way from the other sophisticated New York City men. He looks like he belongs in a café beside the Louvre, reading a novel in wood-framed sunglasses, or on the coast of the Maldives in a caftan.

I arch my back as Carter lifts me onto the bare desk and pushes my legs apart. He's thirty-six—a decade older than I am—and now the guys I used to bring back here feel like boys. We met at a launch party six months ago for *Culture: 1972–2022*, a coffee table art book filled with gorgeous stills from the past five decades of *Culture* magazine. Carter wrote the foreword. He's only been the editor in chief of the magazine for a few years, but he's known for progressive, sharp-tongued commentary and boundary-pushing photography. I suppose Carter is why I fell in love with *Culture*, and why I wanted to shoot for them. I had my pick of magazines at that point, and it wasn't only that I was a natural fit for *Culture*; it was him, too. That's the truth, when I'm being honest, which I'm not always. I was reeling from my brother's death, and then there was Carter at the helm of *Culture*, and it was like he had a bullseye over his chest, like I just had to work for him, like it would somehow mend the things that felt unfixable. He wrought a darker and less polished aesthetic on the masses, made them see what he did—he picked the kind of photos that I've always shot: pain and darkness and beauty all as one thing, not separate. Life is pain; pain is art; art is beauty. I'm not glamorizing pain, quite the opposite; I'm saying it exists for everyone in varying degrees. To not capture that with a photo feels untruthful.

And I was in so much pain after Sam died that I couldn't really imagine working for anyone else.

That night at the book reading when I approached Carter with my copy, I lifted my hand in a shy wave and said, "I'm Anna. I freelance for *Culture* as a—"

"Anna Byrne," Carter interrupted with a grin, holding a cocktail glass with beads of condensation glittering beneath the chandelier overhead. "I know all my photographers."

I acted surprised, even flattered, though I'd suspected as much. "I love that the shot of the woman drinking sangria was included in the book," I said, and I waited for him to say something, maybe to acknowledge how inherently clever I must be for appreciating that photo. I shifted my weight in the vintage heels I'd found at a thrift shop in my neighborhood, four inches high with faux feathers on the ankle straps. Only an hour in them and they already killed. Carter was staring at me, still saying nothing, so I added, "That was the shot that made me want to work for you."

For you.

The words sounded intimate. Maybe I'd meant them that way, maybe I could already feel our future unspooling.

"And what was it about that photo, Byrne?" Carter asked slowly, catching on. We only ever use last names at *Culture*. A wide span of age ranges works there, from nineteen-year-old interns to seventy-something photographers and editors, but no one would dare use *Mr.* or *Mrs.* I guess we do anything to make it seem casual and artistic and the furthest thing from a bank or whatever type of career the people at *Culture* would deem dull. Maybe it's half the reason Carter is sleeping with me—to seem anything in the world besides *dull*. And if that's part of the allure, I can live with it. We all have our reasons.

That night at the bookstore I thought I was ready for whatever it was going to be between Carter and me, but when he leaned in, I faltered and broke his gaze. It was winter then. The city outside the bookstore was already dark, and beneath the streetlights I saw an old man on a bicycle resting against the window like he was lost. When I turned back to answer Carter's question, he was already slipping away; a pink-haired woman in thick black glasses was at his side, saying his name, gesturing toward a corner of the bookstore where someone was waiting for him.

Carter gave me one last small smile, but I didn't speak to him again that night. I was sure I'd lost him, or at least that I'd lost the tiny kernel of something I'd felt spark the air between us. But later that week, on a snowy Friday, he pushed through a big steel door into a stark, metallic room with too many sharp corners, where I was photographing an Oscar-nominated actor for *Culture*'s cover. I was on my knees, camera tipped up, the toes of my Converses pressing the floor for balance. The actor turned to see Carter enter and I snapped a photo, and ironically, that was the one that made the cover. I'm not even sure he knows that, but I do. Carter didn't say much to either of us, but he silently hung around and watched me shoot, which was somewhat performative on my end, because I knew I'd already caught the perfect shot: the one that caught the actor searching and unsure. But I kept shooting photos because I enjoyed the feeling of Carter watching me, his presence like a silvery, magnetic shadow. I stared through my lens, wondering what he saw through his. An artist? A conquest? A someday lover? With his eyes boring into my back, I thought again about the photo that had made the coffee table art book, the one that I told Carter had made me want to work for him. In the photo, the subject holds a joint and a soupy mix of sangria, her head tipped back, laughing. There's a half-drunk pitcher on the rickety wooden table in front of her, and behind her, a scene of brutality unfolds: it's blurry in places because the focus is on the woman, but it looks to be some kind of dogfight with jeering men and teenagers surrounding two snarling animals. One of the teenage boys looks just like the woman in the foreground, enough so that he must be her son or a relation of some sort. In the photo, the woman either hasn't seen the dogfight yet; doesn't care; or worst of all: she's laughing at what's happening. And because it's a photograph—and not a film or a video posted online—the viewer never gets the answer. From the photo, anyone who wasn't there couldn't possibly tell what the woman's role was in the chaos unfolding behind her. When I first saw it in *Culture*, I stared for so long my eyes watered. And it wasn't just me; letters to the editor poured in, digging deeper, *asking*. Readers needed answers, but Carter never gave them, nor did the photographer. During the past few months, the more intimate Carter and I have become, the closer I've come to asking him what really happened on that photography assignment. But the more time that's elapsed since the first moment I saw the photo, the less I really want to know the truth. Life is like that, isn't it? There are some things in my past I need clarity on, real answers. And then there are other things I'd rather leave buried in cavernous graves. And maybe I like my interpretation of that photo too much to really want to learn something different.

The thing about photography (or any art, really) is that the viewer brings their baggage, same as anyone in a conversation or nonverbal exchange. What I suspect—what I *believe*—even now, when I look at that photo in the coffee table book, is that the woman didn't set out with cruel intentions. But her life unfolded in such a way that she just couldn't bring herself to look at things with eyes wide open, to really see things as they were or understand the part her carelessness played in it all. And that's what I'm thinking about as Carter runs his hands over my skin.

I have always hated carelessness.

TWO

Georgia. Waring Ridge, New York.

I'm supposed to be writing up the minutes for the July meeting of the Waring Ridge Library Board (a heated meeting about whether or not we could afford to buy the outdoor furniture on loan to us from the Waring Ridge Garden Club), but instead I'm sitting on the floor of my closet in the house where I grew up, torturing myself like I often do, reading my childhood nanny's handwriting scrawled in a journal.

Confiscate the pills, bring them to the rehab so we'll know what Georgia's on and we can go from there. Call Dr. Akash Bhatt to schedule.

There are other entries in the journal, of course. Letters mostly, and some entries about my brother, Max, and me, particularly when Max was acting up or in a destructive mood about our mom, who'd died four years earlier. But it's that frantic note our nanny, Eliza, scrawled on the very day she herself died that always pulls me back to this dark corner of my closet.

I was only sixteen when Eliza wrote those words, but I'd been taking an opioid called Dilaudid steadily for two years. I'd found the pills in my mother's stash; my dad never cleaned out the back portion of her bathroom closet after she died. I'd seen my mom pop Ativan to sleep every once in a while, so one night when I couldn't take the dark dread

I felt in the middle of every night, I rifled through my mom's stuff and found a pill for myself. I swallowed it before I could think better of what I was doing, just so desperate to feel anything other than despair. But the Ativan made me feel too out of it and itchy with anxiety, so I tried a few of her codeine, which made me throw up. It wasn't until the next night when I found my mom's Dilaudid that everything clicked. Dilaudid was a glass slipper of a pill, tiny and easy to swallow, and it didn't make me anxious or nauseated; it only made me feel like all of my edges were muted, like I was floating somewhere soft and warm. At first, I could still function on the pills, but by the time I was sixteen and Eliza had called that doctor and was trying to figure out what I was using, my tolerance had built up until I had to take a dozen pills each day to feel anything. And I was so constipated that I lived on senna tea and magnesium citrate. My dad had cut off my allowance and I was shoplifting things to sell so I could afford the pills—at first I'd lied to my doctor about a tennis injury so I could get a prescription, but then when he wised up to what I was doing, I found an older teenager I could buy from. I was barely going to school at that point, insisting to my dad that it was more important I stay home and work on my writing. Sometimes he let me stay home and write, wild as that sounds, because he didn't have much will to fight me after my mom died. And I *was* writing—that's the unbelievable part. It wasn't until Eliza died that night trying to find my pills that the words stopped flowing onto the page. I loved Eliza so much, her and my mom both, and all at once I'd lost them.

I close my eyes and breathe into the fury that still plagues me. My guilt over Eliza's death is never ending.

Crunch goes the sound of our back door scraping against the wooden frame. Everything in our Waring Ridge house is old, and doors sound different here than they used to in our modern New York City apartment.

I hop up from my closet floor. "Millie?" I call out, winding my way out to the second-floor landing and down the stairs.

In the kitchen I see my daughter and I can breathe again, the fury and guilt subsiding. I think of her inside my belly, the watery weight of her anchoring me. I got pregnant with her at twenty-four and never relapsed. It's not a common addiction story, but it's mine.

"Mom," Millie says, looking at me like she's surprised to see me, which makes no sense, because this house is where I always am, particularly when she's in it, too. She doesn't smile. She's been like this, on edge and sometimes sullen. She never used to be like this back in the city, and the other mothers I talk to say their preteens have turned sullen, too, and not to blame myself or the move. *It's the age,* they all say. Even our new pediatrician says so. Millie and I don't argue very often, but I can feel that time coming for us. We're on the precipice of her teenage years, still holding hands as we wade together into choppier waters. Now, as it stands, we're both too sensitive to ever want to land a punch, too in tune with each other not to think of what the other one would feel at a verbal slight. Sometimes, when I look at her, all I can think about is how she's the same age I was when I lost my mother. How did I bear it? How does any child?

"Hi, love," I say, and Millie comes closer and wraps her arms around my waist. At twelve years old, her head lands right at my chest, and I hold her snugly against me. "How was camp?" I ask, relaxing against the feeling of her small body breathing. She tightens at the mention of camp, as though she'd momentarily forgotten, even though she just finished. "I called to see if you needed a ride," I say. I bought her a watch so she can call me, but she always forgets to charge it. "I assume Caroline's mom brought you home?"

"Yup," Millie says. "Sorry, Mama. The watch was dead." I love when she calls me Mama; it's such a throwback to when she was a little girl. She extracts herself from my hug, and then moves to the pantry and disappears. "Can I play squash tonight?" I hear her ask from inside, her voice echoey. The first thing my husband, Tom, did when we inherited this house from my dad last year was blow out a side wall and make a pantry the size of half a subway car. He'd love to do many more things to change the house, but I need to go slowly, and for the house to look enough like the one in which I grew up.

"I feel like I need to hit something," Millie says, emerging with a granola bar. "Is that normal?" She unwraps the granola bar without looking at it, her eyes locked on mine.

I shrug. "To me it is," I say. "I can think of far worse urges I've had." Millie loves nuance; she'll understand what I'm hinting at without me needing to spell it out. She knows a PG version of the things with which I've struggled.

"That's reassuring," she says. She takes a bite of the bar and considers me. "Life is definitely kinda hard."

"Life is hard and complicated and wonderful," I say, which is the truth as I see it.

"What about Dad?" Millie asks, chewing carefully.

"What about him?" I ask.

"Do you think Dad thinks life is hard?"

I don't answer. Millie keeps eating for a bit, and then says, "I don't think Dad thinks life is hard, per se."

I laugh even though I shouldn't. "I don't know how you pick up on these things at your age. But I can't say I don't agree with you."

Millie laughs, and I feel a little guilty, having a laugh at Tom's expense, though I'm sure he's had plenty at mine. "I *do* imagine Dad thinks life is complicated and wonderful, though," I say. "I know he thinks you're quite wonderful."

"Does Dad think *you're* wonderful?" she shoots back.

I shrug. "I hope so," I say, unwilling to give her more. It's not exactly something I can figure out with her. It's her father we're talking about, and she's twelve. "I love you, Mills," I say, trying to shut down the conversation. It's been a tame one, but sometimes they aren't. I've probably been more honest with my daughter than I've had any right to be, telling her the truth about nearly anything she asks. My own mother was that way, even during the darkest days of my childhood, and I appreciated it.

"Mama?" Millie asks. I turn, and she reaches into the pocket of her shorts. She pulls out a tightly folded square of paper. "I'm sorry," she says when she sees my face.

"Don't be," I say, trying to look like I'm not scared. I'm her mother. I should be able to deal with the things she does. "Do you remember writing it?"

"I do," she says. "It was last night. I was really tired, but it was just one of those things, like I had to get it out. And then I slept great. No nightmares, for once."

The nightmares started when we moved into the house, which I'm loath to admit. "Do you want to read it to me?" I ask gently.

The staccato chirping of birds at the feeder filters through the kitchen's screen door, and Millie won't meet my eyes as she unfolds the paper. There's a slight shake to her voice as she begins reading what she's written.

> Outside through the window we go
> But they are them and I'm a ghost
> Scratching at the night air
> Trying to find my way
> I see you, with your big eyes
> Seeing me
> You know that I know
> What you did so long ago

I'm quiet for a beat as she refolds the paper.

"It's beautiful," I say.

Millie doesn't say anything. The birds outside have gotten even louder, sounding like they're fighting. "You're a talented writer, Millie," I say over their cries.

"It's not that," she says. "I'm not upset about the writing itself."

I cross my arms over my chest. This whole thing has become so frustrating. "Then what?" I ask.

She still won't meet my eyes.

"This is nothing to be ashamed of," I say. "I wrote all the time when I was your age."

"You're not scared of the poem itself?" she asks.

"Not at all. And if you're scared of it, writing is one of the best ways to go deeper and explore things you find scary. I wish I was still as prolific as I was at your age, and I love that you've become such a writer this past year."

Millie looks out the screen door onto the lawn. I follow her gaze, and I can just make out the corner of an old wooden swing hanging from an oak tree. Our nanny, Eliza, used to push my brother, Max, out there for what felt like hours.

Millie's light eyes meet mine. "I *am* scared," she says. "I'm scared of the poems and how I write them. Something about it feels so weird, it's like I get so sleepy at night, but then that's when I get the unstoppable urge to get up and write them."

"Maybe it helps you sleep, to get out all of these feelings and fears."

"Maybe," Millie says.

I've always known what to say to Millie, ever since she was a baby. But I don't know what to say to her about the poems and nightmares she's been having. I almost mentioned it to the pediatrician at her last appointment, but what was I going to say? *My daughter writes frightening poetry at night and feels deep shame about it?* It barely makes sense to me, and I'm her mother.

"I'm gonna go read," Millie tells me, and I let her go. I watch her tiny frame slink around a corner and vanish. It unsettles me, because these days I'm usually the one ending our conversations or slipping out into a different room. That can't be normal for most preteens and their mothers—aren't most kids her age trying to get some space? Instead, Millie has clung to me harder than ever since we moved to Waring Ridge. It's not like I'm trying to get away from her, it's just sometimes I have things to do.

My phone buzzes with a text from my brother. What are you up to?

I could read this text in a few different ways: maybe he really wants to know how my day is going, to connect, to see me. Or maybe he's bored. Or maybe he wants a free meal.

But more likely, his demons are descending like they often do in the late afternoon, like they have since we were children together sharing this big, rambling house, trading secrets like candy and baseball cards.

Hi Max, I text back. Come over.

THREE

Anna. New York City, New York.

The sun is still glinting through the slats in my shades later that afternoon, and after a long shower by himself, Carter is back in my bed sleeping. After sex I always have so much energy, and the fact that Carter's lying there fast asleep annoys me a little, but we're still new enough that I shrug it off. Nothing festers in an early romance, there isn't the right atmosphere for it; it's all sunshine and fresh air, not dank, dingy corners.

When I see Carter sleeping like this it feels more intimate than sex, the way his beautiful face goes slack, the muscles in his tanned arms soften, and his hands unfurl like he's letting go of something. My white sheets tangle around his legs. His chest is bare, and I want to put my hands on his skin; I want to start everything up again.

A five-o'clock shadow covers the lower half of Carter's face, and without his blue eyes piercing mine I have more time to really look. His dark stubble has been shaved where his pulse would be, and there's a patch of smooth skin over his windpipe. He looks so vulnerable lying there like that, and the thought of him getting hurt sends something hot behind my eyes. I lift my hands to wipe away what feels like tears, but there's nothing there. I push off the bed. My camera sits on my desk like a found treasure, and I lift it gently. I live for the sensation of my camera in my hands. It's how I imagine people must feel about cigarettes or babies; you can spend a lifetime looking for the things you want to hold. I raise the camera to my eyes and see Carter through the lens, and something in me loosens like it always does when I see the world this way. There are borders to a photo, a way of containing a subject and zooming in, and you can see a person differently without the rest of the scene competing for your attention. If consent didn't matter to me, I'd photograph Carter just like this: narrowed in on his face, the set of his jaw, the slit of his lips parting on an exhale. I watch him through the lens for a long time, right up until longing sets in somewhere low in my stomach, and then I put down the camera and slip back into bed. I slide a hand over Carter's stomach and into his underwear, and I whisper things crude and unsophisticated. I need Carter for so much more than what I'm saying, and when his eyes flutter open, I tease, "I thought only the young napped like this."

A smile crooks his lips and I kiss it.

"Goodness," he says against my mouth.

"I can't just watch you lie there any longer," I say, curving my leg over his bare waist. I can feel him beneath me, ready. "I don't have that kind of willpower."

"Does anyone?" Carter asks.

"Do you?" I ask.

Carter lets out a laugh. "I wouldn't be here if I did," he says. I try to figure out how to take that, but then he uses his hands to raise me up and back down again on top of him.

What we do is lightning quick, a thing that makes its own heat and leaves a warm imprint of the scene against my sheets. And when we finish, I turn onto my side, facing away from him.

The neon red numbers on my clock say *5:32*. Carter grips my thigh and whispers into my hair. There's something about his hands, the weight of them on my body, and I already know that when this whole thing is over, it'll be his hands I miss the most.

"I'm going to get away for a bit this summer," I say softly.

"You and everyone else," Carter says, like I'm not saying anything of note. He's wrong. But I suppose this is the world I orbit now, ever since the right person saw my work at the right time and I was lucky enough to score a job photographing celebrities for magazines. It's a world where many people take time off in the summer because they can, because they're soaking waist deep inside a trust fund or they make their own money. Or maybe they're barely making enough, but their family always vacationed while they were growing up, so they scrape everything together so they can live that way, too, because it means something to them. And I can visit this new elite world—I can move among the players and even rearrange them and create consequences—but it's not mine. Being able to move fluidly within the upper echelons shows all the advantages in the way I grew up, and I'm grateful for that, but there's still a sense I have of not quite fully belonging, like I'm not really a card-carrying member. I don't like that feeling, but I'm also afraid of losing the feeling if I stay and play the part for too long.

"Where are you going?" Carter asks.

"Somewhere upstate, I'm not really sure yet. It'll eat up most of my book advance," I say, regretting the words as soon as they're out of my mouth.

Carter doesn't say anything. I'm sure he wants to warn me, but he's careful about our age difference. He won't want to say anything that comes off as too paternal.

I need to change the subject, but I can't find any words.

"Is that smart?" Carter asks carefully. He gives me a gentle tug, turning me toward him.

"I'm sure it's not," I say. I look into his dark blue eyes and imagine what it would be like to see me from his angle. He's making solid money and likely saving it. That feels a lifetime away, and sometimes I wonder if I'll ever get there. "That's why I'll probably end up couch surfing," I lie. "Kingston. Hudson. My college friends settled in so many different places up there."

Carter touches my forehead, the tip of my nose. "That's a good way to do it," he says. "And it'll be good for your headspace. Getting out of the city always is. Change of scenery. And you'll photograph for fun instead of money."

"Those two things don't feel different to me."

"Really?" he asks. "It must be nice to feel that way about your work."

"It's not because I don't need the money," I say. "I do. It's just the actual photographing itself, in the moment, doesn't feel different whether I've been hired to take the photo or I sell it after the fact, or I don't sell it at all. Do you not feel that way about *Culture*?" I ask. "I mean, about the actual work. The editing?"

He laughs a little. "I barely edit anymore. You know that. Now it's meetings and keeping relationships and knowing who to feature and listening to pitches and reviewing ad campaigns."

"But you love the thing of it," I say. "You love *Culture*."

"I do love *the thing of it*," he says with a smile.

"Words are not my forte," I say, smiling back. "They're yours."

"I like how you said it, actually." And then again to himself he says, *"The thing of it."*

FOUR

Georgia. Waring Ridge, New York.

"Tom?" I say into the quiet ether of my kitchen, leaning against the white marble on our island, trying to get my husband to look up from the *New York Times*. "You're absolutely sure?" How is he this hard to read after so many years of marriage?

He's sitting at the kitchen table, his long legs splayed beneath him, dark-framed reading glasses on. "What do we have to lose?" he asks me, voice hushed. He always speaks so quietly when Millie's upstairs reading or drawing, like we're talking about something sexy or embarrassing that he wouldn't want her to overhear, when really all we're doing is exchanging banalities common among married couples with children, stuff so boring, even the world's biggest eavesdropper wouldn't want to listen.

"What do we have to *lose*?" I repeat. "Probably a lot. Our deposit on the Southport house, for one thing." I'm trying to make a joke, but Tom doesn't find me very funny. He used to.

"You worry too much," he says, flipping a page, his fingers already stained with newsprint.

"Says every husband whose wife has children," I say.

Raspberries bleed red-tinged water onto the countertop, and I move to grab a paper towel. This house is the first place I've lived where the care and upkeep feels more like a calling than a chore. It's the house I was born in, and nothing will ever make me leave it no matter what happened here. After the pantry, the next thing Tom and I did was replace the kitchen countertops with glistening marble, which I now regret because everything bleeds into it, like the grocery receipt I left lying out and then spilled water on, *@ $9.99/lb* inked into the marble for perpetuity.

Tom finally looks up from the newspaper. "Just list our house and see what happens," he says. "It's only for a month. If someone creepy applies, you can turn them away. You can always say no."

That's ironic coming from Tom. Almost no one says no to him. And what both of us know but neither of us will say is that if I decide to rent out our home, the whole thing will be on me. Tom won't feel obligated to glance over the contract he had his lawyers draw up for our house, because that's how Tom does life: he delegates and compartmentalizes. If the future renters' contract looks good enough for our lawyers, Tom will be content. He won't give the renters another thought. He won't imagine them sharpening our best knives and pilfering through our nightstands; he won't imagine someone else's kids opening our daughter's closet and finding love letters in the pockets of her corduroys. And he certainly won't imagine visitors gazing into the dark corners and hideaways I played in as a child, somehow able to sense my secrets just by studying the shadows.

I don't say anything. And then Tom lets out a short laugh and looks back down at whatever article he's reading. "Maybe you should list the house as haunted," he says darkly. "You might get more interest that way."

I get cold and clammy, and not at the content of his words but how he said it: there's an endless supply of resentment in his voice; he's righteously angry that I dragged us out of glossy Manhattan for the house in Waring Ridge. Last year, my dad died and left this house to Max and me, and Max needed the money from the sale of the house. He couldn't afford to co-own it with us and split taxes, and the only option

Tom and I had if I wanted to keep the house was to buy out Max. Tom has never liked my brother, and now there seems to be no coming back from the position we're in because of Max being *financially irresponsible*, according to Tom. *He's only thirty-one,* I'd snapped back when Tom said that. *Plenty of young people can't afford to buy a house.*

To which Tom had replied: *Georgia, I'd like to remind you that we're also in our thirties.*

We were just so young when we had Millie, and it forced us to be more responsible than we might otherwise have been. And the truth is that my brother wouldn't have wanted the house even if he could afford it.

I stand there unmoored in the middle of the kitchen, holding a fistful of paper towels, waiting for Tom to apologize about the *haunted* comment, but he doesn't. He doesn't even look up. I study him carefully, the broad shoulders and the deep-set eyes. I love him. That's what makes his discontent with living here the past year in this house feel so much worse. But I can't give up this house—every time I round a corner and the sun slants into the room at a certain angle, I see my mother and our nanny, Eliza, who was like a second mother to me. I don't mean that I'm losing touch with reality or that I see ghosts parading around my home, but I can feel my mom and Eliza in this house. It's why I've always felt the pull back to Waring Ridge on the weekends, ever since I was eighteen and left for college in New York City, and even a few years later, when I met Tom and we moved further downtown to SoHo. I couldn't stay away.

"Tom," I say, squeezing the wad of paper towels until my fingers feel like they'll snap. "I'm tired of the *haunted* jokes."

His eyes meet mine. "It's not a joke to me," he says, shifting his weight so he's standing tall, arms across his chest. "I've been saying it since long before your dad died. There's something in the air of the house, Georgia."

"So poetic," I say. "Reminds me of you when we first met."

His face is blank, like he doesn't remember writing me love poems, these long, flowing things with sentences that curved this way and that, metaphors and dark imagery, always lightening and resolving as they hurtled toward the end. I wish there were always such a clean resolution. It's one of the things I like about writing short stories: you control every ending. Of course, I haven't written anything in years, but it's what I used to love about it all.

"You can't say you don't feel it," says Tom.

"You're mistaking history for ghosts," I say. "I do feel my mother and Eliza in this house, it's part of the reason I love it."

"And your father?"

"And my father. I feel him, too."

I think back to the trips we used to take when we were just out of college, and how Tom wouldn't go into the bathroom where my mom died, or even the bedroom that led to the bathroom. It's the only thing I've ever seen scare him, besides me. And now that it's *our* house, and *our* bedroom, I swear he looks at me differently when we're there, especially when we're being intimate. It's like he can't let go the way he used to. Once he told me he felt like he was being watched, and no matter how bullheaded I am about the house, sometimes in quiet moments, I wonder if I've made a grave mistake dragging the three of us out of the city where Tom and Millie were so happy. I wonder if it's a thing too selfish for a good mother to do.

"Georgia, look," says Tom. "Just press the gas and list the house. I don't think there's too much to be concerned about. I don't think our biggest liability right now is a family from the Upper West Side who wants to rent our house for the month. I think our biggest liability is your brother."

I blink hard. I don't mind that Tom said it—I really don't, because it's true. It's just so incredibly painful.

"Tom," I say, softly.

"He seemed off last night," Tom says. "I don't mean I necessarily think he's drinking or using, but last night he was on edge."

Max is back from a stint in Los Angeles, where he bunked with a friend and directed an independent film. He has a steadier gig on a Hulu series in New York, but it was on break, so he took the LA gig. It wasn't good for his proclivity to drink and party, but he seems better now that he's back. *Grounded* is the term Max used to describe his life here, on the East Coast, near the rest of us. Near me. He's living in the cottage in the back of our property near the cliffs for the rest of the summer until his Hulu series starts shooting again in the fall.

Tom says Max and I are magnets for each other, which means I feel more settled when he's back here, too, and like I don't have to wonder what he's up to thousands of miles away. I remember sneaking into Max's nursery when he was an infant, climbing over the bars of his crib, and lowering my ear to his mouth to make sure he was still breathing. I remember the way shadows clawed the walls of his nursery like fingers. That room is Millie's room now, and sometimes when I go in there, I think back to the way I used to set up my fuzzy yellow blanket on the floor and sleep beside Max's crib, and then eventually his toddler bed, to make sure he was okay in there. And now as an adult I realize how messed up it was that my parents never checked on me while I was checking on him. I was just a child; I could have been doing anything in his nursery, clipping his fingernails or suffocating him with a too-warm blanket. This was before Eliza started staying overnight when she was scared of the state our mother was in, too afraid to leave us alone in the house with her if my dad was traveling. And Eliza was right to be scared—she was right about how dangerous it all was, because my mom ended up drinking herself to death, passing out in a bathroom and bleeding to death when Max was eight and I was twelve. Max was the one who found her. She spent those early years of our lives in and out of consciousness, with a need so big it electrified the house.

"I agree Max was *off*," I say, deciding to use Tom's language. It seems safest. "But he didn't touch anything, not the wine, no weird bathroom trips. I think he was just sad."

"Maybe so," Tom says. He's not a prude when it comes to these things. I've led him straight to the fire, watched his fingertips singe as he reached out for me and pulled me back from the flames. I owe Tom my life. Tom and Millie both.

"You really think you'll have enough time off in August that this will make sense? The whole point is to . . ."

Reconnect. Remember how much we love each other.

". . . spend time together as a family."

Get a break from our house, where nothing seems to be going as I'd imagined. At least I can admit it to myself.

"I'll have enough time off, Georgie."

He hasn't called me Georgie in forever. It's an olive branch, and I reach for it greedily.

"Okay," I say, trying to sound easy about the whole thing. "And you think the price we're listing it for is right?"

Our house in Waring Ridge is one hour north of New York City. For the month of August, we're heading east to Southport, Connecticut, where we're renting a beach house. Southport is only a half-hour drive from here, but being on the beach will feel like an escape for all of us. Tom can still commute into New York City, but I want to make sure he won't be working such long hours that this will be a waste. The beach house in Southport is expensive for the month, about $5,000 more than I think we'll get for ours. Our Waring Ridge house overlooks picturesque woods and rocky cliffs, plus it has a pool, which drives up our rate, but nothing compares to the beach.

Tom doesn't say anything. Sometimes, when he wants to signal to me that I need to manage something on my own, he goes eerily quiet. It makes me feel like a child, and then I say the wrong thing. "So, you think you'll have at least two of the four weeks completely off?" I push. "You haven't taken any time off this year."

We don't say anything for a moment, and I know I've annoyed him.

"You and I both know that I'm going to try my best." His voice sounds so tired. It only ever sounds that way with me. Not with work, and never with Millie. I catch a glimpse of myself in a mirror. Artfully messy blond bun, a preppy J.Crew shirt, boyfriend jeans, even though I resisted them for so long. Loafers. When did I become this person, this mother? When did I stop listening to Radiohead?

I was once a creature possessed by substances, and that lone fact is so terrifying to Tom that sometimes I think it's why he sounds this tired; I've done this to him, I've taken him to darker places than he signed up to go. When we were in our twenties, I was falsely advertised: the shiny girl in the bar who went to an Ivy League school and wrote short stories by candlelight, letting him read a line here or there. I can own up to my part in that. I've tried to make amends, but now I've gone too far in the other direction: Tom never wanted someone this vanilla. That makes two of us, but a bland, watered-down version of myself is how I keep us all safe.

FIVE

Anna. New York City, New York.

That night I'm about to search the vacation rental sites again when I get a text from my friend Bee.

I'm in ur hood. Meet me! Welcome to the Johnsons. Come. Good scene.

K, I write back. Lemme shower. See you in 15.

I open up TikTok. I have a million followers on the platform, and close to that on Instagram, and that's partly why I got the book deal. It's not that my photos aren't good; they are. But now publishers look for the whole package, and coffee table art books are obscenely expensive to produce, so if the publisher is going to pour all that money into you, they want to know you're going to be able to sell books to your followers. When I think about this, I feel a little dead inside, and usually I try to think about something else.

Still, I need to post something, I feel it like the pull of a tide, like an obligation. I find a series of photos I took at an outdoor concert this weekend in Brooklyn on a pier, and I pick a dozen of them and make a montage, and then set that to a trending song. I write a caption at the very top, so that it won't get in the way of the images. I always fumble over this part. I'm way worse with words than with images, but I've got this book contract and I'm supposed to do at least five hundred words with each of my photos. (I could shoot photos of every block in NYC and have it finished before writing five hundred words about one hundred photographs.)

I finally give up trying to write something awesome and settle on boring words that describe exactly what it was that I was photographing: *Last weekend in Brooklyn.* It's not like people follow me for my words. People follow me for a world I've created. Or, rather, for the lens through which I see the world that's already there, and how unafraid I am to look into the darkness.

SIX

Georgia. Waring Ridge, New York.

That night, I'm sitting at a table at the Inn waiting for Ethan, Maya, and Tom. This restaurant always reminds me of my mother and Eliza. My mother loved it here, and the staff loved my mother, and everyone knew Eliza was our nanny and loved her, too. Eliza and I would exchange a knowing glance when one of my mom's many admirers stopped by our table to pay her a compliment about her latest book or short story published in the *New Yorker*. I was so proud, and you could tell Eliza was proud, too. My mother belonged to us, she was *ours*, and we loved her so dearly. Whenever anyone came up to us in public, Eliza would get a stiff look of pride and protection, her shoulders squared like she might have to shoo them away at some point, which she never actually did. By the time I was seven or so, four of my mother's books had hit the *New York Times* bestseller list, the film rights to two had been bought by Paramount, and one was already in production with a bona fide movie star playing the lead. Those years—including when the movie came out with great press and fanfare—were a high point for my mother's career, but they were some of the gloomiest times for our family. It was as though my mother became overstimulated by her success and plagued by a raging case of imposter syndrome and Catholic guilt. And those years, Max was an increasingly demanding toddler prone to tantrums, and my mother was irritable and practically jittery unless she was drinking. After the first few drinks, she mellowed a bit, but she could never seem to stop at the mellow phase. *Mellow* became *drunk*, and then *drunk* became *belligerent*, and pretty quickly *belligerent* became *blackout*. Eliza tried to get us to bed before *belligerent*, but she couldn't always manage it. Sometimes it was four p.m., and we weren't tired. My mom seemed to do better when exterior forces demanded more of her, as though any opposition gave her purpose. Adversity, for her, was a bone to chew, and with her jaw grinding and teeth gnashing, she simply needed less drink to wash down all the rage. I suppose it had a place to go. Even mildly uncomfortable social scenarios seemed to do the trick, like the time she created an uproar in our town because she wrote a story published in the *Atlantic* about a couple practicing polyamory and engaging in frequent threesomes. It infuriated my father. He was normally supportive of her work, but her fiction was so unapologetically detailed that everyone just assumed she and my father were living a polyamorous lifestyle. She literally wrote about the feeling of having two different men inside her, and people absolutely died over it. We went to the country club that summer, and everyone looked at us like we were a traveling circus of prostitutes and exotic birds. My mom, rather than burying her head, seemed filled with purpose. She *tsk-tsked* and muttered about how *pedestrian* everyone was to assume she was somewhere buried inside her book characters. I couldn't formulate what I wanted to ask her because I was only nine at that point, but a part of me wondered: Aren't your deepest fantasies and desires on display in your work? Could you really write about something that didn't already interest you, or call to you in some way? My parents argued that entire summer, and I could never figure out whose side I was on. Eliza was all business, holding her chin high and marching us into the club with a canvas pool bag hooked on her elbow. Fiery Irish hair like a halo, lips set in a prim line.

I loved Eliza like a mother. I've never said those words out loud to anyone.

God forbid I ever wrote about being a bad mother, my own mother once scoffed, not long after the polyamory debacle. Being a bad mother was my mom's worst fear. And I still don't know, all these years after her death, if she died knowing she was never that, at least not to me. I don't know what Max would say. And I don't know how to make anyone, including Tom, understand that even with my mother's binge drinking, blackouts, and subsequent days of guilt, she wasn't a bad mother. She was *my* mother, and no matter how furious I was with her, I loved her endlessly. My father was charming but distant. Max, my mother, and Eliza were the loves of my life. To lose the synergy of that trio had felt like the end of the world as I had known it.

I take out my phone and try to get lost in my texts and forget about my mother. I can't wait to see Maya. Being friends with Maya is like being by yourself in the woods ruminating about ticks and mosquitoes, and then Maya shows up with lighter fluid and a grin, about to burn the whole thing down. I can't think in straight lines when she's around.

When Maya and her husband, Ethan, enter, it's like a light switch is flipped inside the dim restaurant, that's how luminescent they are. Ethan with his unearthly pale skin, Maya with her deep brown skin, both with big smiles, both tall: Ethan's an inch or two over six feet and Maya's an inch or two below it. They met on the set of a student film, and in the hazy lighting of the restaurant, they could still pass for grad students.

"Hey!" I say, standing. I throw my arms around Maya's shoulders and kiss her cheek. "You look beautiful." She's wearing bright orange glasses and a light blue dress that nearly skims the floor.

"Where's Tom?" she asks as we let go of each other.

"He's on a work call in the car. He'll be right in, I promise."

"Young, beautiful Georgia. How *are* you?" asks Ethan in a booming announcer's voice. I smile, I can't help it. I always smile when they're around.

We all sit. Wooden beams crisscross the ceiling, and the gray stone walls make it feel cozy and rustic. Our menus look like they've been printed on scrolls. "We haven't been here in ages," says Maya, and I wonder if she's hinting around the edges of her theory that Tom doesn't like going out with her and Ethan as a foursome. It's not entirely untrue, it's just a little more complicated than that.

"We haven't," I say, not biting. "And the food looks especially tasty."

"And mysterious," Ethan says, reading. "*Sherry reduction celeriac-parsnip mash* . . . I'm not fancy enough to even guess at what that would taste like."

"Has work been busy for Tom?" asks Maya, not letting it go as easily as I'd like her to. How can I really explain Tom to anyone, let alone people he doesn't trust?

"Yeah, probably the same as for everyone else in Waring Ridge," I say with a wave, because that's the truth of any New York City commuter town. Many people work long days and bear huge commutes to be able to live somewhere charming and bucolic. Tom leaves on a six a.m. train and usually doesn't get home until nine or ten. And, of course, I can't really complain about Tom's hours, because I was the one who begged to move up here. Him getting home early enough to go to dinner tonight was an aberration, and he still has work to do. That's why he's still in the car on a call.

Ethan is an academic, teaching film theory at NYU, which is why he has the best hours of anyone in Waring Ridge, and which is maybe why he never understands how often Tom cancels. Or maybe canceling is rude no matter what kind of job you have, and Ethan and Maya are right to fault Tom for it. Maybe I'm rude, too, for condoning it, for not insisting he hang up the phone and come inside the restaurant.

Ethan puts his phone in his bag, and I know he'll never retrieve it during dinner, because he's one of those people who's notably present. Though I suppose it's a luxury to be married to a woman like Maya who would never put her phone away, so you don't have to be worried about whether your kids can reach you, because they can always reach their mom.

"And your brother?" Ethan asks. "How's he doing?"

Maya and Ethan are always engaging Max in neighborly chats, and they probably know the answer to that question better than I do. I start to say that he's fine, but then a waiter comes to our table. One side of his head is shaved, a pencil above his ear. "Hi, welcome," he says warmly. "Can I start you off with anything to drink?"

Ethan and Maya order a bottle of wine, and I'm debating whether to order Tom a gin and tonic when I feel a squeeze on my shoulder. I turn and glance up at my husband.

There's a feeling I have when I see Tom, an experience almost, and it hasn't changed in all these years. Tom has a ruffian quality to him, like maybe there's been a bit of a scuffle right before he got to me, but he's here now and everything's going to be okay. There's something about him that settles me, the set of his shoulders, the crook of his chin, and a way he has of looking at me. And maybe we don't have all the laughs and easiness with each other anymore, but we always have this moment. At least, I do.

"Good evening," Tom says formally to Ethan and Maya. He's always formal with my friends. Really, with anyone he hasn't let into his inner circle. In the moment it all feels charming, and I forgive him for his lateness. Maybe I forgive him too easily in general—Maya would agree with that. But what's marriage if not forgiving more than you ever thought possible? "Sorry about that," Tom says, pulling out his chair and sitting, smiling at me. I smile back. You would think, with our upbringings, I'd be the one keeping people at arm's length and always on the lookout for disaster. Tom grew up with a well-adjusted sister and two doting parents who still live in DC. They visit us several times a year, and it's a picture-perfect family, as far as I can tell. But it's Tom, not me, who suspects the worst in everyone. His paranoia swings from overly trusting and assuming nothing bad will come of any situation—even precarious ones—to full-blown suspicion over things that seem innocuous. It's like his inner barometer for who and what to trust is just slightly off-kilter. It has made for some big disasters—a few work partnerships gone sour that nearly ended his career—and then smaller disasters like this thing that happened with Ethan last year. When we first moved in last July, we met the Campbells, and Tom kept warning Ethan about a dead ash tree on the edge of their property that was close to our house. He texted Ethan the numbers for a few tree businesses in town, but Ethan did nothing. And Tom kept bringing it up every week or so, in a way that I thought was completely obnoxious, until the night the ash tree came down with the force of God and crashed through our dining room window onto the table. It could have killed us if we'd been eating there. We were on the other side of the house in the library, Tom reading a biography, Millie reading *12 to 22*, me flipping through an old issue of *Vogue*. We heard the roof crack and glass shatter like I've only ever heard come from the construction sites scattered throughout New York City. It was so loud I leaped from my chair and grabbed Millie, sheltering her with my body. But Tom didn't move. A beat later, he set down his book, his face transformed by rage but utterly still. He knew exactly what the sound was. He stood from his chair, completely composed, and walked toward the dining room. By the time Millie and I had gathered ourselves, he was striding back down the hall. And then he let himself out the front door in his robe and slippers into the crisp fall night and walked to Ethan and Maya's house. He pounded on their front door until his knuckles bled, but they'd gone out to eat with their boys. He waited for nearly an hour on their front porch while I begged him to come home, to cool down. But he wouldn't leave their porch. *That man could have killed my wife and daughter,* he kept saying, over and over, as though he were in a fugue, and as though Ethan had planned it. And when Maya and Ethan returned home, Tom exploded on him. *Negligent son of a bitch! Careless bastard!* And then to both Maya and Ethan: *You call yourselves our friends?*

We all tried to calm him down. But it wasn't until Millie walked over in her pajamas and wrapped her arms around Tom, saying, *I'm okay, Dad. Let's go back home,* that he finally left the Campbells alone.

It took us months to recover. Maya and Ethan were as apologetic and graceful as they could possibly be about the whole thing, and of course I was upset, too, for a little while, and terrified at what could have happened. The Campbells never really offered an excuse for why they didn't deal with the tree, leaving us to wonder if it was just sheer laziness or overwhelm; or maybe they didn't want to pay for it; or maybe they didn't think Tom was correct that it would fall. Whatever their reasons were, Tom couldn't get past what had happened, and he focused his outrage on Ethan. He kept muttering things to himself and to me: *There's something I don't trust about him. Haven't trusted him since the day I met him.* But he'd never voiced anything like that about Ethan to me before the tree. And now here we are, months later, still trying to mend fences, literally.

Tom orders a gin and tonic, and when the waiter retreats, we do that thing couples do when they first sit down together: big exhales, smiles, looking expectantly at each other like there are so many exciting things to catch up on that we barely know where to start. But the conversation always begins with something boring, and sure enough, Maya asks Tom, "How's work?"

"Ah, it's fine," Tom says, pushing away from the table a bit, looking like he's trying to get comfortable. "What about you? It was a nice write-up in the *Times* about *Watch*," he says.

Maya beams. "I was *thrilled* about that," she says. "Press can go either way, as we all know. I was worried we'd be the butt of a joke."

"And you certainly weren't," Tom says.

"Hmmm," says Maya, and then she sips her wine. *Watch* is her third documentary. It explores the female gaze, the subject on which she wrote her PhD years ago, and specifically the underrepresentation of minorities in films that are traditionally considered to maintain a female gaze.

"We're very proud. *I'm* proud. Of this woman," Ethan says, beaming at Maya.

I watch the glance exchanged between them. I wonder what it would be like to have that careful balance of professional respect, both of you working so prolifically in the same field. There was a time when

Tom and I were a bit closer to that balance, when I'd had my short story published and I was at least making a show of writing in coffee shops. We orbited a professional New York City landscape together, respected each other's work, talked about how amazing my someday novel would turn out to be, and it was mostly lovely. Back when I was writing, I wanted to emulate my mother. After all, she was the person I thought was the most beautiful creature in the world. But I couldn't make the words appear in the way she always could. I published that first short story after nearly two years of work. I'd always been able to write prolifically as a child, even after my mother died. But something about Eliza's death suffocated the words right out of my brain, and they never came the same way again. I'd heard of writers who were slow, meticulous, detailed—and their novels took years to write. But my glacial pace seemed unnatural, stunted, and weighted like a hand on my shoulder. When I was in labor with Millie, there was the feeling that I was coming up against something when I tried to push her out. Like there was a physical force trying to hold my daughter inside of me. The doctors had to make a cut so that I could free her from my body. That's the feeling I have when I write: like I'm coming up against something that I can't push my way through, and there's no doctor there to cut it out of me.

"Georgia," I can hear my husband say, but I can't stop thinking about my mother, about how very prolific she was. I wish that what I'd inherited from her was that lone quality, instead of a love of substances. I imagine myself inside of her, sharing blood with her, using my tiny translucent fingers to grab the genes I wish were mine and discard the ones that almost killed me.

"Hmmm . . . ," I say to Tom. I have no idea what he was trying to tell me. He gives my hand a squeeze, and I turn to Ethan and Maya. "I'm putting the house on the rental sites tonight," I say.

"Really?" Ethan asks, surprise curling his voice. "So, we'll have new neighbors."

"Just for the month of August," I interject.

Maya stares at me like she can't believe it.

"That's right," I say. "Cheryl says it'll go quickly." Cheryl is our real estate agent and a mutual friend of mine and Maya's. She was the one who gave me the idea of putting the house up for rent. Cheryl and I went to high school together, actually. Waring Ridge is the kind of town people move back to, and there's a solid group of us who returned home years after we graduated college. Some still commute into the city, others work locally, but there's an intuitive bond there when we all see each other. My mom died when I was in seventh grade; I was addicted to pills by early high school; and Eliza died during the summer between my sophomore and junior year. So when I see high school friends like Cheryl, I have a feeling of comfort, like they saw me through my absolute worst days and chose to care about me anyway. And now things are better, partly because I have an adult life with Tom and Max and my friends, but mostly because I have Millie and my sobriety.

I went to rehab after Eliza died and stayed sober for junior and senior year, pouring my traumatized brain into my schoolwork and managing to get into college. I relapsed in college a few times, thinking I could drink and smoke pot like everyone else. I got away with it until senior year, when I started back on my old friend Dilaudid, about the same time I met Tom, who'd graduated early and was already working in the city, career savant that he was. I hid a lot of the opioid use from Tom—we never actually lived together before we got married. He proposed as soon as we found out I was pregnant, and we got married three months later. I haven't touched a drug since. When I first got sober, I used to feel like a match hurtling down the black strip of phosphorus—about to catch fire. Like at any moment I could succumb to my desire and combust. But now the wanting has mostly receded, and it's livable like this. Most days.

"Will someone rent it sight unseen?" Maya asks.

"I think so. Or maybe through a video tour? I suppose if it's someone in the city who's interested, maybe they'd come check it out."

"Wow," says Maya, shaking her head. Her gaze is so penetrating I can't look away. "I can't believe you're going through with it."

"Doesn't seem like a smart financial choice to just jet away for the month *without* doing it," says Tom.

This is something I love about Tom. He has zero problem making a statement like that—and I'd bet most of our friends probably wouldn't talk about finances in this way or show vulnerability.

"I suppose," says Maya.

"Not all of us have trust funds," he says pointedly. Maya, of course, has one, and I cringe. He's not even one gin and tonic in.

"Or even two working adults," I say, trying to make fun of myself. But it comes off all wrong.

"You work," says Maya. If she's annoyed at what Tom said, she doesn't show it. That's Maya, unreadable, able to plaster the expression of Mona Lisa on her face when she needs to. I wish I could do that, but I've never had a poker face, or any ability to hide what I'm feeling in each fleeting moment.

"You know what I mean," I say. I *do* work. Part time at Millie's school. And I love my friends who work in the office alongside me, and I love Millie's principal and the teachers who have become friends. Middle school teachers are a special breed of wonderful.

The waiter stops by to take our order. He smiles at us expectantly, but Tom asks for another minute to look at the menu.

"I don't know what you mean," Maya says to me when the waiter leaves. I knew she wouldn't be able to drop it. "Work is work. Don't sell yourself short, Georgia. You always do that."

"She does do that," says Tom.

"And worse," says Ethan. "Because plenty of people make the same hourly wage you do, so to devalue that insults an entire class of working people."

"Jeez!" I say, even though I know he's right. I take a sip of my seltzer. "I'm not devaluing the money I make or saying that there's something wrong with my hourly wage or the job itself. But you all know I'd like to be producing creative work like you are."

"I'm not producing much creative work these days," says Ethan.

"But you're teaching it," I say. "And I never published enough to be able to teach. You've all achieved something." I wave my hand around to include all three of them. "And I haven't had that kind of artistic success. So, for the record, what I was devaluing was *myself*, and my failure at producing what I want to be producing, which is creative work. It's not like I've written novels and they just haven't sold. That would be out of my control. So many unpublished manuscripts are right on the cusp of being good enough to sell, but maybe the right eyes haven't been on them, or it hasn't been the right time, or whatever it is. But I haven't even been able to finish a first draft to have a go of it. I failed at even getting to the full manuscript part that most unpublished writers have already gotten to."

Maya's lips purse. Ethan has deep hollows beneath his eyes that I didn't notice before. It's like I've tanked the night and dragged them to the bottom with me.

"That said, it *is* nice to see you all agreeing," I say.

The men smile. Maya doesn't.

"You're a beautiful writer," Maya says.

"You haven't seen anything I've written."

"Not true. I read the short story you had published, and it was some of the most exquisite writing I've ever seen, and I also read the buzz around it, how everyone thought you were as talented as your mother and would follow in her footsteps. Everyone was excited, Georgia. And they'd be excited again if you turned something else in."

"I was in my early twenties when I wrote that story," I say. "Practically still a baby."

"So, show me your recent stuff," says Maya. Her gold chandelier earrings glitter as she leans forward to take my hand.

Tom is uncharacteristically quiet. This is a sore spot between us, a finger pressing the tender skin of a bruise. "The problem is I can't write anymore," I say. "When I was Millie's age, I wrote pages and pages."

Just like Millie's doing now, I think, though I don't mention it. Tom hasn't even seen Millie's poetry.

"All the way up until I was sixteen, I wrote like that, even when I was high," I say. Maya and Ethan know I'm sober. I don't ever try to hide it, not from anyone. "And then after Eliza died and Max and I were the ones to find her like that . . . I just couldn't make the words come. Even writing those short stories I worked on in my early twenties, they came out like sludge. I had to sit all day even to write a hundred words, and sometimes the words didn't come at all. I don't think writing is supposed to be that way."

"But the story was fantastic," says Maya. "Maybe that's just your writing process. I always read about novels that took years to write, even a decade or two, and nothing's wrong with that. You could still try it."

"I could," I say. "I have. But it never feels right anymore." I don't look at Tom. I'm about to say something I've never admitted to him. "I think a part of me desperately hoped that coming back here to Waring Ridge and my childhood home would somehow help me write again, like I used to, up in my bedroom. Millie sleeps in Max's old room. I set up a desk in my old bedroom, thinking maybe it would happen, but . . ." I shake my head. "Maybe it still will," I say hopefully. I need to change the subject, I'm desperate for it, and Tom senses it.

"Maybe in Southport the words will come," Tom says gently. "I could take Millie on some excursions, and you'd have the house to yourself."

I shoot him a grateful look, and then I try to change the subject. "The beach is going to be great for Millie," I say. "It really is. I can feel it."

"The boys will miss her," says Ethan. Their sons are on either side of Millie, one going into sixth and the other eighth. Sometimes they'll shoot hoops at the Campbells' house, or swim at ours.

"I guess I still can't believe you're all right with a stranger staying in your house," Maya says.

I'm picking apart a piece of salty bread, and I can feel my hands freeze in midair, because of course I'm not entirely all right with it. A sliver of panic slices through me, and I set down the bread and take another swallow of seltzer to wash down the panicky feeling, wishing the seltzer were something stronger. Alcohol has never been my thing, but I understand the pull of it: the way it fuzzes the edges and tamps down the anxiety. I understand what my mother and Max were doing with the booze, at least part of it. I still don't touch alcohol, because God forbid it set me down that path again.

"Please don't do that," Tom says too sharply to Maya.

Maya lifts her hands. "I'm just saying. It's unlike Georgia. She loves that house like a second child."

I was pregnant with a second child once, something Maya doesn't know. Tom knows, of course, and one day I'll tell Millie. A little boy I miscarried at the beginning of my second trimester, right before I was about to tell everyone about him.

Ethan looks between Maya and Tom. Maya lets out a noise that sounds like *phfff.*

"We've just told you we don't think it's financially wise to do the month in Southport without renting out our house and recouping part of the cost," Tom says. "So don't fill her head with anxiety, please."

"It's already filled with anxiety," I say.

"Where's our waiter?" Ethan asks, voice tight. "Shouldn't we order?"

"It's a nice thing, really," Maya says to me, seemingly undeterred by Tom's irritation. "The way you love that house. It's inspiring to me."

"Thanks," I say. "You'd feel that way about your house, too, if you'd grown up in it."

Ethan and Maya's house is the only one we can see clearly from our property. It's a converted barn that once belonged to the property farther down the road, but the owners parceled off a few acres with the barn and put it on the market. Ethan and Maya bought it in a heated auction. They kept the charming red exterior and redid the inside to look like something out of a magazine.

Tom sips on his gin and tonic. Then he sets it down with a *thunk* and says, "Georgia does love the house like a child." I can feel the tension between them ebb until it's gone. Directly to Maya, Tom says,

"Sometimes I'll find her running her hand over a side table or gazing at portraits with her eyes glazed over and a secret smile."

I bite my lower lip. It satisfies me, the way Tom still pays attention. "I've become so nostalgic ever since we moved in," I say. "Each corner has a memory of being little with Max."

"A lot of it's your mother and Eliza, I think, too," says Tom. I look up to meet his eyes, wondering what he thinks when he looks at me now. Waring Ridge has changed how he sees me; I can feel it. This suburban version of me isn't who he married. And I know many couples go through this change, but they go through it *together*. Tom's still on his own island, waving at me from the shore, and it feels like Millie is swimming between us, stuck between our old life and the new one.

I take another sip of seltzer.

"You were born in that house?" asks Ethan.

"Literally," I say. "In an upstairs bedroom. By the time Max came around we went to a proper hospital. We had Eliza by then, helping to take care of me, and my mother was sober from the time she was pregnant with me until a few months after Max was born. I wish I remembered it better, being that little. It must have been lovely to be with her when she was sober."

"Max was only a few months old when she started drinking again?" Ethan asks.

I flinch at the timeline. Sometimes thinking back on our childhood feels physically painful. "I remember how hard she was trying," I manage to say, "and then suddenly she couldn't do it anymore."

"She was sober at other points, though, right?" Maya asks. Sometimes she can't help being a documentary filmmaker at heart, probing deeper than most. I don't mind it, because I love talking about my mother, even when it's painful. Of course, there are many things I'll never tell Maya, no matter how long I live.

"Never for an entire year," I say. "A few months at most." I turn to Ethan. "What about you?" I ask, thinking about how little I know about his upbringing. "What was it like growing up in your house?"

I see Maya tighten, and then Ethan lets out a little laugh that tells me I've asked the wrong thing. "Oh," he says, a slight shake in his hand as he waves it over the table. "Trust me, you don't want to know."

"Really?" Tom asks, and I can feel what he's going to do like a pressure change in the air between us. He's going to do the thing he does, the twisting of a sharp object into a wound. It's not so unlike what Maya does with her questions, but it's much less gentle. "How's that work?" he asks. "What happened to ya?"

"God, Tom," I say. "Leave it."

Maya looks at her husband.

Ethan holds Tom's gaze. "No, no. That's fine. You want to hear it, Tom?" There's a challenge here, but Tom isn't wise enough to back down.

"Sure I do," says Tom.

"My dad hit me with a belt. All the time. Said I wasn't good enough to be his son, wasn't good enough for anyone, wasn't good enough to be on the planet sharing the air with him. His own dad kicked the shit out of him, and he did the same to me, and it was like a thread of violence laced through decades of DNA."

"Except it's not like that," Maya says, "because you put an end to it. That thread stopped with you." Her words sound convincing, but her heavy-lidded eyes flicker, like she's scared to be wrong.

"I don't know," Ethan says. "As of now, yes, you're right: it stopped with me. But who can say what someone is capable of under the right circumstances?"

A nearly imperceptible flinch from Tom. His childhood was cookie-cutter perfect, and now he's out of his depth. But Tom has darkness, too—don't we all?—and it must be what he draws on to say what he does so steadily. "And your mom? Where was she in all of this?"

"Afraid," Ethan said, knuckles strained against his wine glass. "She was very, very afraid. Of him. Of losing him. Afraid of me, too, when I was an angry teenager and lashing out at her. I didn't hurt her—I don't mean that. But the rage I felt at her for staying with him, the things I said . . . there were times I threatened her so badly. In some ways I was just as bad as he was."

"You weren't," says Maya.

"You were a child," I say.

Tom, mercifully, doesn't press further. We're all quiet for a moment until Tom raises his glass and says, "Here's to us all being here now, with all of our flaws and fault lines."

"Well said, Tom," Maya says, lifting her wine. "I'll drink to that."

I swear I see Ethan crack the smallest smile. He clinks his glass with the rest of us. "Cheers to flawed humans," he says.

SEVEN

Anna. New York City, New York.

A chalkboard sign outside Welcome to the Johnsons announces that lesbian, left-handed art directors drink for free tonight. I'm friendly with one of the bartenders, Clarice, and I bet she wrote the sign, and it makes me smile because my best friend Bee is all three. We come here all the time for the relatively cheap drinks and a scene that isn't straining at the seams with trying. It's a true dive bar, with beer from a fridge and a wood-paneled basement vibe. I bartend two nights a week a few streets over on Ludlow, and all of us bartenders in this area know each other. We're pretty friendly, giving out free drinks to each other and that kind of thing. It's a scene, and I like it.

This afternoon, right before I met Carter at my place, I'd stopped by the bar where I work and tried to explain to my boss that I needed August off. It's a delicate dance: My savings account is the highest it's ever been because of my book advance and my freelance work for *Culture*, so I can afford the month off. But I don't want to lose my bartending job, because what if that other money dries up? What if *Culture* decides they don't need me anymore, or, more likely: What if I've made a catastrophic mistake sleeping with Carter, one that eventually ends in my dismissal from the magazine? I'm not technically employed by them, I'm only a freelancer, but everyone at *Culture* would frown on our relationship for so many reasons. I wish I could be less risky with my personal life, but I can't seem to, so the least I can do is be safe with my finances. Bartending makes me between $300 and $400 a night in tips, so figure around $700 a week, give or take. My rent is $3,000, so bartending almost covers it. Which means I use the rest of my money to eat, pay a few other bills, and save something each month. So I can't give up bartending anytime soon. And plus, I like it. I waitressed for a while and hated it because the dynamic is so different than bartending: With waitressing, you're at everyone's beck and call. But if you bartend at a small bar like the one where I do, you have much more power than you do when you're waiting on tables.

I climb the concrete steps, push through the swinging glass door, and step inside Welcome to the Johnsons. Right away I see my friends playing pool. Hayes and Bradley are laughing, Hayes angling over the pool table and sinking an easy shot, then missing a harder one. Bee and Selena are standing off to the side, shimmering beneath the dim overhead light like pearls. Bee twirls dark curls around her index finger, and then leans into Selena to say something up close.

The jukebox blasts Pearl Jam, and Eddie Vedder shakes the place with sound, hitting a low and mournful note that seems to stop time as I walk toward my friends. Selena sees me first. She looks up and says, "Anna!" in that slightly buzzed and happy way girls greet each other.

I raise my hand in a wave, and when I get up close, I give them each a kiss on the cheek. Selena is a relatively new friend; she works with Bee. She's a musician in her spare time, a singer-songwriter who sometimes plays bars in Brooklyn. I try to use her music in my TikToks as a show of goodwill. A funny thing among creative people is that some are competitive with each other, some aren't. I'm not. Bee's not. Selena is.

Bradley hangs back. Hayes comes over, shaggy blond hair falling into his face, skin milky-white and splattered with freckles. He holds his pool stick and gives me a one-handed hug. Bradley makes eyes at me, like he's wondering if we'll ever hook up again. We used to drink and hook up, but then when I started things up with Carter, I told Bradley that I was seeing someone else, and that I thought it might get serious. Which was true, but probably not how Bradley thought I meant it. The night I told him that, he grabbed his phone and jumped off the couch like it was on fire, and then when he hit the doorway, he turned and said something cruel enough to make my stomach twist: *This one will go up in flames like all the others, Anna, won't it?*

I make my way over to him now. "Are you getting beat here, my friend?" I ask, gesturing toward the herd of solid balls on the green felt. Hayes only has a couple of stripes left to sink.

Bradley hands me the pool stick, eyebrows up, small smile. It's as friendly a greeting as I get from him these days. I angle the stick and drop his five ball into a corner pocket.

The bartender bends to get a VHS tape and shoves it into a VCR on a tiny TV from the '90s. Credits roll for a movie I've never seen. Even with this melancholy feeling, at least it's nice to be here with people my own age, with some of my same problems. At the bar, there's a guy all tatted up who reminds me of Sam. Another drink or two and maybe I'll go talk to him.

Or maybe not. Everything feels so uncertain lately.

Bradley watches me play, his eyes roving my body. He was a good guy, and I liked being with him—it felt safe. And he was there for me when Sam died. But in my grief, I ruined things with Bradley to be with Carter, because being with Carter felt like a need far too deep to ignore, and I knew I couldn't, so I didn't.

After the pool game, the girls and I sit. Bee is wearing lavender eyeshadow, and it's gorgeous against her smooth, dark brown skin. "Are you really supposed to be changing that earring already?" I ask, spotting a rose-gold moon in her left earlobe, right in the second hole we both got together a few weeks ago. "Didn't the lady tell us to wait at least six weeks?"

"I think it's okay, *Mom*," she says with a wink. The irony is that, of the three of us, Bee is the most like a mom. Being safe and responsible matters more to her than it does to most twenty-somethings I know.

"Don't come crying to me when you get a situation," I say, smiling.

"*You're* where she gets that word?" Selena asks. "Everything that comes up at work, according to Bee, is a *situation*. Sometimes I don't even know what she's talking about."

I smile at Bee. She's been my best friend since we went to school together at SUNY Albany. We have an understanding all our own; we don't need to say everything on our mind unless we want to, because the other one just *knows*. It's the first time I've ever had that. As a child I didn't understand the patter of friendship banter; I couldn't seem to insert myself. I sat there trying to anticipate the next thing one of the other kids might say, so I could get to it first and say it the right way. But I could never figure it out. It always turned out that the thing the next kid said was something unlike anything I'd imagined they would. I kept practicing, kept straining to understand the things I was supposed to say in a group, and I did eventually get better at it. By high school I was the odd, artistic girl with her camera, but in the eyes of my classmates I'd gotten stealthily beautiful, which meant they could tolerate me. People will forgive you almost anything if they find you beautiful. How sad but true is that?

A Natasha Bedingfield song comes on the jukebox and Selena jumps onto a chair. She has this in her, the desire to be seen. She stretches her skinny pale arms in a V. Her tank hovers above her belly button, and a silver piercing catches the light. There's a tattoo of a cartoon rabbit near her hip. She belts along with the song, and she sounds good. Not as good as Natasha, but good enough for this night. The bartender even looks up from making a drink and watches her. Bee and I clap. I video a clip of it, figuring I'll ask her if I can post it. I'm trying to be extra nice, because the more followers and semblance of success I seem to get with my photography, the more tightly Selena holds on to Bee. I don't think Bee would ever leave me, but it doesn't mean I'm not insecure about it.

I don't have many friends, and as of this year, I no longer have my twin. So who, then, other than Bee? I used to think Bradley and Hayes were my inner circle, but Hayes got more distant when I broke things off with Bradley. I don't think they're mine anymore. Maybe it's all a matter of time before this group will split up, and what if Bee chooses them?

I stop videoing. The guys are immersed in their game of pool, and Bradley hasn't once looked this way. I take a sip of my beer and try to forget about it. "I'll post it?" I say to Selena when she finally comes down off the chair.

She nods, acting casual. But she knows I always link her account, and I'm pretty sure she sings in front of me like this on purpose so I'll post it.

Still, I do. I caption it *Selena at Welcome to the Johnsons*, and then post before thinking about all the reasons I shouldn't blast on social media exactly where we are. Right away there's a weird comment: *Hang tight, Anna. Taking the F train down. Would love to meet u in person.*

There are always weird comments on TikTok and Instagram, stuff that can make your stomach turn no matter how often you tell yourself it's just the game of social media, the new world, the thing you must do if you want your art to be visible and valuable. I recognize the username. I've seen him commenting weird stuff on my posts before. And he must be on social all day long, because he always comments right away, like he's waiting for me to post. I've tried blocking other usernames in the past, but there's always another one who follows, and sometimes in the middle of the night I worry it's the same user, just constantly creating new accounts as soon as I block him, out there waiting to get me. And now I know he lives in New York City, or lived here at some point, because how else would he know the subway system that well to know which train to take down here? He could have googled the subway map and the address of the bar quickly, but he seemed to comment almost instantly after I posted it.

I tap Bee's shoulder and show her the post. "Ew," she says. "Same guy?"

I nod. Selena grabs the phone, and, still high off her singing and dancing, says, "Ooooh, a new fan. Let's stay till he comes, and we can both sign autographs for him."

I try to laugh, but it comes out strangled. I want to act like I'm not scared about stuff like this, but the truth is, ever since my accounts blew up on TikTok and Instagram, I feel vulnerable, like strangers are peering into an intimate world I wasn't ready to share. I don't know how to make it work; I want my photographs out there because I want to make my living as a photographer, but it's still bizarre to have that many people seeing my every move. Obviously, I need to be smart and not post where I am, but I'm one drink in and wasn't really thinking.

"Finish your beer, and then we'll go," says Bee. "Just in case he's being serious."

Selena rolls her eyes. I love Bee more than ever in this moment.

"Okay," I say, leaning back in my chair, taking a sip of a beer that tastes too metallic. I feel a slow, sinking feeling that isn't pleasant, a mix of loneliness and vulnerability. I suppose there's a feeling I have in my relationship with Carter that could be described as vulnerability.

Or maybe something worse.

EIGHT

Georgia. Waring Ridge, New York.

That night, when we get home from dinner, Millie's already asleep. Tom pays the sitter, a friend's daughter who's home from college on summer break. We don't call the young woman a *sitter* in front of Millie, because Millie insists that, at age twelve, she's far too old for one. But I can't imagine leaving her alone for hours at night in a house surrounded by woods.

Tom and I climb the stairs silently, peeking in on Millie. She looks so young when she's sleeping, her face free of any angst, her pale arms folded over a stuffed zebra.

We pad down the wide oak planks to our bedroom. Tom strips down and gets right into bed. I wash my face and change into pajamas, and then I get in beside him. We're both tucked beneath the duvet, eyes open and staring, which isn't really normal for us, because usually when Tom gets into bed we don't really talk. Millie goes to bed earlier than most of her friends, and she's often sleeping by the time Tom gets home from work. And on those nights, when Tom climbs up the stairs and meets me in bed, we have sex. When Millie made that statement earlier today about Tom not finding life hard, she wasn't wrong, but that's only a part of it. Tom's complicated, at least to me, but the best I can figure him out is to think of him as a hedonist who likes life's large and small pleasures, including having sex with me nearly every single night we've been married unless I was postpartum or had the flu. Sometimes it amazes me that Tom's been able to stay faithful as long as he has. I think it's why we have sex so often, because he knows he'd be more tempted to look elsewhere if we weren't. And thinking on Millie's question more, I don't know if a hedonist like Tom necessarily thinks life is wonderful. Maybe it's quite the opposite: maybe he doesn't think life is inherently wonderful at all, and maybe that's why he has the urge to seek out the wonderful by partaking in everything extrasensory and pleasurable: sex, work, cars, clothes, beauty, food, wine, and whatever else it is he gets up to.

"Are you tired?" I ask. He's turned off the bedside lamp, but with the moonlight I can still make out the lovely contours of his face.

He doesn't answer me. He reaches beneath the covers and puts a hand on my body. "I can't seem to forgive him," he says.

"Ethan?" I ask, even though I know who he means. "*Tom.* Come on." His fingers move under my pajama pants, curving over my hip bone. "It was months ago," I try.

"He could have killed my family," says Tom. His palm stills on the flat plane of my stomach.

"But he didn't," I say. "And it's not like he came over here wielding a knife. It was an ash tree. And he had no idea it would fall on our house."

"No, but see, that's the part I can't work out," Tom says, and now his hand is going lower. "Where else would it have fallen, Georgia? It was tilting toward our house at an angle that made it obvious that straight through our dining room was the only route it could take."

His pushes down my pajama pants. I let go of a breath.

"It's almost like he was waiting for it to happen," Tom says, his voice a low growl. And then he takes my tank up and over my head. "I don't know what I would do if something happened to Millie, or to you," he says. "I wouldn't survive." His mouth presses mine. He kisses my lips, my jaw, my neck, but he doesn't feel like he's completely there, or like what we're doing together is about me at all. It's like he's getting off on the prospect of protecting me from a bad guy, or from tragedy.

"Tom," I say, breathless as he touches me. "Are we okay?"

He pulls away and looks at me. I think about him saying he felt watched in this house. Maybe I feel it, too, maybe I know exactly what he means, and I can't admit it, not even to myself.

"I don't know," he says. He lifts my hips, and we don't talk after that.

NINE

Anna. New York City, New York.

The house comes online at dawn.

I could barely sleep after last night out with my friends, and now I'm sitting here snapping back to life when I see the house pop onto Realtor as soon as I put Waring Ridge into the search box. My heart pumps faster when I click on the thumbnail photo. It's an utterly beautiful house, glistening white with black shutters, and stoic like something I conjured out of a dream, like something shot straight out of the middle of my brain. It sits proudly at the top of a hill, with crisp rectangular windows that look onto a rolling front lawn. Hydrangeas burst in white firecrackers, the kind of flowers that usually only look so artfully perfect in a magazine. They run the length of the porch, and along the front of the house they grow so tall they're likely visible from inside the house through the windows. I've searched hundreds of houses these past lonely weeks at my computer, waiting for this moment, and right away I check the price: it's a fortune, just like everything that's commutable to New York City, but it's in line with the other homes I've seen. It'll eat up most of my book advance, but I plan to write the book while I'm there, and what else is money for if not living out a fantasy?

My fingers are a little shaky as I click past the exterior shots and marvel at the interior: checkerboard floors in the foyer and glossy gray paint on the walls, a glimpse of wallpaper and gold-framed photos of birds. You can tell the home has been recently remodeled and redesigned: the style is too current not to have been done in the past few years, but there are still all kinds of old things hanging about that fit perfectly with the new ones. Whoever decorated it did it perfectly; there's a seamless blend of old and new. I check the house's price history and it shows a sale one year ago. There's a shot of a bathroom with herringbone tile and a claw-foot tub, and just above the tub is a window overlooking a private backyard that, according to the map, backs up to one hundred acres of preserved woodlands and cliffs. There are hikers' trails that crisscross from a southern entrance, but this house sits on the northernmost part of the preserve, near the cliffs. You can't access the woods from the house's property—you couldn't get safely past the cliffs to reach the trails—but that doesn't matter too much to me; it's not like I want to escape to a country house so I can get lost in the woods. Next comes a photo of a bedroom with a four-poster bed that looks antique, and a rocking chair in the corner of the room tucked in the shadows. Then there's a shot of the living room, where white couches surround an oak coffee table with legs sculpted in feminine curves, and a deep brown wooden side table holds a studded vase and more framed photos. I'm about to click to the next image when I catch a stack of chunky art books. I squint, almost sure that the top one is *Culture*'s new book, and it gives me a buzz. I squint at the tiny photos on the table, but I can't make out who's in them: most seem to contain the small shape of a child, others a man and woman holding the child. I imagine myself scoring this house for August and gazing upon those photos, obsessing over this family's life together, trying to discern their dynamic from a photograph: their intricacies, moods, backstory. People are mysteries, of course, and nearly impossible to crack, especially from a photo. But it doesn't stop me from trying.

I sit back and try to slow my breathing. It's four in the morning, and I don't want to message the number listed because I don't want them to think I'm some insomniac party animal emailing her at this hour. I'll wait until six so they think I'm a person with a proper job who rises early and gets right to it. And I don't want them googling me and finding my social media, and then showing them to her husband and being like *Can we really rent the house to this young person?* So I decide I'll rent the house under a more common spelling of my mom's maiden name: Smith. It doesn't feel like lying, because I suppose at any point, I could have taken her name instead of my dad's. I never would have, though. My dad was a security guard who worked all night so that he could take care of us during the day while my mom worked, and then when my mom died, he did everything. I don't know when he slept. I loved him so much, and we still talk every day, mostly texting each other photographs of Sam. His heart is broken over Sam, so is mine, and there's no one else left who can really understand what we feel like except each other. Sometimes we call each other at night and run through our days, and we don't mention Sam. But usually, we can't help ourselves. We both blame ourselves in different ways, which maybe happens to everyone who's lost someone they love to suicide.

I scroll through the photos again. Whoever took these doesn't have a bad eye for photography, or maybe they just love the house. That happens sometimes. Deep love translates through the lens, and it's one of the reasons I'm glad I don't have to make a living photographing other people's children. Even the least artistic mother can usually capture a shot of her child stunning enough to be on the cover of *Parents* magazine.

I crawl back to my bed, feeling like I've caught fire. I imagine myself in that house, exploring each corner, sitting on the screened-in porch in the back, listening to birds and crickets. I imagine losing myself in another life, like when you're reading a book or watching a movie and a small part of you escapes to that location, to that story. But this is the real-life version. The perfect escape.

I finally fall back asleep, dreaming of an arching staircase and checkerboard floors, missing six a.m. entirely.

TEN

Georgia. Waring Ridge, New York.

At nine a.m. I already have three inquiries into the house. Millie's at tennis and Tom's off to work, and I'm sitting on our screened-in back porch with my laptop and a lukewarm cup of coffee. I'm nervous seeing each prospective renter's message because it makes all of this very real, and I can feel in my bones that it's going to happen, that we're going to go through with it. I'm going to spend August with Millie and Tom in a beautiful beachfront rental in Southport, and it's going to be a dream. I feel a zing of hopefulness, because sometimes you just need a change of place, and when I think about being there and gazing upon a deep blue sea, I can almost feel the tension subsiding. And if I'm honest, it could be good to have a month off from my brother. I'm sure Max will come to Southport a few times to see us, but it won't be like it is now with him living in the cottage on our property.

I really hope it doesn't turn off these potential renters that Max is living in the cottage behind the main house. But likely whoever these people are, they're coming from the city. The cottage is all the way over by the cliffs. What's the difference between that and any other neighbor?

The first message about the house is from a couple on the Upper East Side with three children. They end their message asking if they can bring their dog, which puts them in a less ideal category in my mind. I love dogs, but it could be the kind of dog that pees everywhere and chews. The second message is an elderly couple from South Carolina who are looking to be closer to their daughter for the month, which sounds ideal. And the third message is from a woman named Anna Smith who tells me nothing more than how beautiful the house is, and how deeply she connected with the photos, and that it's exactly what she's looking for in a summer rental and she'd love to rent the house for August, no tour necessary, and that she can have the money to me via Zelle right away. I'm leaning toward the elderly couple just because I can't imagine they'll be throwing parties each week, and I don't have a sense of the age of this woman, Anna. Or what if she has young children? I just worry so much about the pool and the cliffs. The property is treacherous.

The doorbell rings. Probably a delivery. I walk over the checkerboard tiles in the foyer and swing the door wide to see my brother.

"Max," I say, scanning him, like I always do, trying to assess his state.

He gives me a lopsided grin. "I was in the neighborhood," he says, his favorite joke ever since he started living in our cottage, a joke that's quickly losing its luster. I don't deal well with inflicting tension on Tom, and that's what Max living on our property is doing as of late. I felt that way when I relapsed into drug use in the years before we had Millie. The shame was overwhelming. There have been other small, guilt-inducing things, like overspending or, once, getting drunk and flirting with Ethan. Maya didn't seem to care, but Tom did. And now, Max. My brother living on our property counts as my fault.

"Am I allowed to come in?" asks Max. I can't help but look at him and see him as he was when we were little, when nothing bad had happened yet, when we were like two pennies flicked into a fountain, momentarily shimmering on the surface before sliding down to the bottom and tarnishing.

"Of course," I say. "I just put on coffee. Come, sit."

In the kitchen, I grab him a mug and put a sprinkle of sugar in the coffee, just how he likes. We make our way back to the porch and sit on wicker chairs with red flower-print cushions. I couldn't bring myself to change out those chairs. They were our mother's twenty years ago, and this porch was her favorite place to sit. It's screened in with floor-to-ceiling windows and looks out onto the edge of the cliffs. A long time ago, my dad fenced off the edge of the property from the cliffs, but the fence is low, and you can still see over it to the cliffs and the mountain beyond it. The view is beautiful. Dangerous, but beautiful.

Sort of like Max.

"I saw Maya this morning," Max says, taking a tight sip of coffee.

"And did you have a neighborly chat?"

Max takes a daily run through the neighborhood and stops for small talk with whoever he sees. For a thirty-two-year-old accustomed to bachelor life in New York City and LA, he's taken to suburbia surprisingly well.

"Indeed, we did. And get this," he says, inching forward, his body like a spring about to uncoil. "Maya mentioned you listed the house. She assumed I knew, obviously. Because I'm your brother. And also because I live on the property you're renting out to a stranger." His dark eyes cut into mine. "Why didn't you tell me, Georgia?"

"I *did* tell you," I say. "At the grocery store. While you were palpating avocados."

Max lets out a laugh, but there's an edge to it. "You said you were *thinking* about listing the house," he says. "You've thought about a lot of things and haven't done them. Like Botox."

"Max, come on," I say, and he considers me, his left leg jiggling double time. He's always in motion; he's been that way since he was a boy. His eyes dart out onto the lawn, where acres of green grass span out until the cliffs. My dad had the pine trees removed so we could get a better view of the woods and the cliffs, and Max and I cried for days. We loved those trees. Even Eliza was upset, and nearly nothing ruffled her. My mother was trying to win back my father's affection after she embarrassed him by drinking too much at one of his work functions, so she went along with him and defended the *tree murder*, as Max called it.

"Remember when Dad cut down the trees?" I ask.

Max looks back at me. "Dad was a bastard."

I roll my eyes. "He wasn't. You can't really think that."

Max waves a hand. "Don't dismiss my feelings, Georgia." He's had a lot of therapy, and now he seems able to set boundaries with me, which is ironic, because I thought I was the one who needed to set boundaries. "You and I feel very differently about Dad and Mom," he says. "It's almost like we had entirely different parents. You don't seem to blame them for anything."

"Because what would be the point of that?"

"People don't blame people because there's a point. It's just something they feel." He shifts his weight and wicker creaks beneath him. "You must at least sometimes think about how if Dad had done more to get Mom in recovery, she never would have drunk herself to death, and then we wouldn't have been motherless." He looks out on the pool, runs a hand over his face. "Or how, if he had put up a fence on the roof where we all liked to sit, then Eliza wouldn't have fallen from it. Don't you ever think about that? Because I think about it all the time," he says solemnly. "Maybe he wanted Eliza to fall. She and Mom were so close. Maybe he was jealous."

"Max, come on," I say. I wish I could agree with him and blame our dad for everything, but something changed in me when I had Millie. I stopped looking at the what-ifs and wishing otherwise. And I stopped looking at everything as if it were either good luck or bad luck or even any kind of luck at all. Of course I wanted my mother to be alive, but when I had Millie, I couldn't stop thinking about how any other path my life could have taken might not have led me to her. And then I stopped questioning all the mistakes I'd made. And that, of all the things about Millie, is the thing that saved me the most, the thing that quieted my deadly, ever-present guilt. If I had done anything differently, she wouldn't be here.

"I'm not sure anyone could have stopped Mom," I say softly. I don't want to go here right now, but Max's grief is a freight train that can't be derailed. I remember the way he'd cling to my mother's legs and wrap his pudgy arms around her neck; I remember how she'd sing and nurse him in the old rocking chair that I still have upstairs in my bedroom. Their love was tactile.

"What's your problem with me renting the house, really, Max? You share a driveway, but it's not like you live in the house. You barely need to see the person if you don't want to."

"So, you know who it is? A *person*? Singular?"

"I don't know who it is, yet. A woman was in touch with me. Also, an elderly couple. And a dog lover."

"Then you should leave Tom home."

"That's an awful joke."

"He was rude to me the other night. At *family dinner*, or whatever it is you like to call it."

"He's worried you're using."

"Well, I'm not." Max shakes his head like he's disgusted with something. Me, Tom, himself. It's anyone's guess.

He looks out the window and runs a hand over his smooth, tan skin. Max got our father's coloring. I'm more bleached out, like our mother. "Maybe it's not the biggest deal that you're renting out the house," he concedes. "It *is* your house. Maybe I'm just bummed you didn't tell me, and I had to hear it from Maya." He turns back to me, his dark stare piercing mine. "But also, Georgia, things happened in this house," he says. "Things we don't want anyone knowing or seeing or intuiting."

"I'm not renting the house to a psychic," I say.

"You don't know that."

"Maybe that's the plot of your next movie," I say. He's always tinkering around with ideas, saying he wants to work on a film or TV show with darker storylines instead of the quirky rom-coms he's worked on recently.

"Or the plot of your next novel."

He's the only one who thinks of me as a novelist. It's kind.

"The rental only lasts a month," I say. "What can really go wrong?" Of course, I know even as I ask it that the answer to that question is wide and porous. Max knows I know it, so he doesn't call me out.

"Why do you need to get away so badly?" he asks instead. "It's beautiful in Waring Ridge in the summer. People want to come *here* for vacation."

Something in him has shifted—he's getting melancholy, folding in on himself like he does. Even as the morning sun filters through the screens and the day gets noticeably warmer, even as an orange-bellied robin chirps near the hydrangeas, he's darkening. He has a gravity all his own when he's like this, and I'm a moon to his planet, desperately sticking close as he hurtles through space. "Is it *me*, Georgia?" he asks. "Do you and Tom hate me living here?"

Yes. No.

"I don't," I say, reaching forward to squeeze his arm. But it feels awkward. Now that we're adults, there's so much less physical contact: no more knock-down hugs or high-fives, no sitting hip to hip for a favorite cartoon.

"Does Tom?" he asks.

"He doesn't hate you living here," I say, sitting back in the love seat, trying to look casual, like I'm not navigating a conversation filled with booby traps. "The move has been difficult for him, and work has been stressful, and that's partly why I need us all to get away."

Max gazes out to the lawn, where two robins are splashing in a bird bath, and then looks beyond it to where his cottage sits. Maybe he's worried to be away from us. He hasn't been sober for that long, and it takes a lot for him to maintain a semblance of a healthy lifestyle. I remember those days, how early sober life felt like I was walking on a thin layer of ice with ashen water churning beneath. Max has always been drawn to a fast crowd and a loud lifestyle. No sleep, too much partying, all the trimmings. And now he's here, with us, and I can't really tell if the slow pace is good for him, or if it's driving him mad. Sometimes a fast lifestyle distracts from all the feelings that are too scary to face, and maybe he's afraid to live like this—slow, quiet, sober—without us right here keeping watch on him. And maybe I'm a terrible sister for leaving.

Max turns his gaze back on me. "Are you guys having problems?"

"Oh," I say, realizing I might not have correctly guessed what was on his mind. "Tom and me? No, we're okay."

"Okay?"

"Yeah, we're okay, like lots of people who have been married a long time. We're not amazing, and we're not bad. We're okay. We respect each other, we love each other. That's what matters, right?"

"Respect," Max says. "That must be nice. I really need to find a girlfriend."

"You have, like, six girlfriends," I say, and he finally laughs.

We're quiet for a bit, gazing out onto the cliffs. When my mom was drinking, sometimes Max and I ran out there because we knew that if Eliza was tending to my mother, then no one would be watching us. It was such a steep drop. No wonder my father eventually stopped us with a fence and a locked gate. But I remember the few times we got away with it. We held hands, crept to the edge of the cliffs, and peered six stories down into a rocky ravine.

I shudder to think of it now, of what could have happened to us.

ELEVEN

Anna. New York City, New York.

I look up into the massive mouth of a *Tyrannosaurus rex*.

The Museum of Natural History feels special at any time during the day, but being here with my crew at dawn feels nearly sacred. Morning sun filters into the hall, casting a gentle glow that's perfect for shooting. The *T. rex*'s six-inch-long teeth are bared above us, and its four-foot-long jaw looks massive enough to snatch a small horse. There's a small glass partition near its ankles, and we aren't allowed to go over the partition to get any closer to it. But I tested it out with my assistant earlier, and I'm pretty sure I can get the shot of the actor beneath the bones without any of the partition showing.

It's six a.m., nearly twenty-four hours since I messaged the owner of the Waring Ridge house. I haven't heard a word, and I'm increasingly agitated thinking about all the people who must have already applied. It's a beautiful house, so of course multiple people are going to be interested. I want to reach out again and offer more money, but I'm concerned that would come off as desperate and backfire. Or *should* I do that? It's the kind of thing I want to call my dad and ask, but he's never rented a vacation house, and plus I don't want him to know I'm doing this. I'm frozen, my thumb hovering over my phone, trying to decide what to do, when I hear a shrill *crash*. I look up to see a glass Evian bottle has fallen from the craft services table and shattered. "Someone needs to clean that up," I snap. My makeup artist, Farrah, turns. She's never heard me use that tone before, and I open my mouth to apologize, but it doesn't come out. Farrah's holding an eyeliner pencil in midair, inches above Ava Clark, the actor I'm photographing today for *Culture*. Ava's the star of the newest *Jurassic Park*. She's stunning, with clear brown skin and strong, toned shoulders visible in the Wales Bonner crocheted top and skirt we're photographing her wearing. And she's smart and ebullient, chatting warmly with my crew this morning. Her PR person is here, whispering something into Ava's ear. The PR person hasn't yet looked me in the eye. She only stares at Ava. Neither one of them has acknowledged the broken glass bottle, which is ironic because Ava was the one who insisted she never drinks out of anything plastic. Ava only stares ahead, like a pro who knows not to glance around at loud noises while getting her makeup done.

I'm itching to get going, to catch her in the shy, orange sunlight. We've been here since four a.m., doing wardrobe and makeup. The museum wouldn't close for us to shoot, but they did us the favor of letting us come in before hours. Which means I need to be done shooting by nine and have everything cleaned up by the time museumgoers arrive. Carter was the one who made the call to the Museum of Natural History for me; apparently it helps to have friends on the board of the museum to get this kind of access.

Access. What a loaded word, and surely one of the things that drew me to Carter in the first place. And it's all been good so far. But that's only until something bad happens and we part ways, and then what will happen to me?

"I want to start shooting in five," I say to my makeup artist. "'Kay?"

It's weird being twenty-six and in charge of the shoot. But it's the job of the photographer to oversee the set, to maintain control, and to direct the whole thing. (And, also, to get the perfect photo, of course.) Which is why I have to settle down and get this right. I just need to focus on work, and then deal with the vacation rental in a few hours. I'll message the owner, make my case, and maybe offer more money.

I tip back my head and take in my surroundings, something my mom used to remind me to do when I was little. *See the moment, Anna,* she used to say, her voice singsong and so beautiful to me. I think of her when I take photos. Seeing the moment, catching it, and preserving it forever.

"Ava?" I ask when I feel a little calmer. "Are you ready?" Before she answers, I crank the music louder. It's my favorite mix of badass, empowering songs to play before shooting, and a Heidi Rojas song called "Madre Creator" filters through the hall. Ava smiles at me, a line of perfectly white teeth and a dimple on her left cheek. I watched the new *Jurassic Park* movie last night when I couldn't sleep. I kept thinking of what Bradley had said about things with Carter going up in flames. The remembrance of it started off low, like memories sometimes do. But then his words intensified while I lay there awake, pounding my brain until they were as loud as a subway car on metal tracks. To drown the memory out I turned on the movie screener *Culture* sent me of the new *Jurassic Park*, and there was Ava, somehow gorgeous and sexy even while running from velociraptors. And she was brilliant. Above all, Ava's character was smart and cunning as she single-handedly came up with a plan that would halt world destruction and right the balance. I've always been hooked on this type of cinematic plotline: that a person can right the wrongs and salve the hurts and restore the order. I would do anything to be able to do that in real life for my family, and deep in the middle of the night when my brain feels like it's on fire with insomnia, I get this feverish feeling telling me that even if I can't reverse all the ways we've been destroyed, I can somehow even the score, like a balance reinstated on a scale tipped with rocks. There must be a way. Every time I've called my father since Sam died, I could tell by the gravelly sound of his voice and the whir of the fan that he was sitting in his recliner, and that he probably hadn't stopped looking at photos of Sam on his phone for the past several hours or even days. Sam was so very beautiful and cinematic—he could have been anything. But his disease was a bear let loose at a birthday party. He had edges that wouldn't be tamed, swings he couldn't weather, and medicine that sometimes worked and sometimes failed him. He tried so hard, and so did I. Trust me, I tried. I loved him so much.

I know that reverse engineering the past is impossible, but what if there was a way to avenge the wrong? I suppose in movies like *Jurassic Park*, it's just survival plus glorified revenge. The dinosaur ate Ava's boyfriend, so the movie ends with her spearing the offending allosaurus with a knife sliced through his spongy gray skin and bloody, pulsing heart. And then there's the ending scene where she reunites with her family as the hero she is and mourns her boyfriend while the music swells.

But real life is different than the movies. Who can really pull that off?

Ava finally rises from the makeup chair. My makeup artist looks pleased, and she should. Ava is magical with shimmer high on her cheekbones, black eyeliner and mascara, and matte pink on her lips. "Come stand here, love," I say to Ava. My work persona is my warmest persona. I live to make my subject feel good, which is, of course, partly selfish: I want to get the best shot. Some photographers maintain a level of aloofness because they like the shot they get when their subject is trying to win them over. Not me. I like the shots that come when I've convinced my subject that they can tell me their deepest, darkest secrets. I've shot half a dozen covers for *Culture*, and many more interior pages, and there are a wide range of personalities and levels of insecurities and hang-ups in the people who come to be photographed, and almost always they report back to *Culture* about how thrilled they were to work with me. Except for one time. The actor I was photographing reminded me so much of Sam: sullen, brooding, twenty-something boyish good looks, and even the way he flicked his hair just like Sam used to. There were the tattoos that blazed across his skinny, pale arms, and piercing green eyes that matched Sam's (and mine). *Like cats,* people have said about Sam and me, and I'd say it about that actor, too. He was positively feline. I was photographing the look-alike actor in a Tribeca restaurant with oak walls and shimmering bottles lining the bar, and I'd already had enough of life that day, of being alone without my twin and trying to pretend I was okay. And then in walked the actor, and all I could see was my brother while I was shooting, and I felt so incredibly sad and numb. Apparently, it came off as unfriendly, and the actor's manager reported back to *Culture* that perhaps they should think about getting some new blood in the photography department.

The actor was high profile enough that Carter himself had fielded the phone call. And that night, when Carter came to my apartment, was the first night I realized that he was falling in love with me. "I need to talk to you," he said when the door to my apartment closed behind him. We were new at that point, shiny and gold, a sharp intake of breath. I was wearing a silk tank, no bra, and cashmere pants that I scored from a set when an actor didn't want them. Carter dropped his bag, and his hand went to my waist, and then his mouth was on mine. I said his name against his lips.

"There was a complaint," he said. His hand was under my tank, gliding over my stomach, cupping my breast. "Rob Sampson."

"Oh?" I asked, trying not to sound as scared as I was. I felt sure I was about to be in trouble, but I was excited, too, because here was my new lover in my apartment and it was nightfall, and I've always relished the time of day when sunlight gives way to darkness. I had music playing in the background, something jazzy. And Carter showing up here in this state—a little angry at me, a little scared of me?—made me wonder at the range of things I could make him feel.

"The complaint isn't about the quality of the photos," Carter said, his voice a low growl. "It's about your on-set behavior."

"Hmmm," I said. Now my hands were all over him, too. Everything between us was too warm, and I had the sensation of our bodies melding like wax figures.

"He called you *uninterested* and *polarizing*."

"I think you have to be verbal to be polarizing," I said. "And I could barely talk that day, because Rob Sampson reminded me so much of my brother." I never would have been this bold if Carter had called me into his office. But here, in my apartment, with him wanting me . . . well, it's amazing how quickly you can score the upper hand when you're alone with a man as starving as Carter. "I wasn't polarizing, Carter. I swear to you."

"I know you weren't. And I said so. And I said we stood by the quality of the work, and that we'd be sure to assign him someone else next time. And his manager wasn't ballsy enough to tell me there wouldn't be a next time if you were still working for us. So we left it at that."

"You stuck up for me?" I asked. I knew my question was childish, but I wanted to hear him say it.

"I suppose I did," said Carter.

"Sam's dead," I said. "I was having a bad day."

"I know, Anna, and I'm sorry," said Carter.

"So perhaps that day I was *uninterested*, as he said."

"I'm sorry you lost your brother." He pulled me closer. There are so many things I wish I could tell him about Sam, about our childhood together, about how it broke Sam to lose my mom, and how he never really properly recovered. Within a few years of our mom dying, he was exhibiting signs of a mood disorder, and everything snowballed from there: higher highs and lower lows, a painful delay getting the right diagnosis and the right therapist, and then Sam's inconsistency taking his medication. I want to tell Carter these things, but every time I try to find words for who Sam was to me, about the twin bond that you read about but can't really understand unless you were born one, too . . . I don't have the right way to say any of it. I've shown Carter dozens of photos of my brother, and that's the closest I can get to explaining what a loss it is that he's gone.

I barely ever thought about Rob Sampson again unless I passed a poster advertising his new film. But I knew, from that moment, from the way Carter walked into my apartment and consumed me—even after I'd messed up for *Culture*—that he was falling for me. Which was exactly what I wanted. But I never made that mistake again: letting my personal life affect my work, which is what I'm reminding myself now when my mind keeps drifting back to the Waring Ridge house. *Focus, Anna,* I say to myself like a mantra, studying Ava through the camera, still trying to get it right. We shoot for another hour, but too quickly we're running out of time at the museum, and I still haven't captured the right photo. Ava is perfect—almost too much so. She's glamorous and self-assured, and I worry I'm trying to capture her as she is in the *Jurassic Park* movie: vulnerable but razor smart. And standing beneath the dinosaur is doing nothing for any of us, because she's still *Ava Clark, in a museum.* Nothing about the photo is going to move an audience or even inspire them to go see the movie. There has to be an intangible element, an amalgam of real life, film characters, and the surreal, and I know all of this, and it's running through my head as Ava grins at me.

Snap, snap goes my camera.

This is my job. Not hers. She's already done her job: she's made the movie.

"I have an idea," I say carefully. "What if we went to the shark exhibit?" We've been working for long enough that I worry she's getting tired of smiling and posing and trying to convey who she is to millions of people. "There's a metaphor there that I think can work. Sharks have been alive longer than dinosaurs, haven't they?" I ask, even though I know the answer. "They're misunderstood. Just like Viola."

"You watched the movie?" Ava asks, flattered at the mention of her character's name.

"Of course I did." I don't mention that I watched it last night on a whim. Normally I *do* always make sure to see the work of the people I photograph. I've just been so focused on other things lately: Carter, my summer plans, missing Sam, my dad. "And sharks are threatened, like Viola. But they maintain their strength and their cunning."

I'm reaching here. But it's not like it isn't true. And Ava seems to like the idea.

"Okay, cool," she says. "Let's try it."

We move through the museum, Ava and I. Everyone else on set clamors to move the lighting and get everything we need in order. At the entrance to the shark exhibit, Ava drops her shoulder and spins to face me. There's a massive shark mouth above her—no head, just the teeth in a wide oval. The lighting isn't exactly right, but there's something in Ava's face that I love. I start shooting, and she starts laughing, and somewhere in here it feels like I may be getting photos that will work, and suddenly I'm laughing, too, as Ava gets sillier, the relief of knowing I already caught the shot.

And then there's a hand on my shoulder, and I turn to see Carter. It's the first time he's ever touched me at work, and his hand feels so dangerous there, flaming through the cotton of my shirt. He drops it almost immediately.

"Carter, hi!" I say, my voice too shrill. "I didn't know you were coming."

"And miss a chance to meet Ava Clark?" Carter asks. He's a bottle of charm, pouring it all on Ava, but it's the kind of professional charm that comes off as sunny, not smarmy. You never once think he's flirting with you, only that he's delighted to be in your company. It's part of what made him so incredibly attractive: zero waft of desperation, only confidence and reserve. I had to put my cards on the table first.

Time seems to slow as I listen to Carter and Ava talk. I can feel a few members of the crew watching Carter, trying to figure out what he wants and why he's here.

Ava seems extra alert beneath Carter's gaze, like she's just had an espresso. Carter has that effect on people, and I wonder what Ava sees when she stares back at him. A man at the highest echelon of the media stratosphere? Someone she needs to impress? Or someone who should be trying to impress her?

I think about lenses, like I always do, and about how each of us humans have our own lens tainted by years of living life, being crushed, and picking ourselves back up again—a lens clouded with loss and cracked with slights. And we're still trying so hard to really see each other, and maybe it's a miracle we still can.

"Welcome to my world," Ava says to Carter, gesturing at shark bones with a manicured hand that glitters with gold rings.

"It looks like you're all having some fun this morning," says Carter, seeming pleased.

"Anne's *amazing*," Ava says, pulling her attention from him to shoot me a beaming smile.

I don't really care that she's messing up my name. I take the compliment and hold it close like a keepsake. Carter is my boss, and the need to impress him still runs through my veins like something molten.

At this point, the rest of the crew has set up a few lights. Even Ava's PR person has caught up to us, lugging a glass Evian bottle for Ava, her face pinched. I have a feeling we won't get too many more photos, but at the sight of Carter, the crew scurries around and tries harder. A gaffer stops slouching; Farrah the makeup artist stops texting. Everyone's like that at the magazine's editorial offices, too, but Carter's different at the office than he is out here meeting a celebrity in the field. In the office, his features often draw together like he's solving a puzzle laid out in front of him, and there's an intensity about him that translates to everything within his orbit. The room at *Culture* is entirely different when he's in it, partly because he has a way of seeing everyone and everything, and a way of absorbing energy and deflecting it into something new. He's looser out here in the field with Ava and me, less on guard. In a twisted way it feels like flattery.

Or maybe he's just trying to make Ava happy. She's A-list these days, and that matters to Carter and to *Culture*.

Carter watches me shoot a bit, and it feels like heat on my skin. Everyone's so quiet. The balance of power on a set has always felt like a turn-on: no one would ever dare to interrupt my work; not even Carter would offer a suggestion. This shoot is mine, only mine, and I'm high on it, telling my crew how to light Ava, bending and crouching to snap photos. When we finish, I feel out of breath. Ava seems equally exhausted, but we exchange a glance and I think she's feeling pretty good. "We got great stuff," I say, smiling. Ava isn't that much older than I, and for a moment I can already see the gift she'll have sent to *Culture* for me if she likes the photos: something youthful and hip that she might not have picked out herself, but could have.

"We're done here," I say to everyone with a clap of my hands. "Awesome work." I take my camera off my neck and the energy changes: now it's all about Ava; we cheer and congratulate her and make a big fuss. I avoid looking at Carter, because I'm so worried someone will see something forbidden in my stare. Carter gets a phone call and takes it, waving a curt goodbye and hightailing it for the exit. I feel a tug of longing when he's gone, like a shiny piece of treasure has been snatched from my hand. Everyone cleans up, and when the museum looks exactly like we found it, I say goodbye to my crew and take my phone out, needing to check my messages and see if there's anything about the house. But first I see a text from Carter.

Meet me in gems and minerals.

My heart picks up speed. I love the secrecy, but I don't know how much longer we can stay hidden, and I don't want anyone at *Culture* finding out about us right now.

No man has ever said that to me before, I text back, trying to be funny, but he doesn't write a reply. He's not one for emoticons or really anything frivolous over text.

My sneakers squeak against the floor. Museum staff filters through the halls, but there's still fifteen minutes until they start allowing customers through the door. It's so very quiet. I curve right into gems and minerals and see Carter standing with his back against the glass case of a display glittering with sapphires and rubies. His dark curls are thick and mussed, and he's looking down at his phone, his expression tight.

"Hey," I say. I give a cursory glance around us, but I can only see a janitor, his head down, pushing a cart with cleaning supplies. The air smells like lemon when he passes us.

"Hey," Carter says. His shoulders drop. He's becoming increasingly easy about this, which makes me nervous. Anyone who saw us standing this close and relaxed with each other could guess at what's going on.

"Some of my crew could still be here," I say, inching back. The air-conditioning is blasting, and the patrons aren't here to warm up the air with their body heat. Whenever I'm working, I'm always warm—with nerves, excitement, movement—but now I'm just freezing, almost bordering on coming down with something. I suddenly don't want to be here having this conversation with Carter. It's not safe.

Carter's long lashes flutter, dark blue eyes hard on mine. I don't like this feeling inside of me—I haven't been in love in so many years, not since a college boyfriend who broke up with me on a grassy quad, saying, *I feel like I don't know you. No matter how long we've tried this. You still lie. Little lies. White lies, even. But they add up.*

It broke me. I never felt serious enough about anyone else, including Bradley, to call it love. But there's something about this thing with Carter that's becoming too heavy to carry.

"A break will be good for us," I say, and then I flinch, because I didn't mean to say the words out loud.

His eyebrows go up. I can't believe I've just blurted that. "I don't mean a break for *us*, for this," I say. "I just mean me leaving, couch surfing upstate, like I told you. I still want to talk if you do. I just mean I need a break from the city."

"That's not what you said," Carter says. He's no fool. He straightens up, all six foot three of him. He's another shark on exhibit in this museum. Always hungry, always in motion.

"I don't know where that came from," I say carefully. I reach out and take his hand in mine, but then I drop it and say, "Someone could see us."

"I don't care anymore," he says, and that gives me all I need to just come out and say it.

"I didn't expect to fall for you," I start, "and I'm worried it's getting too complicated. We're hiding among gemstones." I try to smile, but suddenly it all feels a little sad. "I don't expect you to do anything, or to say anything. Actually, I think I'd prefer you didn't. I need next month to clear my head."

"And then, when you're back?"

"What do *you* want with me when I'm back?" I ask gently.

"I can't stop seeing you," Carter says. "I can't stop thinking about you. I can't stop wanting this, and I don't plan to. I haven't felt like this in years."

The words reach somewhere deep inside me, and the sensation isn't pleasant. The weakest part of me, the part that's gotten in too deep, wants to hear these words, of course. But my head, my *knowing*, as my mom used to call it—that part of me is telling me to run.

"So, then what?" I ask, trying to keep my cool, trying not to show any hesitation. "What do we do?"

He rubs a hand over his jaw. "Maybe we'll spend next month apart and clear our heads. In September, life will start back up again, work will get hectic, but maybe after the time apart we'll know what to do with *this*." He gestures between us.

I nod, but things will be so changed after this month away for both of us. I know it like a warning shot in the dark, and the feeling is so unsettling that I want the conversation to be over.

"So it's goodbye for August, then?" I ask. Impatience has trailed its way into my voice. Somewhere in the last hour of photographing Ava Clark I've realized something: I'm getting myself to Waring Ridge on a vacation no matter what it takes. I'm escaping the city; I'm escaping this ill-fated romance; and I'm getting where I need to go. I can already feel how much clearer my head will be.

"It's goodbye for August," Carter says, like he wants to make sure I'm not really going anywhere too far. "In September, we'll talk. But

Anna, you don't understand what you're doing to me, honestly. Please don't doubt it." He leans forward and kisses me. It's startling. We've never kissed anywhere other than my apartment. "Carter," I say against his lips.

"I don't know what I'm going to do without you for a month." He's never spoken this plainly, and it throws me off balance. I kiss him back, but everything feels slippery, like I can't get my footing.

"You'll miss me," I say, and then I wrap my arms around his waist and arch onto my tiptoes, kissing him deeply, scared that it might be the last time. My phone buzzes, and I see a 914 number. My nerves spike, sure that it's a call about the house in Waring Ridge. Carter's arms are still around me.

"I have to take this," I say, breathless from the kiss, and from the prospect of being told the house is mine to rent. But Carter doesn't move. "It's my doctor," I lie, and he raises an eyebrow. He's probably terrified I'm pregnant or something, so I quickly add, "Nothing's wrong. Routine bloodwork." I motion my hand in a shoo, which I know is rude. "I hate goodbyes, Carter," I say. "You have to go."

"This isn't goodbye," he says, and kisses me gently. He gives me a long look, and then finally turns and walks away. I duck farther into the gem exhibit and wind my way quickly toward the back. I swipe at my phone, my voice catching when I try to say hello.

"Is this Anna?" asks a voice on the other end of my phone.

"This is she," I say, still shaky.

The first museum visitors have arrived, chatting among themselves. A woman with a fanny pack and an umbrella ushers two tanned children toward a case with diamonds. I duck behind a wall near the restroom.

"I'm calling about the house on 34 Wilmington Lane in Waring Ridge," says the voice, and electricity fires up my veins. "This is Georgia."

Georgia. "Hi!" I say, my voice going up an octave. I'm just so nervous. Please don't let her be calling to tell me I didn't get it. "I love your house," I gush before she can even say anything. "I love the checkerboard floor in the kitchen and the claw-foot tub overlooking the property. I love the way you've decorated it with a nod to the past." Am I going too far? "And the pool, the diving board."

"There isn't a diving board," Georgia says.

"Oh," I say quickly, feeling foolish. "Sorry. That must have been from another house I was looking at." My blood is moving too quickly—I can hear it in my ears. Georgia is so quiet I get nervous, and then I find myself saying something that I think she'd want to hear, something someone in her social circle might say. "I've searched so many houses online since I started looking for a summer rental . . . ," I start, and then I let my voice trail off, and in a lower, more conspiratorial tone, I say, "It's been exhausting, really. But when I saw yours, it was almost as if I felt awash with relief. I knew it was something special."

I can hear Georgia breathing. And then she says, "We used to have a diving board when I was little," and I know I've won her back over. I keep quiet so I don't ruin it. "But my dad took it down after my brother cut his head open on it," she says.

"Was he all right?" I ask. "Your brother?"

She pauses too long. "Yes. He was."

Lucky her.

"But he had to go to the hospital," she says. "And all the blood freaked everyone out, and then it was over and done for the diving board."

Her voice is more casual than I'd imagined it would be for someone like her, and I'm sure that's wrong of me to guess at what kind of adult she is, but I can't seem to help it. I imagine her there in that beautiful house, padding around the kitchen, organizing her spice rack, waiting for her offspring to come home. *Tall. Blond. Beautiful.* I can picture her, and I know I'm right. I imagine her moving through the rooms with a wistful air about her, deciding who will be lucky enough to rent her glorious castle in the woods. I imagine the tilt of her chin as she looked over the applications for the contestants. *Who wants to live my life for the month of August?*

Maybe that's not fair, and I'm sure people guess about my circumstances, too, especially when everything looks glamorous at work. I guess none of us really know each other.

"So, is it available?" I ask. I can't wait another moment—I'm too worried I'll blurt out the weird stuff in my head and ask about her hair color. "The house? Can I rent it?"

"It *is* available," Georgia says, and my entire being lifts. "I'm calling you because the last person I interviewed . . ." Her voice trails off. "Well, I called this other woman thinking, actually, that she'd be the person I'd rent the house to. But during the conversation, I suddenly felt as if I were the one being interviewed . . . something felt a little off about the whole thing."

"Yikes," I say.

"Yeah," says Georgia. "So, tell me about yourself. What drew you to Waring Ridge?"

Now I'm nervous again. I don't want to say the wrong thing. It must be nerve-racking, renting your house to a stranger, letting them inside your most personal space. All I need to do is give her the wrong vibe, like the last woman did, and then I'll be out, too. "I searched a few different towns," I say, carefully crafting the tone of my voice to sound reasonable and smart. "Bedford, Katonah, Pound Ridge, Waring Ridge, I've been looking in that general area. I live and work in New York City, and I really wanted to get far enough away that it would feel like an escape. I love New York, but it's a grind." I don't want her to ask about my job, because I really don't want her googling me and then not finding me under the name I gave her. I don't want her finding me at all. The last thing she needs to see is my TikTok, with my friends and me out at bars or whatever else we're doing. Right now, she seems confident that she's talking to a fully functional adult who can properly afford her home and not ruin it somehow.

"I know what you mean about the city," Georgia says wistfully. "My husband and I lived there for years. I miss it. My husband misses it even more than I do."

"Oh, really?" I want to ask more, but I can't figure out the right balance for this conversation. I don't want to come off like a prying weirdo, because why would anyone want someone like that in their home?

"So, we'll be out on August first," Georgia says. "Would you be willing to wait until August second? Or at least until August first sometime after three? That's the time we're allowed to get into our rental. We're just going to Southport for the month."

"Sure," I say. "And Southport is beautiful. You're lucky."

"We are," she says, but she doesn't sound so certain. "And one thing I'd like to mention before we talk business is that my brother, Max, lives on our property in a cottage about a hundred yards from the main house. It's back by the cliffs, and while he shares the driveway with you, he doesn't use the main house."

Georgia sounds really nervous, and my heart rate picks up speed.

"So I guess it's not much different than any other type of neighbor situation," she says with a chirping laugh. "We also have the Campbells down the road, and either they or my brother, Max, can help you with anything you need, but I did just want to mention it so it wasn't a surprise, and . . ."

"Oh," I say, and I can feel the subtle shift of balance in our conversation, as though Georgia thinks I'll lose interest in the house now that I know someone else lives on the property. "I sleep about ten feet from the person in the apartment next door, so I think I can handle it," I say.

Georgia laughs, and we talk a little more about business arrangements, like the money and how to get it to her. "I'll leave the Wi-Fi password in the kitchen along with some emergency numbers," she says. "You'll need to be on Wi-Fi to get cell service, it's really spotty in Waring Ridge. And I can leave you a list of fun places and things you might want to try while you're here, if that would be helpful."

"I'd like that," I say.

"You'll have the pool, of course. But the town itself has a lovely library and coffee shops, a vegan bakery . . ."

A brick theater; a home goods shop; a rustic, upscale restaurant called the Inn; a small art gallery that doesn't carry photography . . .

I know all these things. Of course, I don't say so. I just try to sound gracious. "I'm really excited," I say, squishing against the museum's eggshell wall to avoid four kids laughing at something on one of their phones. "Thank you so much for this."

"Thank *you*," Georgia says elegantly. "I'm happy you'll be the one enjoying the house." Her mood sounds like it's lifted a notch or two since we started talking. "Anything else you think of, feel free to text or call."

"Thanks," I say. "I will."

We get off the call and my legs are shaking. I feel like a month in Waring Ridge could really do it; it could be the thing that helps me process Sam's death and move forward. And then I could feel like myself again, and then maybe I could help my dad, or just somehow try to make things a little bit less painful.

TWELVE

Georgia. Waring Ridge, New York.

A few days later I still can't believe it. Anna has already wired the money into my account, and it's official: we're spending August in Southport. Tom and I are in our bedroom packing, and the whole thing still feels surreal. Tom's been skittish, almost like he's suddenly getting cold feet about Southport, which doesn't make much sense, because usually he's the one who loves excitement and change. He's avoiding my glance, bending to grab swim trunks from a pale wooden dresser. I used to love early weekday mornings with Tom. He's always so alert in the early-morning hours, so ready for the day to begin. In the city we'd wake up and trek to the bagel shop down the block and get hazelnut coffees, and then we'd walk back to our apartment holding hands. Tom would sit at a tiny table in our apartment and drink his coffee and read the paper. And even with everything that's happened, having Millie, moving to the suburbs, feeling the marriage age as we do—I still love being alone with him in our room, carefully sidestepping each other as we dart in and out of our closet, rummaging through drawers. It's like a dance only we know how to do, a middle space between moods. We're not stopping to kiss and paw at each other like we used to when we first got together, but it's not totally lost, either. There's still something that delicately hums between us.

"Was that Millie?" Tom asks, cocking an ear for a sound I didn't hear.

"I don't think so." We both listen, but there's nothing. "She'll probably sleep in after last night," I say softly. Millie comes into our room at least five or six times per week in the dead of night after one of her nightmares, drenched in sweat. Last night I eventually got her back into her own bed, but sometimes I can't.

Sunlight filters through the window and splashes the light oak floors. Tom's hand hovers over a pair of boxer briefs, and he asks, "Do you think you should be getting her to bed earlier?" He picks up a stack of underwear and a diving watch I haven't seen him use in ages. He shoves it in the bag by his feet, turns to face me.

"During summer break?" I ask. What an odd thing to say. He almost never has feedback on anything I'm doing with Millie. The one area of my life in which I know Tom admires me is as Millie's mom. It's not that he explicitly tells me he's disappointed in me as a writer or anything like that, but how could he not be? He was so proud when that short story came out in the *New Yorker* all those years ago. He sent it to everyone, and he kept taking me out for celebratory dinners and toasting to it—we must have celebrated that story's publication a dozen times. And even though he knew it had taken me years to write, much longer than it should take anyone to write short fiction, he kept saying things like *You have it, Georgia. Your writing is exquisite. Everyone thinks so. You're going to be a huge novelist, I can feel it. And you know I have a sixth sense about these kinds of things.*

Tom does have a sixth sense about those kinds of things. But I suppose everyone's wrong sometimes.

"It just seems like the nightmares are nearly every night," Tom says. "And she never had them in New York."

It twists like a knife, because he's right. Millie never had the moods before we came to this house, never the nightmares. How can I argue with him?

"So what should we do?" I ask. "Move back to the city?"

"Maybe," Tom says.

Tears spring to my eyes. I'll do anything for Millie, I really will. But how am I supposed to know if it was the move that was bad for her, or if this is all just normal adolescent stuff?

Tom's eyes meet mine. Have I done the wrong thing by bringing us all here? Tom hasn't been the same since we moved here last year, and certainly neither has Millie. And I wouldn't say I'm exactly thriving, either. I have a steady group of friends who grew up here, plus the friends I've made working at Millie's school and joining the library board, but not everything about this move has felt right. I haven't been able to write here, for one thing. And then there's Max, living on the property, which helps nothing in my marriage, despite how much I love Max. And I'm so focused on Millie and Tom's adjustment that I can't seem to truly enjoy it. Last week I tried to take Tom to a barbecue that Millie's friend's parents were hosting, and he hung out on the fringe of the party, barely interacting with the other dads, even though all of them were trying to talk to him. He keeps telling me he can't stand to meet yet another suburban dad who loves to golf at the country club, and it comes off as such reverse snobbery I don't know what to make of it. He's always been the kind of person who cares more about achievements than memberships, and I love that about him, but we have to try to make a life here.

"Maybe Southport will be a reset," I say. "It's what I want for us, it's part of why I was so eager to do it." I want to talk about all of this with Tom, about the distance and loneliness I've felt between us ever since we came here, but he looks away from me and then switches the subject.

"You're absolutely sure they have a washing machine?" he asks, going back to packing, first his oxford shirts and a beloved pair of corduroy shorts we bought in Barcelona, and then a thick, white knotted bracelet that Millie made him that he somehow pulls off, especially when we're on vacation and he's tan. He's always been so surprising to me, the way he moves through the world: intense, but also steadily in love with Millie and me, and seemingly in love with our life together, right up until we came here. I know he never would have left the city. Because even though Waring Ridge is the idyllic countryside and not overly suburban, it's still too suburban for Tom. I don't think he ever saw me joining a garden club or driving a tennis carpool for Millie and her friends. But wasn't that his own fault, not to imagine something that seemed so obviously in our future?

The house itself gives him pause, which makes it even worse. He's never been at ease with the history of everything that happened here, with Eliza and my mother dying so tragically. Once Tom told me that if any house had a right to be haunted, it was this one. He said it in passing, so cavalierly, like laughing and spinning in a circle with a knife. It was the only thing he's ever said to me that made me stop speaking to him. It took days before I could look him in the eye again.

"Tom, please," I say now, trying not to let exasperation leak into my voice. "Of course it has a washing machine." I shove deodorant into my suitcase and then turn to face him. "We studied every photo of the house together. What's with you right now? Have you changed your mind?"

He could choose to be unfair if he wanted to; he could say something like *Southport was always something* you *wanted, not me.* I'm sure he would have preferred we did a month in New York City, if anything.

"I want to go," he says. That can't be entirely true, but maybe these little moments of someone taking the higher road are one of the reasons marriages work. He sits down, and our bed gives a sharp *creak.* "It'll be a good month," he says. "And it'll be good for Millie, that's for sure. A change of pace before going back to school will be good for her."

"It's hard to believe she'll be in seventh grade," I say.

A small smile lands on Tom's face. "Sit, Georgie," he says gently. I sit next to him on our bed, the sheets still strewn about like a tiny hurricane. "I love you," he says. And then he takes my hand like a teenager. His palm is warm. It always is. "And you're a good mother."

"And a good wife?" I ask with a smile. I think that I am, but it wouldn't hurt to hear him say it.

"And a very good wife," he says, his voice sliding lower, kissing me gently on the collarbone. But then we hear footsteps, and I stand quickly, smoothing my bulky cardigan.

"Millie?" I call, stepping through my doorway onto the upstairs landing. This house is filled with nooks and hideaways, and upstairs there isn't one long hallway, it's more like a square landing with four bedrooms scattered haphazardly, all different sizes. A tiny side table with an antique compass and books sits next to a chair I had reupholstered when we moved in. The staircase is treacherous, an incline so steep we had to gate it every time we visited my dad until Millie was at least four. She appears now, clutching the porcelain doll with the crinoline blue dress in whose pockets I used to hide my stash of Dilaudid. The doll's unearthly blue eyes stare at me. She's missing nearly all of her top lashes because Max and I used to pull them out with tweezers, but her bottom row of lashes are still painted onto her peachy skin. I shiver to remember the years I'd pull pills out of her pockets, and the way it felt to get high and sit on the roof with the wind in my face, like nothing could ever touch me.

After Eliza fell from the roof and died, Max told the cops that Eliza had gone out to the roof to retrieve my doll. Which they probably would have figured out anyway, because the doll was lying beside her body on the patio. I never asked Eliza to go get my doll, the cops just assumed I did, so I sort of played along. What I never told the cops was that Eliza had gone out there to get my doll because she realized I was stashing drugs there. And this is the reason I've never been able to stop blaming myself for her death, even though none of it makes sense. My mom, Max, Eliza, and I were out on the roof all the time—it had such a beautiful view of the cliffs. On that part of the house, the roof was completely flat. And the doll wasn't even on the edge of the roof. For a while I kept the doll out in plain sight in my bedroom so no one would suspect I kept the drugs hidden there, but eventually I was going out to the roof so often I just left her in my hiding spot on the roof. It was easier that way, and I didn't want Eliza to get suspicious if she saw me carting a doll around the house. I tucked her away inside a stout brick chimney so she wouldn't get wet, but the chimney was at least ten feet away from the edge. It just doesn't make sense that Eliza would have found the doll, and then walked up to the edge of the roof and fallen off. But I'm absolutely sure that the doll is the reason why Eliza went out there, because after she died, I read her journal, which I know was wrong of me, but I was missing her and desperate. In the journal, she wrote about my drug use, and that she knew the doll was my hiding spot. She wrote about her plans to confiscate the pills and take them to a professional so that they'd know exactly what I was using and what kind of help I should be getting. And because I was sixteen and terrified, and never wanted the police to know I was using and certainly never wanted my drugs taken away, I hid Eliza's journal in my things. I still have it, hidden somewhere Tom and Millie could never find it.

Millie follows me into my bedroom, carrying the doll, making me feel a little sick just like I do every time I see it. The strange thing is how the doll's porcelain face never broke when Eliza fell. Eliza's body must have cushioned her fall.

Thinking about it makes me want to vomit.

Millie found the doll in a closet when we moved back here and took a liking to it, and I didn't have the heart to tell her it bothered me.

She sits on the bed, still sleepy. Her honey-blond hair is sticking out at impossible angles, and her skin is pale and flushed high on her cheeks. She's wearing an old nightgown of mine that I used to wear at her age, and when I see her in it, it's like seeing an apparition of myself, pacing the house, looking for my mother in the middle of the night. Sometimes I'd find my mom having sneaked out the window of this very bedroom onto the gray shingled roof, drinking from a wine bottle. Our bedroom is all angles, and in the middle of one of the navy-wallpapered walls sits a bow window that leads out to the roof. Whenever I'd find it open, I'd crawl out there and usually find my mother drinking. Sometimes Eliza was already out there, trying to coax my mom back inside, worried she was getting too tipsy and could fall to her death. The irony of that always slays me; that Eliza would be the one to eventually fall feels so cruel after the years of delicate care she gave my mom. Sometimes Eliza and my mom would sit together on the flat expanse of the roof and gaze onto the pool and the cliffs, and I'd watch them from inside my mom's room, trying to eavesdrop on their conversations. The bow window onto the roof had a light-green cushioned bench, and I'd sit there and listen, overhearing tiny snippets like small birds twittering, some of it lost on the wind but much of it reaching my ears.

It's hard, you know, my mother would say. She always started with a line like that when she was drinking early and feeling tipsy. *And you know he judges me, he wants to send me away again, Eliza.* These were the kinds of things she said about my father.

And then Eliza would say something like *He wants you to be well, that's all he wants, because he loves you, we all love you, and you're going to be okay,* the Irish lilt in her voice making everything sound like a poem, something beautiful but too dangerous to believe.

Sometimes Max joined me at the window. He was skinny and knobby kneed in that way of little boys, and my mom used to say that whenever we stood next to each other, his dark-brown eyes made my blue ones look even paler. It was like that for our personalities, too. Max could be difficult when we were little—prone to striking out at her during wild tantrums and spinning out of control without much warning—and all of it, in sharp contrast to the people-pleasing child I was, made me come off as angelic in my mother's eyes. She worried about Max all the time, saying things like *I knew a child like this once,* and then Eliza would have to calm her down and assure her it was normal for children to act out. If only my mom could have seen what became of me after her death: the substance abuse, the way I treated my family, even Eliza—especially Eliza—then maybe she would have been less worried about Max and more worried about my impending fall from grace.

In these moments of eavesdropping at the window, I always sided with my mom when she talked about my dad wanting to send her away, because the thought of losing her to yet another rehab was more than I could bear. When I became an adult, of course I knew my father was right to try to get her help, but she'd already tried rehab three times by the time I was ten, and the months she was away from Max and me were agony.

After my mom passed out and died in her bathroom when I was twelve, it was obvious that my mom had needed way more help than we could ever have given her at home. The difference between Max and me is that I eavesdropped on those conversations and knew my dad was trying to get help for her. I've asked my brother, and he doesn't remember my dad saying anything like that. Our memories of our childhood diverge like a path in the woods at too many of the important moments. Whenever I try to remind Max that our dad was trying, Max just says he wasn't trying hard enough.

And then we lost Eliza four years later, and even though everyone assumed that Eliza lost her balance on the roof when she went to retrieve my doll, sometimes I dream horrible, unspeakable things about what happened on that roof. My father was jealous of Eliza and my mom's relationship, how close they were, how easy it was for them. And though my mom had died four years earlier, my dad never really let go of his one-sided rivalry for my mother's attention. There was a tightness between Eliza and my dad, no matter how much he depended on her to help raise us in the aftermath of my mother's death. Eliza was saving us, really. And my dad was never cruel to her, but there was tension between them every time they were in a room together. If I didn't know better, I'd have thought it was romantic. And in my dreams sometimes I see my dad going after Eliza on the roof. I can't see my body when I dream, but it feels like I'm pressed hard against the window; I can feel the cold pane of glass even though I can never see my skin. And then I'm forced to watch as my dad places two hands on Eliza and shoves her off the roof. And every time, the ensuing crack is what wakes me up.

Those nightmares nearly kill me.

I try to remind myself that they're not real, that my dad wasn't even home when Eliza died. But I can't remember any of it well enough, which I'm sure is mostly because of the pills I was on. I want to remember that afternoon so I can reassure myself that Eliza was alone on the roof and simply slipped, but it's as though a part of my brain has entirely shut down the memory. It's like a curtain closing over the stage actors, and it feels eternal, as though I'll never get the true memory of that afternoon back, even though I know it would reassure me. There are so many things my drug use robbed me of, and my family, too, and that afternoon is one of them.

"Sweetie, we should finish packing you for Southport," I say to Millie, sitting on the bed beside her. I wrap her in a hug, feeling her tiny ribs inside my embrace, trying to ground myself in real life, in what's really happening here, inside this bedroom. It's the best strategy I have for trying to forget.

THIRTEEN

Anna. Waring Ridge, New York.

As the driver sweeps through Waring Ridge and pulls into the long driveway at 34 Wilmington Lane, I can hardly catch my breath. The house is more beautiful than any photo could ever be, standing proudly at the top of a hill in bright white paint, black shutters, a gray shingled roof, and an inky front door that glistens in the sunlight. It's a proper colonial with no front porch, but there's a screened-in porch visible on the left and a covered portico off to the right. Roses climb a trellis that leads to the backyard, and the hydrangeas lining the front of the house seem even bigger than they did in the photos. The evergreens and fully mature trees give it a supreme air of privacy. The driver stops at the top of the driveway, and when I thank him, my voice is hard with emotion. His face looks drawn and apprehensive as he spies me standing there on the driveway, like maybe he's made a mistake, and this is the wrong address, and something in his rheumy eyes sends goose bumps over my skin. I force a smile and wave at him, signaling that all's well and he should go. And he does. He retreats over the driveway to the main road, and I watch as he slips into the dense landscape. On the way here we passed woods, meandering streams, purposefully wild gardens, ponds, and wetlands. Most of the properties are cordoned from each other by evergreens and stone walls.

The lawns aren't perfectly manicured—it's not the style of the town; most of the people who live here have made their exorbitantly expensive homes look as quaint as possible.

I grind pebbles with my heels as I turn to take in the house. It's hard to believe I'm really here, standing somewhere so chillingly beautiful, so elegant and complex. Like an onion with layers to peel back, rooms to explore, things to feel, a town to infiltrate, photographs to take, memories to make. All the things. The house sits up straighter than any house I've ever seen, like it's the kind of house that has witnessed things and survived and will stay standing long after Georgia and her family are dead. Not that I'd ever say something that morbid to Georgia. And I do plan to text her—we've had quite a friendly exchange going in the few days since our phone call. There's a rolling grassy hill in front of the house and it makes me think of Sam and the way he used to love to roll down anything hilly when we were little. We'd be playing a game, and then out of nowhere he'd drop to the earth and cross his arms over his chest and let gravity take over. It brings tears to my eyes to think about him, especially now, when I'm here at this house getting to experience an adventure. He won't have any more adventures, and something about that desperate truth steels me. It pulls me from the moment in which I was trying to lose myself.

Georgia's house is a little more perfect than most of the others I've seen in Waring Ridge; it's beautifully maintained, the lawn and gardens are lush and well taken care of. You can tell by looking at the house that Georgia is not the kind of person who would want anything to look like it was falling apart, which doesn't really surprise me. Why would she? Many adults seem to believe that the perfect facade is an important thing to show the world. I should know; I spend my days photographing extravagantly beautiful human beings, all with imperfections they think are best kept hidden. One of the things I like so much about Carter is that he lays it all out for me. He's never lied to me. We've had difficult conversations, but I'm pretty sure he's always told me the truth. Of course, there are things I've kept from him. Dark things that would blow his mind wide open and tear the seams. He texted me to say he wanted to come up and meet me this month, but I wrote him back reminding him we said we needed space to see where we wanted to go next. He must know being with me is dangerous in some way, between our work together and the age difference, and the list goes on, of course, but it's like sometimes he forgets. I don't.

On Georgia's front steps is a single potted geranium. I pick it up and retrieve the small gold key she left me, but I find my hand shaking when I go to enter the house. Something doesn't feel right, almost like I can't bring myself to enter. I exhale. *It's just anxiety,* I tell myself. *I'm just nervous.* But it feels like a physical force, a pressure in my chest. I'm sweating even though it's a cool summer morning—I can feel it trailing along my spine. I push the key into the lock and twist, and the second the door opens and I step inside, the feeling passes.

The foyer is dim and cool. The scent of lemon and lilies wafts through the air, and I set down my bags on the checkerboard floor and gaze about. There's a black iron side table with a ceramic lion and a shellacked green vase filled with fresh flowers. A brown bench sits off to the side with an ikat-print cushion. The most beautiful staircase I've ever seen arcs up the side of the house like a question mark, with an ebony railing and sisal carpet on the stairs. I kick off my sneakers and move down the hall into the kitchen. The kitchen is beautifully renovated, all crisp and sparkling white cabinets and marble countertops, and big enough to fit a pale wooden table with navy leather chairs. A bowl of lemons and oranges rests on the center of the island.

My legs are still a little jellylike as I move to the cabinets and open a couple to find a drinking glass. Georgia has rows of mason jars, and I fill one at the massive Sub-Zero fridge.

I move to the table and sit on a leather chair. The cold water slides down my throat, over the hard lump I've felt ever since I left the city this morning. I know deep in my bones that coming here was the right choice, that it's exactly what I need. I look around me, at the morning light hitting the bright white marble and making it glow. I want to go upstairs, but when I think about going up there, I get that same feeling again. It's a heavy, anxious feeling in my heart, like a warning. But it's fleeting, too, and in a few more moments I feel all right.

I stand on shaking legs, thinking maybe I'll go upstairs and rest.

I make my way toward the staircase. I steady myself on the railing and start to climb.

FOURTEEN

Georgia. Southport, Connecticut.

We wake on our first morning in the Southport beach house and the thing that strikes me is that Millie didn't have a nightmare. Or at least, she never once cried out or came to our bed.

I turn instinctively toward the window that looks out onto the ocean, and the view is as breathtaking as it was yesterday. From this position, lying in the bed, I can only see the bright blue sea. I exhale and think about how it's as wonderful as I thought it would be. I can breathe easier, as though someone stopped stepping on my chest.

The bedroom, along with most of the house, is outfitted in crisp whites and blues, much of the design from Serena & Lily. If the decorating is a little short on imagination, it's still very beautiful. And the sparse interior design lets your eyes flick to the windows, where the real showstopping scene unfolds. Along the back of the house, all the windows look onto the water. The front windows look onto a small front lawn and the main road. The drive through Southport was scenic, filled with charming and picturesque homes. In Waring Ridge, we can barely see our neighbors, but here on the beach the houses are closer together and the vibe is entirely different, more of a village feel with sidewalks and white picket fences. We're only thirty minutes away from Waring

Ridge, but it feels like a true vacation, like being somewhere coastal and New England instead of Waring Ridge's woodsy, secluded vibe. (Which, don't get me wrong, I love. But the contrast is so nice.) In a few hours I'm thinking Tom, Millie, and I can walk downtown for breakfast and explore the art galleries and antique shops we passed on the drive in.

I roll over to face Tom. His back is to me, and I can tell by the way he's breathing that he's still asleep. He's wearing a thin gray T-shirt, and when I shift a little closer, he turns sleepily. "Hey," he says.

"Did you sleep well?" I ask.

"I did." He rubs a big hand over his eyes. "Millie never came in."

A pit forms in my stomach. "She was exhausted last night." Why can't I just admit the strangeness of her sleeping through the night without one of her nightmares for the first time we've slept away from our house?

Unfortunately, I wasn't so lucky. Last night I dreamt I was up in my mother's bedroom, playing with my porcelain doll, and then I heard something out on the roof where my mother used to sit and drink. I went to the window and peered outside, but instead of my mother I saw my brother and my dad, and they were arguing. And then Eliza emerged from the shadows, and my brother cried, *You don't even see what's coming for you,* his face contorted with emotion for her. Every time I dream about Eliza, I wake up so panicked I can barely breathe.

"Maybe Millie feels safer in this house," Tom says.

Tears prick my eyes, and Tom edges closer to me in the bed. For a second, I think he's going to pull me into his arms, but he doesn't. The inches between us feel like kindling, like something dormant about to spark and burn.

"Maybe she's afraid of the woods, or something else we don't realize," Tom says. "The setting here is different, there are so many more people and houses around. It's much less remote."

"Maybe," I say, my voice soft.

Millie has always been a seer of things. She's been prescient since she was a small child. When she has her nightmares, she'll sob in my arms, but she doesn't usually tell me what they're about, and I'm too scared to ask her. I'm not sure I'd really want to know.

***

At breakfast, Tom, Millie, and I are seated around a circular oak table in a kitchen with bright white cabinets, pale wooden shelves, and a light blue shimmery backsplash beneath a wide silver hood. Stylish containers hold wooden spoons and spatulas, and a ceramic jar that says *COOKIES* sits next to the aqua toaster. A vase of purple wildflowers rests in the center of the kitchen table along with a plate of pancakes Tom made. It smells like maple syrup and ocean air, and I feel choked up, like I might let loose a flood of tears. "I love you guys," I say softly, spearing a pancake. Tom looks up from the *New York Times*. "We love you, too," he says. And then he goes back to reading an article about a foreign war. And how can I compete with that, really?

"Mom, pass the butter?" says Millie. "And I definitely love you, too." She smirks. "You guys should go on a romantic walk," she says while she chews pancakes.

"We're not going to leave you alone in the house," I say. To Tom, I say, "Pass the creamer, please."

"Why not?" asks Millie. "I'm twelve."

This is what gets Tom to look up from his paper. "Really, Mills?" he asks.

"Yeah. I think I'm ready."

Tom passes me the carton of cream and we exchange a glance. Millie has never been okay with us leaving her alone, even though all her peers stay by themselves, and even though Max is often close by in his cottage. Some of Millie's friends even babysit their younger siblings. "What's so different about this house?" I ask.

"Leave it alone, Georgia," Tom snaps. "If Millie feels ready, we should go. It'll give her good practice."

"Do you even have your watch charged?" I ask Millie. "I don't know if there's a home phone here . . ."

"I don't," she says, "but I remembered my charger and I'll plug it in."

"Okay, but this seems hasty," I say. "We don't even really know where we are."

"Nine-one-one works wherever you are, Mom," Millie says.

"Okay, smarty pants," I say. "And what's the address you plan to give them if there's an emergency?"

Millie frowns. "You got me," she says, backing down a little, which plunges me into a cold pool of guilt. Why am I trying to talk her out of something she wants to do, something that even I want her to do? Maybe she'll love it, and then continue to do it when we're back in Waring Ridge. It always seems silly to me that she drops her homework and comes along on every mind-numbingly boring errand I have to run just because she's too scared to be alone.

"Millie, I'm sorry," I say. "You're definitely old enough to know when you're ready to stay alone."

Tom stands up and strides to the kitchen island. He scrawls something onto a slip of paper. "And now you have the address," he says, handing it to Millie. "Problem solved. Put it in your pocket."

They're both triumphant as Tom kisses Millie's cheeks. There's a pink flush to Millie's face, and she looks so grown up I have the desire to cradle her in my arms like when she was little. I settle for a hug. "Have fun," she says into my ear, smelling like her strawberry shampoo.

Tom holds the patio door open for me to pass. There's a rocky path through a trellis, and then we're on the beach. It's only seven thirty, not too hot or sunny. Perfect, really. Tom walks a step ahead of me until he gets to the water's edge. And then he kicks off his shoes. "Wild to be so lucky that the ocean's your backyard," he says. "Don't you think?"

I nod. But I also think about how I can't really imagine raising a child directly on the beach. What would the rules be about swimming? I don't say any of this out loud. I'm trying to be more relaxed in Southport, a more palatable version of myself for Tom.

"Maybe when we're older we could afford a cottage somewhere like this," I say.

"But you always say you want to move somewhere that's warm in the winter," Tom says, an edge in his voice. "It's got to be frigid here on the water come January."

Tom was raised in DC, the child of two professors at Georgetown. I don't think he can really picture himself moving too far from a big city—an hour out into Waring Ridge is nearly killing him—and I wonder what will happen when we're at the age when most people start seeking warmth for their bones. Charleston? Miami? LA?

I shrug. "I don't know. We have a while to think about it."

We start walking along the surf, the water washing in and out at our feet. Maybe it's the gentle rhythm of it all that gives me the guts to ask what I do.

"Do you want to move back to the city, Tom?"

I'm so afraid of the answer that I start to walk a little faster. Tom picks up the pace, too. Walking and driving are always the best times to talk to him. He does better when he's looking straight ahead and doesn't have to hold my gaze.

"I don't know," he says, a gentle shake of his head. He looks down at the wet sand passing beneath our feet. To the left of us is the expansive sea; to the right is fifty yards of beach serving as a front yard to exquisite waterfront homes, mostly shingle-style, with some bungalows and even a few Victorians with wraparound porches. "I just haven't felt like myself since we moved there," he says. "You know how much I love the city."

"I do."

"And it's not just that I love the city, it's that I love *us* in the city. I love the energy between us there, how we were so swept up in it. I love *you* in the city. I loved seeing you with your to-go coffee and heading out to yoga with your hair up, and even how you used to try to write in bookstores."

Try to write. I don't even bother getting offended by it, because the other things he's saying are so illuminating.

"I loved being in our apartment and the view down to Mercer Street," he says, "where everyone was rushing along the sidewalk, because it felt like we were really doing it, like we'd made it somehow, having an apartment in SoHo like we'd always dreamt about. I liked dinners out with you and Millie, and I liked reading the paper by the window and drinking coffee. And mostly? The thing I liked most of all was how happy our daughter seemed."

This makes me start to cry, the sound of it mercifully drowned out by a pair of unruly seagulls squawking near a pile of shells.

Tom stops walking. He turns to face me. "I'm worried that we raised a precocious city child, and now she's a fish out of water, and all of the things we thought were special about her in the city are just quirks here, and we're losing her to these nightmares and increased anxiety."

"But she doesn't seem that anxious day to day, at tennis, or with her friends. I see her interacting socially more than you do."

Tom shrugs. "You know how anxiety is. People can hide it well. Millie hides it well. But we both know she's different alone in the house with us than she ever was in the city. She barely leaves the room you're in, Georgia."

I start crying so hard that my shoulders shake. Tom wraps his arms around me, squeezing me against him.

"There are these poems she's started writing," I say into his T-shirt. He pulls away and looks me in the eye. The sun burns brightly behind him, forming a white-hot halo around his head.

"What kind of poems?"

I'm squinting to hold his gaze, his face shadowed, his eyes hard on mine.

"Dark stuff. She writes them before she goes to sleep. They're not violent or anything explicit, but they're usually about someone witnessing a death or an accident."

"*What?*" Tom growls. "Why haven't you told me about this?"

"Well, at first I thought she was just a writer like my mom and me," I say, my words high and defensive. It takes a lot for me to call myself a writer these days.

"Did she ask you not to tell me?"

"No," I say. "She didn't." I shift my weight on the sand, suddenly feeling like my feet are burning even though they aren't.

"Then why would you keep it from me?" he asks.

I don't have an answer. At least not one I want to share. But he's staring so hard I finally blurt it. "Because you already think there's something wrong with the house. I think you honest-to-God think it's haunted, and I worried the poems would be just another reason you'd hate it there."

His blue eyes are on fire. "So you kept something from me about my daughter? Haven't we been in this together long enough now not to do that?"

I know he's right. "I'm sorry," I say, and I really am.

We're still just standing there. The sun is getting warmer by the minute, and suddenly I'm desperate to retreat to Millie and the shade of the house. But Tom is staring hard at me, and I know what he wants me to say.

Let's move. Let's go back to the city. We'll sell the house.

Why can't I get myself to form those words?

Tom and I don't say much more as we walk back along the beach and up the path to our rental. When we get to the house, Tom swings open the screen door and barely holds it open for me. I slip through, the back of the door scraping my heel. I let out a little cry of pain, which Tom either doesn't hear or ignores.

Millie isn't in the kitchen.

"Millie?" Tom calls out.

Nothing.

"Mills!" he yells louder.

My heart beats a little faster when she doesn't answer. I do a quick search of the living room and dining room, but she's not there. I wind up the staircase, my quads burning from the beach walk and the sprint up the steps. I fling open the door to Tom's and my bedroom, but it's empty, and she's not in her room, either. My heart pounds. "Millie!"

"Mom?" I hear her call, and I follow the sound into a tiny room filled with bookshelves.

"Tom, she's up here!" I shout back over my shoulder.

Millie's leaning against a fluffy white beanbag chair, her hand poised with a drawing pencil over a sketch pad. She yanks out her AirPods. "You okay?" she asks me.

"I'm fine." I don't mention the bile in my throat. "I just didn't know where you were, and I was calling your name, and you didn't answer . . ."

"Sorry," she says, gesturing to her AirPods. "I was listening to music."

Tom is in the doorway now. "Millie," he says, out of breath. It makes me feel better to see that he's shaken, too.

"You're drawing?" he asks.

Millie nods. "Yeah, I packed my pencils. I thought vacation would be a good time to start up again."

Tom smiles. He's always loved her artistic side. She's really quite talented, and I know I'm her mom, so of course I think that, but so did her teachers in the city.

Millie stays sitting on the beanbag, but she flips the book toward us. I nearly faint at the image she's created.

"Wow, Millie," says Tom, but he must recognize the likeness of the drawing, because suddenly he looks a little unsteady.

I don't even understand how it's possible. The drawing looks exactly like Eliza, but I've never shown Millie a photo of her before, and I haven't had pictures of Eliza displayed anywhere we've lived, because passing by them would be too painful. It's hard enough to look at the ones of my mother, but I feel like I'm required to display those photos so that Millie can see her history and who she comes from.

I can't bring myself to say anything about the likeness. Finally, Tom says, "What a gorgeous drawing. She looks just like your mother's old nanny, is that what you were going for?"

Millie's eyebrows go up. "Really?" she asks. She reexamines the sketch and looks at it from another angle. "She does? Sorry, Mom. I hope that doesn't upset you."

Millie knows that Eliza died four years after my mom did, and that it felt like an exceptional and devastating thing to lose them both, but she has no idea that Eliza fell from the roof and died on the property. I think Millie just assumed Eliza was old and died of natural causes, but Eliza was only thirty-seven at the time.

"The drawing is beautiful, Millie. Have I ever shown you a photo of her?" I ask. Surely I must have at some point, or maybe Millie stumbled upon one.

Millie won't meet our stares. She's suddenly consumed with staring at her work. She won't take her eyes off it.

"It looks just like Eliza," Tom says, pushing. "Are you sure you haven't seen a photo?"

"I can't believe *this* is Eliza," Millie says.

"Well, it looks like her," I say quickly. "But maybe you were drawing someone else, like a fictional made-up character, and it just happened to be influenced by Eliza because you once saw a photo of her somewhere, maybe in one of my old drawers, or something like that."

Millie can't stop looking at the picture. Tom shifts uneasily. It's so awkward to watch her consumed like this, and then finally she puts the drawing down and looks up at us, saying softly, "It's just so strange. This is a drawing of the woman I see in all my nightmares."

FIFTEEN

Anna. Waring Ridge, New York.

Halfway up the staircase, I feel so sick that I have to sit down again. I'm in cutoffs and a Lakers T-shirt, and the carpet is scratchy against my bare legs and feet. My palms are drenched with sweat. I try to breathe, but I feel like I'm choking. I lean back against the staircase, my eyes gazing up to the light blue shiplap ceiling of the second floor. Everything feels wet and fluid, like I'm going to melt into the staircase and be forgotten forever.

I lift my head a few inches, and through the glass panes along the side of the door I see a red pickup truck whiz over the driveway past the front of the house. Is someone coming here? I try to hold this thought in my head, but I feel so dizzy that I have to lie my head back down against the stairs. I feel like I'm about to pass out, and I'm scared I'll roll down the stairs and split my head open.

Behind my eyes I see a glimpse of my mom. She always comes to me when I'm the most panicked: I can hear her voice whispering all the things she always taught me: *Breathe, Anna. Focus on your surroundings, on the here and now. Look. Listen. Stay in the moment. See what's really there.* I open my eyes to glimpse the photos lining the side of the staircase, each one showcasing Georgia's daughter, Millie, who she told me about on our last phone call. Even when I was as young as Georgia's daughter is now, I was always so concerned about the future. Maybe I had a right to be.

Ding dong.

I don't move. I don't even think I can. But then there's a hard, insistent knock on the front door, followed by another ring of the doorbell.

I try to raise my shoulders up a few inches and prop myself on my elbows. Another knock.

"Just a minute!" I call, the words like marbles at the back of my throat. I get myself into a seated position and take a few steps down the stairs on my butt. At the bottom of the staircase, I use the railing to hoist myself upright.

There we go.

I'm all right—I'm standing. I walk a few unsteady steps to the door and swing it open, and standing in front of me is a very beautiful man with deep, dark eyes, inky hair that's a mess, broken-in Levi's, and a vintage navy-blue Van Halen concert T-shirt. He looks startled to see me there, and his eyes hold mine, widening just a little. It makes me nervous. And then he says, "Hi!" in a voice that comes off a little too friendly for the circumstances.

"Hi," I say.

"Uh, I'm Max, Georgia's brother. I'm staying right over there, in the cottage." He gestures toward the side of the house. "If you need anything, just come knocking, I guess."

He's got a city vibe to him. Maybe LA. Friendliness with an edge. A part of me wants the conversation to be over because I feel so overwhelmed in this house, but the sight of him standing there in the open doorway, plus the fresh air and sunlight, keeps me anchored to the moment. "Thanks, Max," I say.

"You're up from the city," he says, like a fact and not a question. "My sister told me." He's got a wide smile on his face, a dimple on his left cheek. His lashes are thick, and his lips are a pretty scarlet. Mouths are important to me. I always think about them when I photograph. People love the eyes, and I do, too, but the mouth holds secrets.

Sometimes when I shoot, I can see an emotion that wants to come out, a truth that wants to be spoken. When I can see someone's mouth tense, it's almost like they're trying to put up a wall between us, or at the very least, conceal their truth. And it's my job to set it free, if not verbally, then emotionally.

"I am," I say, but it comes out too short and clipped.

"Oh, sweet," says Max. Definitely LA.

He seems like he doesn't want to leave yet, and I'm a sucker for not being rude and shutting doors in people's faces. You never know what someone else needs in a moment, and if you can give someone a second of kindness, then why wouldn't you?

"Georgia told me this is the house you grew up in," I say.

"Yup," he says, his skin paling. He breaks my glance and looks up to the second story windows. "This is the house," he says obscurely.

"Cool," I say. "I mean, it's cool you kept it in your family. It's so meaningful, isn't it? To be able to visit the house you grew up in anytime you want?"

He shrugs his broad shoulders. He's a little over six feet tall, but he comes off as smaller than that. There's a gentleness to him.

"There are positives and negatives to moving back to your hometown, just like anything else, I guess," he says.

"Where'd you move from?"

"LA."

I smile.

"What?" he asks.

"I figured," I say, and he grins.

"Well, that's where I was most recently," he says. "But I'm usually in New York City. Maybe I was just mentioning LA first to impress you."

"I'm impressed," I say, and we both laugh.

He runs a hand through his inky hair, somehow making it even messier.

"Okay, well," he says. "I should go."

"Thanks for coming by," I say. "Kind of you."

He smiles and gives me a wave before turning and walking along the driveway to the side of the house and then disappearing from sight.

I shut the door and step farther back inside the foyer. Through a window at the side of the house, I see Max walking across the yard, his handsome face rising over the hydrangeas. He's gazing darkly at the ground, like his mind is heavy with something he can't figure out.

I turn back and head up the stairs, and this time I make it to the second-floor landing. This time there's no fear, no shaking legs, no sweat on my palms, no hesitation at all. I fling open the door to the primary bedroom. The bed is neatly made with pillows fluffed to perfection, Georgia-style. God forbid we don't have a flawless facade in this home.

I make my way across the white rug, the wool scratchy beneath my feet.

At the window is a bench. Books are stacked on it, and I shove them to the floor and listen to the crash they make against the wood. I'm not exactly planning to read and relax on this vacation.

I peer out the window. So many times during this past year I imagined what the view might look like from all the different windows in this very specific house I sought out to rent.

34 Wilmington Lane.

An address I said so many times as a child when asked for my address, sometimes adding *cottage* to the end of it so that our mail wouldn't get mixed up with Georgia's family's mail.

And even though I've waited ages for it to come online so I could rent it, I can still hardly believe it.

Right in front of me is *the roof*, the very roof from which my mother, Eliza Smythe Byrne, fell to her death.

SIXTEEN

Georgia. Southport, Connecticut.

My heart stops.

Tom lets out a hard puff of air, and the three of us don't speak for a moment. We all stare at each other in this quiet room with its books and antiseptic white walls and black-and-white photographs of letters and a quill pen. I hear a tiny desk clock ticking in the silence, triumphantly marking the seconds of agony unfolding inside this room. I press my back against the wall and slide down it.

"Are you sure, Millie?" asks Tom, still standing.

I sit against the wall with my knees up. I rest my hands together in my lap, but they're so sweaty I end up wiping them against my shorts.

"I'm absolutely sure," says Millie. And then she turns to me. "Mom, in my dreams, this woman, *Eliza*, I guess, is screaming for someone to help her. And in the dream, I try to go to her, but she always puts her arms up like she's terrified of me, like I'm going to hurt her, like I'm a monster."

I gasp. Tears fill Millie's eyes.

"What does she say to you?" Tom asks. "Keep talking, Millie, please."

I want to help my daughter, but I don't know if I can do this.

"Mom," says Millie, starting to cry harder now. "I don't want to make you upset."

Tom kneels beside her. "This isn't about your mom, or about trying not to make *Mom* upset." There's venom in his voice. "This is about you, Millie, about helping you feel like yourself again."

Millie sniffs. She exhales a shaky breath, and then she says, "In the dream, I can't really tell where we are. Usually we're in your bedroom, but sometimes it's like we're on top of the house."

"On the roof?" I can barely get the words out, but I make myself, because this is my daughter. I've done this to her. My haunted family and me.

Because wasn't I raised by Eliza to believe in this kind of thing? Eliza was a natural storyteller who believed in the possibility of ghostly visitors. She couched it all in being spiritual, in being a weekly churchgoer, but it was so much more than that. Eliza didn't believe that life stopped at death—not even close—and if anyone could figure out how to break the barrier of the human world and the spiritual world, wasn't it Eliza?

I watch the fear contort Millie's features. Do I really even believe in any of this as a possibility? I believe in an afterlife, but not necessarily one where ghosts revisit houses and launch themselves into the dreams of a twelve-year-old. I want to think of my mother and Eliza resting in peace. So if this is real (which is a stretch), if Eliza is somehow visiting my daughter in dreams, then is she warning Millie about some impending doom, or is she trying to right some unsolved part of her death?

Or both?

My heart thuds. I'm going way too far. There has to be another, more sane explanation. I think of the dreams I have about Eliza's death—they feel like dreams, unsettling, sure, but not paranormal.

"Yes, on the roof," says Millie. She grabs her legs and holds them tightly against herself. "In the dream, whenever I try to help Eliza, she gets this terrified look on her face, like I just told you. It's like she thinks I'm a murderer, or some kind of criminal—that's how scared she looks when I walk toward her. And then, in every dream, she throws her arms up to shield herself, and then she starts screaming, and it's just so scary, Mom. I'm sorry . . . I mean, it sounds so silly when I say it out loud . . . but I can't even explain to you how scary it is in the dark."

She's sobbing now. I go to her and wrap my arms around her shoulders. "Don't be sorry," I say. "It's gonna be okay, Millie. I dream about Eliza, too. There's nothing to be scared of, I promise."

SEVENTEEN

Anna. Waring Ridge, New York.

I sit on the bench in Georgia's bedroom and can't take my eyes off the roof. The section where my mom used to sit with Georgia's mom is entirely flat, just like I remember it from growing up in the cottage on this very property, the cottage in which Max now lives. I haven't been back since I was six, the year my mom died. It's hard to imagine why my mom ever would have gone close enough to the edge that she could have fallen. Max was only twelve, and he told the police that my mom went out on the roof to retrieve a doll for Georgia, and that neither he nor Georgia saw her again for hours. Max and Georgia were inside the house, but they never suspected that something terrible had happened to my mom. They thought maybe she'd gone out to do some grocery shopping, but then eventually, when they realized her car was in the driveway, they checked the property and found her dead, lying there with that hideous doll on the stone patio, having gotten horribly unlucky with the way she fell, cutting her head on a jagged stone. In the pocket of my mom's pants was a cryptic note from Georgia's dad: *Be here by eight. We'll talk then, Liza.* No one called my mom Liza. Georgia's dad was either too wrapped up in his own tragic world to write her name correctly (unlikely), or he had a different relationship with her than we realized. I don't really mean anything untoward or romantic—I don't think my mom would ever do that. But when I was a child, my mom and Georgia's dad always seemed pointedly uninterested in each other, almost too much so, like they were making an effort for things to seem that way. And after I saw that note and thought about it more as I got older, I wondered if I'd read the situation incorrectly. Maybe my mom and Georgia's dad had gotten close while taking care of his difficult children together.

Georgia was sixteen when my mom fell, her own mother had been dead for four years, and she was already a mess at that point. She was hauntingly beautiful, with light blue eyes and milky pale skin just like her daughter, Millie, in the photos downstairs. As a sixteen-year-old, Georgia ruled the house with harsh demands and an air of self-involvement so thick you felt like you were entering an atmosphere where you might not be able to find your own oxygen. I felt it every time I visited this house—*the main house*, as we called it back then. You could say that my family and I were lucky recipients of free room and board in that cottage, but it felt more like golden handcuffs. With living expenses paid, plus a decent salary and health insurance, my mom insisted that we could never leave Georgia's family.

My dad once told me that Georgia's family had already nearly exhausted my mother to death while she was pregnant with Sam and me, having her work long hours taking care of Georgia and Max, who were ten and six at the time. My dad promised my mom that if she wanted to leave the job, he could work overtime and they could afford a small apartment on their own. But my mother loved Georgia and her family no matter how difficult they could be, and she argued she'd never find a situation that good, one that paid so well and covered living expenses. She told him she was fine, and that she could feel Sam and me happily kicking around inside of her all day long. And she was right, I guess. She carried us until thirty-eight weeks, gave birth to us one morning at dawn, nursed us, and loved us, and then went back to work eight weeks later. My mother had the biggest heart of anyone I knew; she'd raised Georgia and Max, and she'd loved them, too. And when we were born and Georgia's mom was still alive, my mom knew that Georgia's mom's drinking had gotten so bad that she couldn't leave her alone to raise Georgia and Max. So my dad switched to three night shifts per week so he could take care of us during the day. And it was okay for a while: we had plenty of time with both our parents; we had enough food and a warm, safe home—we were lucky. And then it all went to shit.

The afternoon my mom fell from the roof, my dad protected Sam and me from seeing her dead body. I'll never forget the look on his face when he heard the sirens. It was nearing the end of summer vacation; Sam and I were about to go into first grade at Waring Ridge Elementary and were home with my dad in our cottage. When my dad heard the sirens coming closer, he set down the book he was reading to us and said, "You're both going to wait right here in this room until I come back to get you. No matter what, you are not to leave. Do you understand?"

We promised him we understood. My dad probably thought it was Georgia who got hurt or overdosed, but it was my mom's body he found when he ran across the yard.

Sam and I waited alone in our bedroom for him to come back, but he didn't, not until what felt like hours later. We were huddled together, pressed against each other, not saying much. In my six-year-old brain, I think I knew it was my mother who'd been hurt. Why else would my dad have been gone for so long?

Those hours Sam and I spent side by side sealed us for life. We'd already felt that way about each other—the naturalness of our twin connection—but that afternoon, waiting in a tiny room for the news that would change everything, took our bond to the next level. If there was any photograph I'd like to have of Sam and me, it would be that one: an image of us together in that tiny bedroom, preparing to face our fate. We would spend the rest of our lives doing just that, over and over. When Sam's moods were at their darkest, it was that tiny cottage bedroom I thought about. I knew I could weather anything if Sam and I were together, and I prayed that he could, too. But ultimately, what we had wasn't enough to keep him alive. His disease was too pernicious, too dangerous, and when the guardrails that he needed weren't entirely in place (the exact dosage of meds; a backup therapist for when his was away last summer; a *mother*), bipolar disorder killed him in cold blood.

I was only a toddler when Georgia's mom died, but when I got older, my dad told me that when she was still alive, sometimes he'd peer out the window of our cottage and see my mom on the shingled roof, trying to drag Georgia's mom back inside. And when Georgia's dad wasn't there to help, my dad would stick Sam and me in our bouncy seats and race out the door to help my mom. On those nights, they'd fight well into the night, my father telling my mom that nothing was worth living with the demons of this particular family. But my mom could never let them go, and Georgia and Max's mom dying sealed the deal: now my mom would never leave—not until they killed her.

It wasn't all bad while my mom was still alive. In addition to remembering Georgia's erratic behavior, I also remember the kindness of Max and how he'd bring us small treasures and leave them on our front porch. He was always getting into trouble, acting out, destroying property in town once and having it caught on video by the owner of the hardware store—he once snuck a beer into middle school, and his dad was mortified, screaming at him that he'd turn out just like his mom had. But with us Max was different. And when we were suddenly six and old enough for building forts and playing tag, he sometimes played with us in the yard, even though he was twelve. I think he liked the freedom of running around with us without any other middle schoolers around to judge him or demand he act his age and be any cooler than he already was. Back then, I was a chubby kid with bangs and a bowl cut, who didn't know any better, who didn't understand all the ways in which Georgia and her parents demanded too much of my mother until the very moment she broke. It's twenty years later, and my face looks nothing like it used to: now I'm all angles and sharpness, cunning and razors, and the only thing left of that innocent little girl is the green eyes. I'm unrecognizable as the sitting duck I was back then. At least I hope I am.

We left that cottage, of course, when my mother was no longer employed by Georgia's family, on account of her being dead. A year or two ago, when we found a picture of my mom with her arms around Georgia, Max, and their mom, my father said a low, grumbled sentence that ended with *beautiful, poisonous people.*

I suppose two can play that game.

EIGHTEEN

Georgia. Southport, Connecticut.

I'm sitting upright in the bed, staring out at the Southport sea and the stretch of beach where Millie and Tom are sitting on a towel. I want to join them, but I need a minute alone to think. I need to stop entertaining the ideas of ghosts and supernatural visitors, and instead focus on the facts, because if I'm being rational, then the only way Millie could have drawn Eliza's likeness was if she saw a photo of her. There's a stash of photos I keep hidden in a drawer in Max's cottage, hundreds of them, dating back to when I turned thirteen and got a camera for my birthday. Eliza's own children were still young, and most of the photos are of Max and them playing, and of course Eliza was always with us, so there are a bevy of shots of her, too.

Millie must have found them at some point, but why would she lie? As far as I know, she's never lied to me about anything, so why this? I suppose she could be making it all up to scare me enough to leave the house and move back to the city, but that would mean scheming, lying, and cunning beyond anything I've ever seen from her. And Tom hates Waring Ridge, but he'd never put Millie up to something like that. I can't entertain either one of them fabricating all of this, because that option is the only thing worse than Eliza's ghost haunting us.

I suppose there's a possibility Millie saw the photos a year ago when we first moved in, and forgot about them, and Eliza's memory lingered somewhere in her subconscious enough for her to recall it and dream about her. It makes me want to drive back to my house and find just how visible those photos are in the cottage. Maybe Max happened to go through them recently, and they're laid out on display somewhere for Millie to have seen them.

I think about texting Anna and seeing if I can come by. Or would I even need to ask? I wouldn't be going to the main house, just Max's cottage to get the photos, so I can probably just show up. I need to see if any of the photos show Eliza in the pearlized earrings Millie drew. Eliza wore those earrings so often that I'm sure one of the photos captured it. That's probably how Millie knew to draw them.

I grab my phone and shoot off a text. Hey, Anna! Just checking in to see how it's all going over there. I hope you're having fun!

There we go. I don't think it's too creepy if I stop by at some point and she sees me. I could just say I'm checking on things, that I just want to be sure it's all going fine.

NINETEEN

Anna. Waring Ridge, New York.

I'm rifling through Georgia's drawers when my phone buzzes with a text. I check it to see a missed text from Carter: September can't come soon enough, and another from Georgia checking in to see how it's going.

I ignore both texts and keep searching through Georgia's stuff. I can't believe she's trusting enough to leave so many of her things out. She transferred one of her closets into another so I'd have a huge, empty closet to unpack my clothes into, but she didn't bother locking up her family's clothes. That can't be normal for vacation rentals, but I guess it's probably her first time doing it.

I'm looking for the journal that my mother used to write in, one I'm convinced Georgia has in her possession. It was white with a purple dahlia on the front, and my mother only ever stored it in her handbag, which meant that the journal went everywhere she did. But after my mom died and we got the bag back from the police, the journal wasn't inside. I've asked my dad about it, but he says he never found it. It makes no sense, not unless Georgia, at age sixteen, had reasons not to want anyone in the police department reading through my mom's journal—which she did—and took it. Georgia got high on all kinds of things, and then dragged my mother down into her black hole, and if my mother was writing about her days in that journal, then I'm sure Georgia was worried there would be things in those pages that shouldn't see the light of day. Maybe, among her other brash and selfish acts, Georgia stole the journal. And no matter what that journal revealed about her, I feel absolutely sure that Georgia wouldn't have thrown it away. She loved my mother, even I can admit that; she loved her far too much to throw away her deepest, innermost feelings. The journal would have been one of the only things Georgia had to remember her by.

Two years of my mom's life is held among those pages. We gave it to her on the Christmas Sam and I were four, and she carried it everywhere and wrote daily for the next two years until her death. It was a massive journal, way bigger than the kind she used to write in so diligently, too quickly needing another. We found it while Christmas shopping in TJ Maxx, and I have an early memory of my dad, Sam, and I standing in line, Sam clutching the journal to his chest like a prize. We knew she'd love it. And the possibility that I could find it now, and then triumphantly return it to my father, is nearly too overwhelming to bear.

Georgia's drawers are filled with expensive tanks, leggings, and jeans. They're all so nice it makes me wonder what clothes Georgia chose to take with her. There's a stash of papers, but they're mostly drawings signed by Millie. The drawings give me pause; they're very good. I'm pretty sure Millie is only eleven or twelve, and these are really something. Most are of objects: a vase I noticed downstairs; a tennis racket leaning up against a doorframe; a stack of playing cards with the joker facing up. But there are people, too, and they're exceptional. One drawing shows an old man with a cane, and I wonder if it's possibly Georgia's dad. He's dead now. He never protected my mother by trying to put up boundaries between her and his family. He was a grieving widower with a drug-addled sixteen-year-old, and when my mother offered help, he took too much. My dad used to warn my mom about Georgia's dad, insisting that he had no boundaries with her. Once, when they thought I was sleeping, during the worst fight I'd ever heard them have, my dad said: *He thinks you're his partner. Maybe he doesn't think you're his wife, but he thinks you're their second mother.*

And then my mom said, so deadly soft I could barely hear it, *I am their second mother.* After that, a door slammed and there were no more words.

Georgia's top drawer is filled with cocktail rings, perfume, and colorful yarn friendship bracelets her daughter probably made. I slip on a few of the friendship bracelets and spritz my wrist with Chanel No. 5, a scent my mom sometimes wore. It hits me right in the gut. I close my eyes and try to forget, but when I do, an odd feeling descends on me, like my mom, or someone else, is right there, watching me. I open my eyes and turn around, but there's no one there, of course. I go to the window, peering out onto the bright green grass, my eyes scanning the woods. I swear I see movement in the brush on the side of the house. I stare at the leaves quivering in the trees—maybe it was just the wind moving through? I take a deep breath, and I'm about to go back to searching Georgia's stuff when I see a pale man in a navy baseball cap emerge from the brush. It's not Max. It's someone I've never seen before, and he glances up to my window and locks eyes with me. What the *hell*? I back away from the window, my heart pounding.

Should I call the police? Is he on Georgia's property, or does the side of the house have a different property line? Maybe he works at the house and Georgia forgot to tell me about him?

I want to call Max because I know he's back at his cottage, but I don't have his number. Maybe the guy is a friend of Max's and he was just leaving?

I pick up my phone and reread Georgia's text. Should I call her?

I go back to the window and the man is gone.

I stare down at my phone, my heart still pounding. How odd is the concept of *setting*? Back in New York, thousands of men pass beneath my window each day and I don't think twice about it. But out here, in this remote setting . . .

I decide not to do anything about it. There has to be an explanation, and maybe I'll casually text Georgia back and mention it later. I don't think anyone is trying to stalk me in broad daylight.

I move a little slower, trying to calm down. Next to the bangles in Georgia's dresser are two folded pieces of paper. One is a poem, also signed by Millie.

In the darkness
We go out there together
You first, I follow
A full moon hangs swollen in the night sky

I'm only there to help you, no matter how much
you protest
And I can sense what awaits you, so I keep trying
Your head whips round
You're so very scared, and that's when you start
screaming

And me? I wake to a black room and childhood
things

The poem gives me chills. There was a full moon on the night my mom died, and I always think of her when I look up into the sky and see one shining like an iridescent bowling ball. I miss my mother so much, and Sam missed her even more. In the four years between when Georgia's mom died and my mom died, there were so many nights when my mom stayed overnight in the main house with Max and Georgia. *They've lost their mother,* she used to tell us, and we were too young to come up with a retort about how we were losing ours. We didn't totally understand why, but those sleepovers in the main house increased when Georgia's drug use started at fourteen, because my mom was terrified to lose Georgia the same way she'd lost Georgia's mom. All we knew was that my mom was in the main house with Georgia and Max, and not in the cottage with us. And on those mornings at dawn when Sam woke us both up, he used to stand at the door, whining, his hands pressed against the glass panes, waiting for our mom to walk across the yard between Georgia's house and our cottage. I'd usually draw or read on the floor next to him, but he never left his post. He stared, expectantly, waiting to be in our mom's arms again. When he saw her exit Georgia's house and start off across the lawn toward us, my brother lit up like a Christmas tree. He'd bounce on his toes and paw at the window. On those mornings, my parents wouldn't be speaking. They'd go about the business of feeding us breakfast, giving each other a wide berth, and only talking to each other through us. *Anna, did you tell your father you want us to pack raisins for lunch this week? Sam, remind Dad you have T-ball practice this afternoon at the town park.* The tension was palpable.

My mom died when Sam and I were six, and even though he could mostly understand that she wasn't coming back, he still waited at that window. By then his whining had turned to shrieks and sobs. My father moved us out of the cottage as soon as he could secure an apartment where we could live, but it wasn't fast enough for Sam. He spent those weeks mourning my mother so viscerally it terrified me, and probably terrified my dad, too. My dad was devastated beyond words, and so was I, of course. But Sam? Sam was a shipwreck, an injured animal, a fireworks display of grief. He couldn't stop crying out for her. I remember the little red dots on Sam's skin—petechiae, the doctor called them—and the way they lined the skin around his eyes in a red halo. The doctors said the dots had arisen from the sheer trauma of crying so very hard. They lasted for months.

Next to Millie's eerie poem is another piece of folded paper. I open it to see a handwritten note.

Dear Georgie,

Tonight, in the bar, you were radiant, a diamond among imposters. All those drunk bodies swarming, and you with your vibrant smile, giving me a private look telegraphing that you needed to get out of there. I will always see and honor your little glances. No one has ever looked at me like you do, with such complete love and understanding. Every time I'm with you, I have the desire to sweep you off to somewhere better. I want to be with you forever. I mean these words with my whole heart.

Tom

Is he really so in love with her after all of these years together? I check the date.

2/10/09

So maybe not. I can't help but imagine all the ways their love has faded, because isn't that just the natural course of things? I imagine it's like most relationships, where there are too many tiny injuries to come out unscathed, to feel fresh love like this one. Or maybe I'm just trying to make myself feel better, because the only true love I've ever known was for my parents and Sam.

Buzz.

The vibration from my phone startles me. There are two texts, one from Bee and one from Carter. Carter's reads: I'm lonely without you, and I ignore it again. Now that I'm in Georgia's house, the need for Carter feels less pressing. I miss him, of course, especially the zing of excitement I feel sneaking around with him. But I have so much to do here.

Bee writes, How's the rental? When are you inviting me for a visit?

I'm not inviting her for a visit, but, of course, I don't type that. Ha, I type. The house is so beautiful! How are you?

Bee knows everything about my mom dying. But she has no idea I rented the same house where everything happened. I hate lying to her, and I almost told her that I was going to rent something near Waring Ridge and spend some time in the town for closure on Sam's death. But in the end, I didn't want to make it even worse with a half truth. And anyway, if I don't have closure on my mother's death nearly twenty years later, then how am I ever going to have closure on my twin's?

I move back from the dresser. I'm about to head into Georgia's closet to search for the journal there, but there's a slant of light across the armchair that's too perfect not to photograph. Two vintage books rest on a shagreen side table, and the whole scene sits against the backdrop of blue-and-white swirling wallpaper. I shoot a few photos, and then I post them as a montage on TikTok to a SZA song with the caption: *The perfect escape.*

Right away I see another comment from the same username who commented that he could come meet me at the bar with my friends.

Vacation? U alone? I could come find u

Gross. The amount of creepy things people have posted on my TikTok could fill a book. I put my phone down and head into Georgia's closet.

TWENTY

Georgia. Southport, Connecticut.

Somehow, even after everything that happened with Millie and her drawing, we get ourselves out to dinner at a seafood restaurant in Southport overlooking the beach. Tom's been chilly with me all day, of course, because all of this—this damage to our daughter—is directly the result of me moving us to Waring Ridge, to the messed-up family home from where I came, which may or may not be haunted by the ghost of a woman who was my nanny.

We're seated on the patio, the sea stretched out before us. Paper napkins and wine glasses scatter the table, along with a small vase of purple flowers. The wind has picked up, verging on making dining outside seem like a bad idea.

"I forgot my doll in Waring Ridge," Millie says, expertly snatching up a piece of sushi and popping it into her mouth.

Tom's hand is slung protectively along the back of Millie's chair. All day at the beach house, he stayed closer to her than ever, boxing me out.

"I can drive back to get your doll," says Tom.

"Do you really need it, Millie?" I ask.

"Georgia," Tom snaps.

"What? Maybe not having the doll is why Millie slept through the night last night without a nightmare. Maybe it's the doll's fault."

Millie flinches. I'm being so awful.

"Or maybe it's being away from your house," says Tom.

Your house.

I gaze out to the water. A dock juts out in the navy sea, white sailboats tied up and undulating. Seagulls squawk, and everything smells like salt, and isn't this why everyone loves the beach? I'm suddenly regretting everything about coming here, and the feeling is so unsettling that I speak without really thinking. "So then let's sell our house and move back to the city," I spit out, like a petulant toddler.

"Mom, no," Millie says.

Tom takes a swig of his beer. "We'll do whatever it takes, Millie, for you to feel better. Your mom and I both feel that way. Right, Georgia?"

My heart picks up speed at the thought of losing my beloved home. "But how can we even know that *the house* is the problem?" I ask. I feel slurry, like I've had wine, even though I haven't. Anxiety mixed with exhaustion, maybe. "We can't exactly afford to experiment. We'd have to sell the house to someone else."

"Maybe we could afford to rent for a bit in the city," Tom says, "just for six months or so."

Millie perks up. "Really? Could we do that?"

I want to cry, but I know that I can't. I have to be the grownup, the *mother*. I have to be the person who only wants what's best for Millie, because that's truly who I am.

"Could I go back to my old school?" Millie asks, clapping her hands together like the child she really is, rather than the grownup I sometimes see her as. I remember all those music classes I used to take her to in the city, and how she'd light up with glee at every new instrument the instructor brought out to play. It didn't matter whether it was an electric guitar or a shoddy plastic recorder. Millie loved it all, and I loved *her*. It was a far simpler time when it was just the three of us in New York City and she was a baby, when my biggest worry was lack of sleep. I didn't even feel the pressure to publish anything those first few years of

Millie's life. It wasn't until she went to preschool that I started feeling guilty about my lack of creative work.

Tom frowns. "I imagine we could get you back into your school," he says, but I'm not sure I agree. I don't know how easy it would be to get her back into the New York City academic ecosystem. It's already August. Possible, sure. Easy, no. Tom goes on, "We'd have to figure that out, but look how good it is to be out in Southport getting a change of place. Maybe we can start by you and me doing some weekends back in New York City."

"Sorry, am I not invited on these weekends away?" I ask, my voice so cold that Millie snaps her head up.

"Mom, of course you're invited," Millie says, pulling nervously at a stack of blue and neon-yellow friendship bracelets.

I want to push. I want to repeat Tom's phrasing back to him. *You and me . . . weekends in New York City . . .* But I don't want to upset Millie. Suddenly I have the sensation of something slipping through my fingers like water, and I feel sick to my stomach.

I stare at Tom. He lifts his glass to his lips and takes a long drink.

TWENTY-ONE

Anna. Waring Ridge, New York.

So far, tearing apart Georgia's room has turned up nothing. I decide I'm ready to see the cottage.

I trail my hand down the shiny black railing. In the foyer, I slip on my sneakers and grab my sunglasses from where I left them on the entry table. I cross the checkerboard floor toward the back of the house, and swipe the bottle of wine Georgia left for me in the kitchen. I remember the back porch so clearly from when I was little, and I wind my way down the hall to find it. Halfway there, my voicemail alert shows me a message from Carter. The cell service is strange here—voicemails from Bee have popped up when the phone never bothered to ring as she called. Same for this message from Carter—it's marked 4:04 p.m., but I had my phone on then and it never rang. I press his name and the call connects. My heart pounds as it rings. We haven't spoken—we've only texted since that morning when we said goodbye in the museum, but I'm desperate to hear his voice.

He picks up right away, and the sound of him saying my name sends something hot streaking through me. I miss him—I don't want to admit it, but I do.

"How are you?" he asks before I can say anything. "Are you all right?"

I shiver hearing his voice while I'm in this house. I feel so far away from the life I was living just days ago.

"I'm okay," I say, trying to sound normal, like I'm the same person he's used to talking to. "Are you okay? All's well?"

"I am," he says. "But I miss you desperately. I want to see you. I know we said we wouldn't. But I could come into the city. Or have you left yet for upstate?"

"I have," I say. "I'm already up here. Visiting friends," I lie.

I wonder what he'd do if I told him I was staying on the same property where my brother and I were raised, where my mother died. It all feels so elaborate, and he knows nothing about any of it.

"Where are you?" he asks. "I could come to you. Just for the day. Maybe tomorrow?"

"I can't, Carter," I say. "It won't work. And we said we would take time to think. I miss you, too, I do."

I can't let him distract me—I have too much to do to Georgia in this house, too many reparations to make for my dad and for me. For Sam. For my mom.

"I know what we said," Carter says.

"I need time," I say, pressing my back against Georgia's deep gray wallpaper.

"I understand, I do. But I—"

I cut him off. "I'll call you in a few days." I can't do this, not now. "We'll talk more then."

"Okay," he says, letting go of a long exhale. "We'll talk then."

"Goodbye, Carter," I say, and then I disconnect the call and make myself keep going. I push on toward the back of Georgia's house and freeze when I see the porch. It's the only room I've seen so far that's unchanged from twenty years ago. It's as beautiful as ever, overlooking the yard, cliffs, and Max's cottage, and outfitted with the same wicker coffee table and chairs with red flower-print cushions. Sam and I used to bounce on those cushions, jumping from one chair to the other, squealing that the floor was lava, just like every other child on Earth.

Sometimes when Georgia and Max stayed late after school for sports and their dad was still at work, my mom used to let us come hang out in the main house while she cooked and cleaned. It was only for the last two years of her life when we were five and six and didn't need constant supervision and attention, but it was heaven. Once, I overheard my mother tell my dad, *This is a whole new chapter. I'm going to be able to spend so much more time with Anna and Sam.* But my dad was often wary to let us out of his sight, knowing that Georgia was unstable and using, and he usually only walked us over to the main house when Georgia and Max weren't there. And then he'd see Georgia's Jeep pull in from whatever trouble she'd likely gotten herself into, and he'd be back round to scoop us up and take us away from our mother and home for dinner.

I exit the sunporch through a screen door and step into the yard. The outdoor air smells like summer, the scent of roses mixing with a hint of chlorine coming from the pool off to the right of the property. It's about seventy-five yards of lawn to get to the cottage. I'm shaky with the anticipation of seeing it, but I know I have to do this. That cottage is the last place I ever saw my mother. And we were cozy there, even though the tension between my parents sometimes skyrocketed, we always knew they loved us and they loved each other. A unit, a team. Intact, we were likely the only team Sam needed to survive this world. But Georgia broke us. Sending my mom on a fool's errand, and then letting her body lie there for hours until she and Max finally decided to go look for her. She could have been *alive* down there, if only they'd thought to check sooner.

Tears fall down my cheeks as I make my way to the cottage, which is the last thing I want, but I can't stop them. Right as I'm about to pass the pool, I see the dead body of a small, furry possum among a cluster of Georgia's perfect pink hibiscus. I turn away, unable to look at its ugliness, which isn't how I usually behave in the face of things that are less than beautiful. But I don't feel like myself on this property, and the fear that descends upon me as I head toward the cottage is strange and unsettling.

I try to breathe, to let my eyes settle on the cottage, to face it.

The cottage is still painted a dull white stucco and dotted with light blue shutters. You can tell Georgia has tried to make it as charming as possible with window boxes filled with purple zinnias and an antique-looking metal planter next to the door. There's the covered porch, one of my favorite parts. I loved being out there in the shade with Sam, playing jacks and card games while sheltered from the hot midday sun (Irish skin is no joke—you have to be careful in the broad daylight). Now the evening light lends the porch a warm glow, and I remember the pre-bedtime hours when my dad would sometimes bring us out here to the rocking chairs to read a book before our baths. Upon closer inspection, I can see that it's the same two rocking chairs standing sentinel, but someone has painted them pale green.

Before I can chicken out, I knock hard on the front door. The sun is hot against my shoulders. I hope Max isn't napping or entertaining someone else, but I didn't see anyone pull in.

Behind me, a bird calls out from the trees. You can't hear any road traffic back here, and I'd forgotten how peaceful it could be. The cliffs are to my left, and I can see from here that someone has installed a fence at the edge of the lawn. Probably Georgia. Smart. You could easily fall to your death out there, especially on this cursed property. A shiver creeps over my spine when I think about how protective my mom and dad were of us, never letting us out of their sight, and how lucky we were to have had that. Georgia and Max didn't. I remember my mom being freaked out that they'd sneak back to the cliffs when she was off duty and they were in their dad's care, because he was always so distracted. I start to feel a little sympathy for Georgia, but then Max opens the door.

"Hey," he says. He runs a hand over the same head of messy hair. My initial nerves have passed, and now when I see Max with his soft brown eyes, I just feel fondness for all the ways he showed me kindness when I was little.

"Hey," I say back. "Sorry to be weird, but it's lonely in that big house. Can I see your digs?"

Lonely. The same word Carter used with me in his text. Maybe we're all the same, maybe we're just trying our best not to feel starkly alone in crowded rooms.

"Come on in," Max says, swinging open the door. I follow him, and then I do the last thing in the world I wanted to do: I start crying again. I'm so furious with myself I try to swallow it all back, but I can't. Unlike every room in the main house except the porch, the cottage is unchanged from when I lived here with my family. The same brown leather sofa is laid out in the living room in front of the same standard wooden coffee table on which Sam and I used to draw pictures, our legs tucked beneath us. It's an open floor plan, and I can see that the kitchen has the same butcher-block countertops, and I can practically see my dad hunched over, chopping vegetables, and I swear I can still smell the licorice scent of the fennel he always added to the big boiling pots. To the right of the living room are two small bedrooms. Sam and I shared a room here, and then shared one again at the apartment my dad rented, until we turned eleven and Sam started sleeping on a pullout couch in the living room. He said it was because I snored, but I knew he was just doing it to be gracious.

I can feel Max's eyes on me. And I really don't think, even with my sobbing, that he could ever have any idea who I am, but I'm still freaked out. I move to the kitchen and grab a paper towel, noisily blowing my nose. "Sorry!" I say. I turn to face him. "I lost my brother this year. This month was supposed to be an escape from the city and a way to slow down and process what happened, because I don't think I ever properly did that."

Max's dark eyebrows go up. He's tall and lanky, and he gestures with a long arm for me to come sit on the sofa. "I'm so sorry," he says.

"He would have loved it here," I say, and I mean it. As adults, Sam and I always reminisced about this little cottage. It was our happiest time as a family, even though we didn't know it then. It was when we had *her*, our beloved mother, Georgia's beloved Eliza, a woman whose love felt like sun on your face. Losing our mom when we were little was a tragedy we couldn't bear. And Sam didn't.

By the time I was eleven I'd figured out Google and looked up Georgia. I was curious about her, because the more things my dad told me about her family, the more I began to piece together what had been happening with Georgia's drug use and the strain it'd had my family under as my mom tried to navigate it. The first thing I found online was a blog Georgia wrote. She published her college application essay there, a beautifully written piece about losing her mother to alcoholism, and then losing her nanny, who was like a mother to her. Her writing was incredible, but the part that nearly killed me was the way she told the story like she was the real victim. Of course I agreed that Georgia was the victim of a terrible drug addiction, but at least she was still alive. My mother was the true casualty, and as I got older, it was hard not to view the entire scene from a bird's eye: a privileged sixteen-year-old left her doll on the roof, and a work-for-hire nanny who was trying to do her job when said sixteen-year-old demanded her nanny get her doll, went out to the roof to get it. The nanny died, and the sixteen-year-old wrote a college essay about it to get into an Ivy League school.

I have empathy for what Georgia went through, but she still caused my mother's death and destroyed my family. When Sam died, the rage I felt for Georgia altering the balance of something that could have actually saved him (my mother being alive) grabbed me by the hair and shook me awake. It fueled everything I did, kept me going so that I could eventually ruin Georgia's life just like she ruined mine.

I don't know why I never thought to bring Sam here while he was alive. Probably because I couldn't have stood the sight of Georgia. And now I don't have to.

"Sit, Anna," says Max.

I sit on the worn leather couch. It's warm and perfect, just like it was twenty years ago. I plop the wine bottle down too hard on the coffee table. "Do you want some?" I ask. "Your sister left it for me."

"I'm sober. Or, I'm supposed to be. It's only been a few months. My sister's sober, too, actually."

"Good for her," I say. A little too late for my family, unfortunately.

"You can have a glass if you want," Max says. "It won't bother me."

"Nah," I say, waving a hand. "I'm not much for drinking."

"Lucky you," says Max. "It's my favorite thing."

"Why?" I ask.

"The numbness, I guess. Probably the same for everyone, right?"

I shrug. "Maybe."

He looks at me carefully. I don't like it.

"So, what did you need to get numb from?" I ask. "Something you wanted to forget?"

Unlike in my conversations with Georgia, when I felt like I was talking to a proper adult, Max gives off the kind of vibe I get when I'm with colleagues at work, like we're all the same age, even though we aren't. Max is only thirty-two, so I guess it's pretty close.

"Lots of things," he says, crossing one leg over the other. "There are things I've seen that I'd like to forget, of course. Things that have happened, little slights and big tragedies. But mostly I think it's an oversensitivity to the world. It's like I was supposed to be born with a better outer shield, like I don't have the right layers of skin to just let things bounce off and settle."

"I get that," I say.

"Really?" His dark eyebrows arch. His eyes are a deep, soulful brown. He's got a fisherman sweater on even though it's warm out, and he looks like a poet. "You seem like you have a tough outer shell," he says.

"You can tell that in five minutes?" I ask with a smirk.

"We've talked for like seven minutes total today, if you count this morning," Max says. "So yeah, that's my read."

I laugh. "You're probably right. Tougher shell than most."

"Though you *did* just cry," he says. His voice is careful, like he wants to make sure he can joke around with me.

"I did," I say.

"I'm really sorry about your brother," he says.

"Thanks," I say. "I appreciate that. So, what do you do in LA? Or New York? You live in both places?"

He nods. "I work on film sets. I'm not like a big deal Hollywood person or something, so if you're looking for your big break, it's probably not through me."

"I'm not an actor," I say.

"Oh. Yeah. I just thought maybe."

"Really?" I ask, amused. "Why?"

"You're beautiful and you dress like an artist," he says matter-of-factly.

"I *am* an artist," I say. "I'm a photographer." I'm feeling a little more reckless now that I'm here renting the house. I don't really care what he tells Georgia about me.

"Oh, no way," Max says. "That's cool. Can I see your stuff?" he asks, gesturing to my phone on the table between us.

"If you're lucky."

He laughs. "Come on," he says.

I open Instagram. Nerves race through me, but there's nothing on my account that could out me. I once posted an old photo of my mother, but you could barely see her face, just the side of her neck and the delicate pearl earrings she always wore, and anyway, I deleted it before contacting Georgia, just in case. And my last name isn't anywhere on the page.

"Oh, wow," Max says, taking the phone from my hand. "This is amazing. These photos . . ." He scrolls, stopping sometimes to make the image bigger. "You're really talented."

I don't put any of my celebrity work on my account, even though I know it would get me more followers. My page is all close-up photos of people on the street, mostly New Yorkers, because that's my favorite kind of work, and the subject of the book I'm under contract for. I feel a little guilty looking at my page, thinking about how I'm supposed to be writing photograph descriptions for the book.

"I love this one," Max says, zeroing in on the wrinkled face of an olive-skinned woman wearing prayer beads around her neck.

I inch next to Max on the sofa. There's something so magnetic about him, and I want to go closer. "She's a beauty, isn't she?"

"She is," he says, clicking on the next photo of two children playing in a fountain in the Boston Public Garden. Children aren't usually my thing. Partly because it's harder to get permission to post the photos, and the permission is important to me, but mostly because I'm more interested in adults. But Bee and I were in Boston visiting one of our friends from college, and these two boys had climbed into a fountain and started splashing around with such devious joy that I had to snap it.

Max smiles down at the photo.

"That's one of my favorite things about photography," I say.

He looks up. Raises a dark eyebrow. "What is?"

"How you can recognize and experience an emotion just by seeing a photo. When you looked down at that photo, you smiled right away, like you recognized or connected with that pure spirit of childhood. Right? I saw it on your face."

He nods, but a small, nearly imperceptible sadness flickers, and he hands me back my phone. "You're really good," he says. "Do you sell your photos anywhere?"

"Sometimes," I say vaguely. "So, do you like living here?" I ask, gesturing around the cottage.

"I do," Max says. "It's a little complicated. I mean, I'm kind of freeloading off my sister."

"I thought Georgia said you both grew up here."

"Yeah, but she owns the house."

"Why not you, too?"

"I couldn't afford to buy my share of it, and I needed the money from the sale, so she bought me out. We would have lost the house otherwise. And frankly, I didn't want to buy the house."

"Oh?" I ask.

"My mother died in that house, I'm not sure if you maybe know that, I can't imagine my sister would have mentioned it. In a bathroom."

My heart pounds. I'm shocked he's mentioning it, first of all. Why would you ever tell something gruesome like that to the person renting your sister's house? Is he trying to sabotage the rental in some way?

"Georgia didn't say anything, but I'm really sorry to hear about your mom." I'm quiet, waiting for him to go on. I want him to mention my mother, to give weight to her death with his recognition of it, but at the same time I'm not sure I can bear hearing the words from his mouth.

"And then our nanny, Eliza, died four years later. She fell off the roof."

Tears fill his eyes before they can fill mine. The strangest thing is that he didn't start crying until he mentioned my mother. I jump up to get him a tissue from a box in the kitchen. I hand him a couple, and even though my throat feels choked, I manage to say, "What a tragedy, I'm so sorry."

He wipes at his eyes, and I do something I never thought I would. I wrap my arms around him and pull him close. I can feel our heartbeats. Warmth radiates between our bodies, and I pull away first, surprised not only by what I've done, but how right it felt. It didn't feel like two strangers embracing, I guess because it wasn't. Even if Max doesn't know that.

Max looks down into his hands. "The thing is, I was only eight when my mom died," he says. "My sister was twelve. She remembers so much more about my mother than I do. Of course I remember my mom. But so many of the memories are blurry. Our nanny raised us after our mom died, because my dad was wrecked with grief and barely home because he worked such long hours. When our nanny died, it felt like I'd lost my mother twice."

I swallow. "I wish I knew something I could say that would make it better," I say.

"Are you close with your mother?" he asks.

"My mother died when I was young, too," I say. "It's completely awful. The worst kind of tragedy for a child. It broke my whole world."

"That's exactly what it does," Max says, steeling himself. "And I'm sorry about your mom."

We're quiet for a minute, and then Max sighs and says, "I guess my point is, why in the world would I want to live in that house? All I can feel is death and spirits there. It shocks me that Georgia wants to live there."

"Spirits?" I ask. "Like ghosts?"

"How could there *not* be ghosts? My mom's and Eliza's deaths were so sudden. Unresolved. And then my dad dropped dead there. He was old, but still."

"Why do you say their deaths were unresolved?" I ask.

He shrugs, averts his eyes. "It's just how they feel to me," he says.

"How did your nanny fall from the roof?" I ask, my words so steady I'm worried I've turned into a pathological liar. Maybe I have. And maybe Georgia and her family deserve it.

But even as I think it, it doesn't feel true for Max. He was a child.

"It's a long story," Max says.

"I have time," I say.

"Okay," Max says. "Well, first, my sister became a prescription drug addict after our mom died, which is something she'd tell you herself if she were here, because she's not secretive about it. When she was using, her favorite hiding spot for her pills was in the pockets of her doll's dress."

"What?!" I let out a small shriek, and then immediately clamp my mouth shut.

Max gives me a strange look, like I've spoken out of turn.

"Sorry," I say, my heart pounding. "It's just an odd thing to do."

He shrugs. "It's not that odd. My mom gave her the doll when she was little, and I'm sure she thought my dad and Eliza never would have thought to check a doll for drugs. I guess it was as good a hiding spot as any. And that's what addicts sometimes do—they hide things and lie. It's part of the disease. I've been there myself."

My heart feels like it's shattering inside my chest. "I-I guess you're right," I stammer. And of course I'm sympathetic to substance abuse disorders; of course I believe it's a disease like any other. But drugs in the doll? That's why Georgia asked my mother to fetch it for her?

"One afternoon, Eliza went to go get Georgia's doll from the roof where she left it, but somehow she fell, and Georgia and I didn't realize it right away. We thought she'd just gone out to run errands, and we waited in the house for her to come back. We were bored, lying around reading and playing card games, stuff like that. And then at some point Georgia went and looked out the window onto the roof, but the doll wasn't there, and Georgia started freaking out, thinking Eliza got the doll and took it somewhere—I'm sure she thought Eliza was on to her. So we went to look for Eliza, and we found her dead on the patio," Max says, his words speeding up like he can barely get through saying these things out loud, "and we called the police right away, and we told them about the doll and the roof, but Georgia didn't tell them about the drugs, and neither did I, because I was scared that then I'd lose Georgia, too. I asked the police a million times if I had gone to look for Eliza earlier, would she still be alive. They promised me she wouldn't, that she was dead because of the way her head hit a sharp stone, which caused her to bleed out quickly."

I want to say, *I highly doubt they could really know that, and they were probably just trying to make you and your selfish sister feel better.* But, of course, I don't say that.

"What was your nanny like?" I ask, the slightest tremble in my jaw.

Max takes a moment, seeming to calm down a little as we sit there together, the warm air in the cottage stilling.

"She was wonderful," he finally says with a shrug, like it doesn't really matter, or like it couldn't possibly matter to me. "Hugest heart. She loved my mom, and she was devastated when she passed. She saved my sister and me, really. She was strong. You know, stiff upper lip and all of that. But so loving. What about you? What was your mom like?"

"Similar," I say. And I leave it at that.

"Oh," he says, smiling.

"I should get going," I say. "But this was fun. Thanks for being good company."

"I cried and unloaded on you. I'm not sure I was good company."

I stand up, brushing my hands over my shorts. "Actually, that's the kind of company I prefer," I say.

He smiles wider, exposing a line of straight white teeth. He had braces the last time I saw him. He used to play this game with Sam and me, baring his teeth like he was a wild animal, arms outstretched, emerging from bushes and pretending to chase us while we screamed. We loved it. He was trying to be terrifying, but there was an energy about Max, like he wouldn't hurt a fly. We'd laugh and scatter like jacks dropped on a floor, and Max would pretend like he couldn't possibly catch us. *You're too fast!* he'd shout, and Sam and I knew that wasn't true, no matter how much we wanted it to be.

"Goodnight, Max," I say, and then I hug him for the second time tonight.

"See you tomorrow?" Max asks.

I make myself pull away. "Maybe," I say. "I'm planning to go into town tomorrow."

"Not much of a town, if you're used to New York."

"Yeah, but that's the whole charm of it, isn't it?"

"I guess," says Max. He yawns, looking almost relaxed. A good cry will do that to you.

"See you tomorrow," I say. I close the door behind me. I find myself wanting to head toward the cliffs, but I'm too worried Max is going to watch me from the window. So, like a well-behaved child, I head slowly back in the direction of Georgia's house.

TWENTY-TWO

Georgia. Southport, Connecticut.

Around eleven, Millie's asleep, and I'm texting back and forth with Maya to keep myself from passing out cold. I need to be awake when Tom comes up. He and Millie watched a movie together, which is not what they normally do back home in Waring Ridge, because Tom can't sit still long enough to watch an entire movie. He's usually texting, reading the paper, or catching up on work in his office. Maybe Southport has already put him in vacation mode, or maybe he's trying to avoid me.

When he finally enters our bedroom, he asks, "You're still up?" He's in an old college sweatshirt and looks ten years younger. I would probably love this vacation version of him, if things weren't so tense between us, and if all of this wasn't happening with Millie.

"I figured we should talk," I say, pushing back on the bed so I'm sitting up against the cushioned headboard. He doesn't move from the doorway. "Come, sit," I try.

"I need to pee," he says, and then he heads into the bathroom. The white-marble-tiled floor sparkles beneath the overhead light. He shuts the door, takes an exorbitantly long shower, and when he emerges, he's back in his sweats and using a fluffy white towel to dry his face. He tosses the towel onto a silky blue armchair, and then he shuts and locks the door to our bedroom. I take this to mean he wants to have sex, which I'm not opposed to, because it seems to be an area of our relationship that works. But when he sits on the edge of the bed, I realize I've read him wrong. He doesn't get under the covers; he just sits there, facing me, staring, his eyes drawn and tired. He might be in vacation mode, but there are still circles beneath his eyes that look darker than they've been in a while. My entire hope for this month was that it would help the three of us, but now we seem worse than ever.

"Millie needs her doll," says Tom. "She keeps mentioning it. And you'll be thrilled to know she's now calling it Liza."

A chill runs through me. "Seriously?"

Tom nods.

"No one ever called Eliza that except my dad," I say.

Tom shrugs. "And now your daughter has named her doll after your nanny. We can't seem to get away from everything that happened in that house, even now that we're finally out of it."

"Millie's drawing of Eliza is too weird."

"It is." Tom comes a little closer to me on the bed and says, "I don't think Millie wants to come out and ask us to go get the doll. Maybe she's embarrassed. She's a little old for a doll, isn't she?"

I shake my head. "Maybe. Though I kept that doll around for much longer."

"I can go get the thing. Can you just text the woman renting our house to leave the doll outside on the steps? Millie says it's right in her bed."

"Sure, yeah," I say, trying to shake off the weirdness of it all. "She actually just texted me a beautiful photo she took in our bedroom." I open my phone and show Tom a shot Anna took of a stack of books on a night table next to the flowers I'd left her with a note. Thanks for the note and flowers! The house is so gorgeous and special, she'd texted along with a photo. At first, I thought it was strange that she'd texted me a photo of my own house, but the photograph itself was so pretty I couldn't take my eyes off it. The time of day must have been perfect;

there's an orange glow and a haze that's bordering on magical, making the books look enchanting and the flowers like something in a magazine. Tom stares at the photo longer than he normally would. "Makes our bedroom look ready for *Elle Decor*," he says.

"I was just thinking that," I say. Tom puts my phone down and looks at me. I'm about to open my mouth to say something, but everything feels so nebulous that I don't know where to begin. I start with what I hope is the most important part, the concession. "I'm open to us moving back to the city for some time to see if it's better for Millie," I say. I sit up a little taller in the bed, ignoring the hard knot in my lower back. "I've run some of the numbers, and I think we could be okay for a little while if we found somewhere cheap to rent. A small two-bedroom on the Upper East Side, maybe?"

Tom comes a tiny bit closer to me, which I take as a good sign. But then he says, "You heard Millie say she wants to go back to her school." The bedside lamp is turned on, and the dim light casts a shadow over one side of his face.

"But I don't think we can afford a two-bedroom downtown. Not if we still want to keep our house."

Tom looks out the window, where a full moon hangs high above the glittering black water. "There are other ways to do it," he says.

"Like what?" I ask, pulling a white knit blanket over my legs.

"We could rent something small. Just a studio. Millie could sleep in a proper bed, and I'd take the couch. And we could stay a few nights in the city together, and then a few nights in Waring Ridge and commute."

My head is spinning. "Commute from Waring Ridge to her school? It could take nearly two hours to get all the way downtown." He looks away, and I replay his words in my head. "When you say *we* could stay a few nights in the city together, do you mean you and Millie, or all three of us?"

He can't meet my eyes. Bile rises in my throat.

"I meant Millie and me," he says. "It would make my commute easier."

"Tom," I say.

"I'm not happy, Georgia," he says.

We stare at each other. We've been together fifteen years. Didn't I know this was the truth? Didn't I maybe even ignore it a little, so I could get my way, so I could keep my family in the house I was desperate to hold on to?

"We can sell the house," I say, my voice breaking. "We can move back. It's best for you and Millie, and I love the city, and I guess this whole thing was a mistake, and I'm sorry."

He's quiet. Too quiet.

"Why aren't you saying anything?" I ask. "You just bent me to your will. Are you hearing me? I'm giving in."

"I don't want to bend you to my will," he says.

"It's what I did to you, when I begged you to buy the house."

"I understand why the house is so important to you, Georgia, I really do."

"But what else do you want from me? Because I don't know what more I can give you. I'm telling you we can get rid of the house, we can sell it to the highest bidder and watch someone else's family move in. I would do anything for you and Millie, if that's what you need." Fear has its claws around my throat. I feel like I've lost track of something vital, like somewhere along the way I dropped a family heirloom and now I don't know how to get it back.

Tom puts a hand on my knee and gives a gentle squeeze. "I love you, Georgia," he says. "I want to make it work, I do."

My eyes fill with tears. "I love you, too," I say. "Do you think we can get back what we had?"

"Our life in the city?" Tom asks.

"Yes, that, but also the way we felt about each other. You've been so distant, and I know you're upset with me for making us move, but that can't be all of it."

"I feel lost and unnerved in that house, and completely unlike myself in that town," Tom says, the words coming down between us like the slam of a gavel. "I know you don't want to hear it, but it feels like the air is heavier whenever I enter our bedroom and catch a glimpse of the roof through the window. Once I went in there in the dark and the shingles seemed to be glowing in the moonlight and I thought I was having a heart attack. I went to the ER, you remember that night?"

"Of course I remember that night," I say. It was a few months ago. I'd been out to dinner with Maya, and I'd accidentally put my phone on vibrate. Millie was over at Maya's house, and Ethan had put a movie on for her and the boys. I'd felt awful when I realized I'd missed Tom's call from the ER. And by the time I called him back, he was already being discharged.

"The doctor told me I was having a panic attack," Tom says.

I swallow. He never told me that. He told me his chest hurt, and that he'd gone to the ER just to be safe, and that everything had checked out all right.

"You really think it's all the house?" I ask, my skin going icy.

"I do. I've never had a panic attack in my life before we moved there, Georgia. Something is *wrong* with that house."

I'm crying now. It's just so awful to hear. I believe him, because Tom isn't dramatic, but it still rattles me. "Okay," I say, nodding, letting it all sink in. "Let's make some changes and see what happens." Isn't this what marriage is all about? Making sacrifices? I think back to my parents' marriage. I can't really think of any sacrifices my mom made for my dad, but maybe that's because I was still only a child and didn't know what to look for. Or was she morbidly selfish and I just didn't realize? The drinking was a disease, I know that. And people aren't selfish because they have a disease, no matter what the rest of the world thinks.

Tom gets under the covers and puts his arms around me. "I know I've been distant, and I'm sorry," he says. "If we can try this, if we can try to get our life back . . . that's what I want, Georgia. And being here and seeing Millie struggling, it's obvious that she needs us together, and strong like we used to be."

I don't want the reason for my marriage to work to be Millie—I want it to be because Tom is still desperately in love with me. But at this point I'm scared, which means I'll take whatever his reason is, because it's better than him wanting to give up on us. Tears fall down my face, and Tom's embrace feels like everything I need, even more than the house in Waring Ridge. Tom and Millie are my entire world, and wherever they are, that's where my home will be.

TWENTY-THREE

Anna. Waring Ridge, New York.

In the morning, I wake to the objects in Georgia's bedroom, and it takes me a minute to sort myself and remember what I've done. The doll faces me. She's sitting on the nightstand, staring. After Georgia texted asking me to leave the doll outside on the porch today, I went to Millie's bedroom and nearly died at the sight of the doll. Her dress is old and tattered now, but I recognize her shiny porcelain face, staring dark blue eyes, and the two quarter-sized dots of blush high on her cheeks. I want to rip her head off, but there's something so haunted about her that I don't think I can. Plus, she saw my mother die, and it gives me a sick satisfaction for her to cast those same seeing eyes on everyone inside this house. I don't know how Millie stands it, but maybe I'm not giving her enough credit. Maybe she's built of tougher substance than I'd guess from looking at her angelic image framed in the photos downstairs.

I look out Georgia's window to the cottage and the cliffs. I wonder what Max does all day long in Waring Ridge now that he's between jobs.

I get out of bed and slink down the winding staircase to the kitchen, where I find a sleek cream coffee maker next to a Nespresso machine. Inside Georgia's cabinets, I pick an oversized blue mug with flowers. I open the fridge, but there's no regular milk, only cashew milk, which sounds gross. I'll need to walk into town and pick up a few groceries.

It's nearly ten a.m. It took me forever to fall asleep last night, but I still didn't expect to sleep this late. I check my phone and see a text from Georgia. Hi, Anna! We'll stop by at eleven to pick up Millie's doll. Please don't worry if you're out. You can leave her on the front steps. Thanks so much again. Sorry about the hassle!

Sounds like a plan, I text back. I need to get out of here—I'm not ready to see Georgia face to face. I find a to-go cup for the coffee, and then I grab my wallet, keys, and sunglasses. I race back upstairs to get the wretched doll and hold her between two fingers. Out on the front steps, I sit her down and mutter *good riddance* beneath my breath. She stares up at me with glassy, hollow eyes.

I lock the front door. Georgia was adamant about me keeping the place locked, which I thought was interesting, because it's not exactly a high-crime area. But I don't want to piss her off, and I'm sure when she realizes that I'm not here, she'll check to see if I've done what she said.

I walk down the driveway and onto the main road that leads to town. The closer I get to the small downtown, the closer together the houses are, and even under the circumstances, it's hard not to appreciate the beauty here. Every house and garden is charming and well loved. In one of the front yards, three children play, two girls chase a little boy who's squealing with happiness. I think about Sam and how even though he was only seven minutes younger than I was, it always felt like more. In the same way Max described himself, Sam felt fragile to me, like he, too, was born without the armor he needed to bear the tragedies of the world. I miss being able to text and call and know he was right there in the city, his apartment just down the block from mine, a teeny-tiny studio with one of those murphy beds that folds into the wall. He was funny over text, and in person, too, especially when we were alone together and he was comfortable. Sometimes in a group he was more like me, hanging back and not really knowing how to keep up with the pace of the chatter. But when it was just us talking or texting, he always dropped in private jokes, or little funny things about mundane stuff. Sometimes, when he was feeling well, he joined me when I went out with Bee, Selena, Hayes, and Bradley, and I always liked those nights the best. There were long stretches when his meds seemed to be well balanced and really working, but there were other times he was in crisis, and that was terrifying. Sam and I spent many nights in the ER together, and my dad would drive into the city to meet us, sweaty and panicked by the time he got to Sam's curtained-off room. Sam always called me when he was feeling scary depressed, until the one time he didn't.

As I walk along the side of the road, nearing town, the style of the houses change: there are smaller colonials and antiques that you can tell have been here since Waring Ridge's early days. American flags fly on a few porches, and around the next bend, the town itself appears. It's classic and pretty, and I feel tears start when I see the library where my dad used to take Sam and me. Sometimes my mom would show up with Georgia and Max in tow. Georgia was a teenager at that point, and though she loved books, she always acted too cool to be in the children's section with us, slinking upstairs to the young adult books. Not Max. He joined in the mix with us and the plastic toys. There was a whole veterinary play station with stuffed animals, plastic food, and pretend medical equipment, and Max would sink to his knees and start playing. Which, of course, Sam and I loved, because it made the game so much more fun.

I cross at the crosswalk and spy a brick theater that's new to the town. **Waring Ridge Playhouse** says the banner at the top. Big glossy movie pictures line the front, and inside the glass doors I can see a proper box office and a glamorous interior lined with mirrors and luxe velvet couches. We would have loved a movie theater here when we were growing up. I keep walking down the red-brick sidewalk past a candy shop exploding with color, a quaint interiors shop with antique armchairs out front, and a cooking shop my mom loved. She took me here sometimes, always whispering, *Remember, Anna, we break it, we buy it. Be careful, my love.*

I push open the door. I need to see the shop again, to remember my mom in here, the way she would carefully run a finger over porcelain vases and thumb through cookbooks. I enter and see a front table with coffee table books—they even have *Culture*'s art book, which brings tears to my eyes, because what would my mom have thought to own that book and be so proud of the place where I worked? What would she have thought of me finding success in New York City and trying to make things happen on my own? I was so young when she died—I didn't get the chance to know her well enough to know what she would have thought of me being a photographer, but I think, like most mothers, she would have been proud. If she were still alive, these were the kind of moments we'd have together. My mother dying the way she did feels like being robbed at knifepoint. One minute she was there, and then the next she wasn't.

I try to move among the knickknacks and cookware like a typical shopper would, but I can't stop thinking about how awful it would be if my mom knew what I was doing now at Georgia's house, and all at once I need to get out—I need fresh air. I start toward the front of the shop, but then I stop dead, because through the glass door I see Georgia sitting on a wooden bench with Millie, who I recognize from all the family photos. I nearly gasp at the sight of Georgia. I haven't laid eyes on her in person since I was six. Her fine blond hair is tied up into a high bun, and her face is narrower than when she was a teenager. It's sunny out, but she's not wearing sunglasses, and I can see her pale blue eyes and the way she stares at Millie like she's the most beautiful thing she's ever seen. She probably is. Maybe Millie is the person who helps Georgia forget everything she's done.

Millie's blond hair hangs prettily over her shoulders, and she eats her ice cream like a true young adult: small, guarded bites, not the kind of abandoned freedom you have when you're little and you're attacking it with big licks. She looks just like Georgia did at her age. Seeing them together feels like staring into my future and my past, and I can hardly catch my breath. Millie looks up and locks eyes with me through the glass. I'm just standing there, frozen, so I turn quickly and pretend to busy myself with a few items on a front table. When I glance back over my shoulder, Millie isn't watching me anymore; she and Georgia are deep in conversation. Georgia tucks a piece of Millie's long blond hair behind her shoulder, and then Georgia's husband appears and bends to kiss the top of her head.

I'm not sure what comes over me when I see them all together like that. I push open the front door of the shop and step onto the sidewalk. "Georgia!" I call.

TWENTY-FOUR

Georgia. Waring Ridge, New York.

Millie, Tom, and I are in Waring Ridge when I hear someone call my name. It's a unicorn of a day, all clear blue skies and bright sun, and I turn away from my family to see a pretty woman in her midtwenties staring at me. Something about her is familiar, but I can't place her. I scan my memory, not wanting to insult her. I have no idea who she is. "Yes?" I ask. "Hi?" My voice is high pitched and uncertain. I really hope it's not one of Millie's middle school teachers. So many of them are young like this woman, and sometimes they all blend together with their unlined skin and thick-framed glasses. This one is pale, especially for summer, with skinny limbs, raven hair, and the kind of high breasts that would make any mother who's nursed a child feel envious. She's wearing a vintage Coca-Cola T-shirt and those wide-legged jeans everyone her age wears, even though it's too hot out for jeans.

She smiles and says, "It's me, *Anna*."

"Oh my goodness!" I say. "Anna, hi!" I rise from the bench and Millie hops up, too. Now the four of us are standing, but Anna backs up a little, instead of coming forward to shake my hand. It takes me aback. "Tom, Millie," I finally say, "this is Anna Smith, the *Anna* who's staying in our house."

I can tell Millie's admiring Anna's insouciant cool. Anna has a camera slung around her neck, and her face is pretty and makeup-free. She can't be more than twenty-five or twenty-six. I scan the friendship bracelets lining her wrists, and I freeze when I recognize them. Millie made those bracelets. They're mine.

I avert my eyes.

Is she seriously wearing my bracelets? She would have had to look through my dresser drawers to find them.

"Hi," she says, dropping her left hand behind her back, making me think she saw me notice the friendship bracelets. How could I not?

I look up at Tom, and I'm pretty sure he's looking at Anna's wrist too. Tom is the kind of man who would notice something like this, but I can't be totally sure, because his eyes are unreadable behind his sunglasses. "It's nice to meet you, Anna," he says, and I can tell he doesn't really mean it. He'll hate everything about this. I don't think Tom wants to think about anyone else staying in our house. Not because he likes the house—clearly he doesn't—but because even though everyone acts like vacation rentals are normal, it's weird to have someone staying in your house, and even weirder to run into them in town and realize they've gone through your things. "Are you enjoying the house?" he asks Anna, doing a piss-poor job at masking how much he hates small talk. He sounds like a combination of irritated and bored, like he has to force the words out.

"Oh, I *really* am," Anna says, smiling.

"Maybe you'd like to buy it from us," says Millie. "We might sell it."

"Millie!" I say.

"Sorry," Millie says, grinning.

"You're really thinking of selling it?" Anna asks, the sun so bright against her dark hair it looks metallic.

"It's just something we're starting to talk about," I say. "We're thinking of moving back into the city, but we haven't made any definite plans yet."

"The city's the best," Anna says, sounding younger than she is. "Do you work there?" she asks Tom.

Tom doesn't answer right away. Maybe he thinks she wants something from him. Tom is guarded like that. He's the kind of person who doesn't bend over backward to give someone a leg up unless they've proven themselves. We've had a few friends in Waring Ridge ask Tom for internships for their college-age children, and Tom always says to me, *How can I hire someone I barely know, just because I've been to a cocktail party with their parents?*

It's refreshing, actually.

"I do," Tom says.

"Well, then it'd be nice not to have the commute," Anna quips.

"Though we do love the house," I say. "And we love Waring Ridge . . ." My voice trails off. Why am I trying to sell her on the house? She's already there, and she's already made herself at home with my things.

"The house is magical," Anna says.

"You can say that again," says Millie. "It also might be haunted."

Anna laughs. "Do you believe in ghosts, Millie?" she asks.

"How can anyone not?" asks Millie.

I glance over at Tom, and I can tell by the small fake smile on his face that he's still entirely unnerved by the ghost thing. Millie drawing Eliza's likeness was too much for both of us. If there was ever a thing that made me realize it was time for me to give up the house, it was that drawing and Tom's response to it. Last night in the dark of our bedroom, I swear I'd never come so close to losing my marriage. But today, I feel more hopeful.

"Is there anything else we can help you with?" I ask Anna. "Do you need directions anywhere, or something specific?"

"Nah, I'm good. I just came for some groceries."

"Okay, well, it was so nice to meet you," I say, ready for the conversation to be over, ready to get back to Southport with my family and forget about Anna going through my things. Maybe most people would have spoken up if they ran into their tenant and noticed them wearing their stuff, but how awkward would that confrontation have been? And it's not like the bracelets are valuable . . .

"Nice to meet you," Tom echoes, followed by Millie.

"You have such a beautiful family," says Anna. Her eyes linger on me a beat too long, and it feels strange. "So lucky to have each other," she says.

"We are lucky," I say softly, but then Anna's turning her back, already walking away from us in the direction of our house.

TWENTY-FIVE

Anna. Waring Ridge, New York.

Back at Georgia's house, my hand is shaking as I turn the key in the lock and let myself in. I shut the front door behind me and make it to the couch and sit, hugging my legs against my chest. I feel like I'm going to be sick. I try to put my head between my knees, but it's useless. Everything feels overwhelming, like I made a huge mistake by doing this, by coming here. I close my eyes, but memories of my parents and Sam and who we once were on this property come flooding back: I can see my mom wearing an apron and cooking on the days Georgia and Max were still at school; and I can hear the way she would lightly sing a Welsh song about a character named Taffy while my brother lined up army soldiers near her feet. I used to watch them from the kitchen table while I was coloring, always coloring, just so happy to be in my mom's presence, to smell her sweet vanilla smell and feel the warmth of her arms.

I exhale, try to steady myself.

Knock, knock.

I wipe tears from my face. Is it Max at the door, maybe? I hope it's not Georgia and her family, because I can't do it again.

I swing open the door, and I see Carter standing there with a look of fury that could kill a grandma dead.

Tom Carter. Georgia's husband.

"What the fuck, Anna?" he says, visibly trembling.

"What are you doing here, Carter?" I ask sweetly. Like I said, we use last names at *Culture*. "Or should I call you Tom, now that we're at your house?"

TWENTY-SIX

Georgia. Waring Ridge, New York.

Millie and I are sitting across the table from each other at Bubby's diner on the far edge of town. Everyone calls it *town*, even though Waring Ridge's downtown is only a few blocks long. It's quaint and perfect, smacking of history, filled with little nooks, and what it might lack in size, it makes up for in charm.

Bubby's is an old-school diner with lace curtains and plastic menus. Maya and I come here for lunch or coffee sometimes, and Millie loves the pancakes. Tom didn't join us after we parted ways with Anna. He started furiously texting, and I tried to tell him about the friendship bracelets, but he cut me off, saying there was an emergency at work he had to deal with, and that we should order for him and have his food made to go if he wasn't back in time to eat.

Sometimes, when I'm fed up with the amount of hours Tom has to work, I think back to how excited he and I were just a few years ago when he got the offer to become editor in chief of *Culture*. I'll never forget the feeling I had when I saw the headline in the *New York Post*: *Tom Carter, former features director at* W *magazine, snaps top spot at* Culture *magazine.* It was the first place I saw it made official, and then it was everywhere. And it's meant a lot of late nights working, and times like this, when Millie and I think we have his attention and then, suddenly, we most certainly do not. But it's not about us, and I don't even think we have the right to take it personally. Running *Culture* is a big job, with a big salary and big job perks. And a very large time commitment.

These are the things I try to remind myself of when I want him back, all of him: his attention, his focus. And when we eventually move back to the city, which I already know in my heart is the thing I need to do for my family, maybe some of that *will* come back. Last night, after we talked about selling the Waring Ridge house, we had sex, and for the first time in a long time it felt emotional, something done with care and longing, and not like something we do routinely for a thousand other reasons. Tom held me as I fell asleep, which hasn't happened for months.

"Ooooh," says Millie as the waiter places the pancakes in front of her. "Thank you!"

I smile up at the waiter, a college-age kid I recognize from when he worked here last summer, and when he leaves, I feel myself tear up at the prospect of losing the house.

"Mom?" asks Millie.

"I'm fine," I say, waving my fork around. "I just feel emotional."

"About moving?" Millie asks, using her knife to push the slab of butter off her pancakes. She takes the maple syrup and douses the top pancake in a heart shape, just like she used to do as a tiny girl when we'd take her for breakfast in SoHo.

"Yeah," I say. "About moving." I slice into my omelet. "But I feel hopeful, too, like maybe it will be a new start for us."

"That's what you said about Waring Ridge," says Millie.

"Did I say that?" I ask, suddenly feeling a little panicky. I always look back on our life in the city as some kind of idyllic dream, but maybe even there, things were starting to break.

"I think so," says Millie, chewing.

"Hopefully not," I say. We eat in silence for a bit, and then I say, "I don't know, Millie. Something has to give. Your nightmares, Dad's stress."

"Your worry," says Millie.

"Well, part of the reason I'm worried is because of your nightmares and Dad's stress," I say. "I'm not blaming you, but I'm the mom, and I care about what's happening with you and Dad, and it feels like a weight when I can't fix any of it."

"Yeah, but I'd say you've been more anxious ever since we moved to the house."

I stop chewing. "Really?" I ask.

Millie shrugs. "Just an observation," she says, sounding more like an adult than I've ever heard her sound before.

"Well, then maybe it will be good for all of us." I think about the wretched nightmares I have of Eliza's body hitting the patio, and the way the crack of it always wakes me from sleep, drenched in sweat. I've always had those nightmares, even when we lived in the city. But even I can admit they're more frequent in the Waring Ridge house. In the daylight, when I think of Eliza, I can separate the terrible accident from every other golden moment she spent with us. She single-handedly saved me. I would be dead without her, long overdosed on a bottle of pills. But at night, deep inside my unconscious, the scarier memories claw their way to the surface.

Millie fidgets with her straw, bending it to different angles, stirring around the ice. When liquid flicks free from the straw, I bite my tongue to keep myself from scolding her. "Dad's the one who really seems off," Millie says softly.

A creeping feeling of dread settles like a blanket over my shoulders. I reach across the table and take her hand. "It'll get better," I say. "I promise."

TWENTY-SEVEN

Anna. Waring Ridge, New York.

"Come in, Carter," I say, steadier now that he's in front of me, now that my hand is forced, and I have to confront the consequences of my vile plan.

"What the *fuck* are you *doing*, Anna?" he says as he enters the house and slams the door behind him. We stand in the foyer, my eyes adjusting after the bright sunlight outside.

"Carter, language, please. Or, wait, sorry. *Tom.* Or should I call you *sweetheart*, or one of the other names Georgia calls you up here in the countryside?" I gesture behind me like I'm a *Price Is Right* model and his house is a prize. "Your house is so beautiful, by the way, and I'm absolutely *loving* it."

He stands a few feet away, like he's scared to get any closer, and then he snarls, *"What the fuck are you doing in my house?"*

"I told you I was looking to get away," I say innocently, and I feel the unreasonable urge to laugh.

"You sought out my house to fuck with me? How did you even know where I lived?"

Because I grew up on this property with Georgia. Because originally I found you to mess with Georgia's life. Because I knew you were married to her, and I knew there was a chance that if I could get a job at Culture, *I could make you want to cheat on Georgia with me.*

Of course, I don't say any of that. I need him to think this whole thing is about him, not Georgia. He has no idea I'm Eliza's daughter, or that I have any connection at all to the house or to Georgia. "Addresses are pretty easy to find online, *Tom*," I say. It's fun calling him by his first name. It feels a little naughty. He's technically my boss.

At first my whole plan was just to get a job at *Culture* and get him to fall in love with me, or at least sleep with me. I thought that would be enough to inflict the kind of damage on Georgia's life that she inflicted upon mine. But a few weeks ago, when he told me that he and Georgia were considering renting out their house, I couldn't resist checking the rental sites every day until it finally came on. And then I couldn't resist going through with it. It's nearly the twentieth anniversary of my mom dying here, and all my plans have actually worked. And now Tom Carter is standing here, looking sick to his stomach.

"I can't believe you would do this to me," he says, his deep blue eyes steely. And then, almost to himself, he mutters, "What a fool I've been."

I shrug, keeping my cool. "What's so weird about it? Now we live even closer than when I was in the city. You can come over here to sleep with me whenever you want. It's only, like, a half-hour away from your new beach house in Southport. Georgia was actually the one who told me you were renting in Southport. Is it nice there?"

He looks at me like I've slapped him. "Anna," he says, his voice so low I can barely hear it, "are you insane?"

"Not any more than I was last week when you were fucking me behind your wife's back. What's the big difference?"

"If you think I'm going to—"

"No, I mean it, *Tom*." Why does the word feel so delicious in my mouth? "I want to do it here. In this house. In your bed. The same place you make love to Georgia."

His mouth drops, and he starts slowly backing away from me. I've scared him for the first time, but not for the last.

"What's the matter, *Tom*?" I ask.

He stops. I can see him visibly trying to regain composure. He straightens to his full six foot three or four inches. "I'm calling our lawyer, Anna. You need to get out of this house."

"Surely you're kidding," I say. "I just got here."

"Dammit, Anna."

"See, but here's the thing," I say. "If you call your lawyer and get me kicked out, then you'll have to tell Georgia why. You'll have to admit to our love affair. And it *was* a love affair, I mean, right? We were falling for each other, whether either one of us wants to admit it. You might still be in love with me right now, even though we're obviously over."

"I'm not in love with you," he says, and I laugh. He looks so old standing there, so harmless. He looks nothing like the man I see running *Culture*, tearing through the city in his fancy suits and taking me in an apartment above Houston Street at sunset. Maybe this is just what the suburbs do to some people.

"I don't know what kind of game you're playing, Anna," he says, his hands clenched into fists like a cartoon. "But it won't work."

"Maybe not," I say. "But you're right, Tom. You have absolutely no idea what kind of game I'm playing."

TWENTY-EIGHT

Georgia. Waring Ridge, New York.

Millie and I are waiting for the check when Tom bursts into the restaurant like he's on fire. He scans the tables wildly, and when his gaze finally lands on Millie and me, his blue eyes are burning. He strides toward our table, and it's almost like his body is leaning left as he navigates the diner. At our table, he yanks a chair over the floor with a *screech* and sits down so hard I'm worried he'll bruise his tailbone.

"Sweetie?" I ask.

He runs a hand over the stubble on his face. He's not looking at us.

"You okay, Dad?" asks Millie, fiddling with her napkin, staring at him.

His body is tilted in the oddest way, like his back has been readjusted a few degrees. "There was an emergency at work," he says, voice gruff.

"Is everyone all right?" I ask.

"Everyone is *not* all right," he says. And then he lets out an oddly incongruent laugh. His hand goes back to his face, like he forgot something there. I can see a shake in his fingers. "But we will be."

"What are you talking about, Tom? What happened?"

"It's confidential," he says. He leans farther back in his chair until it looks like he's about to tip over. "But you've got nothing to worry about, Georgia, darling, *nothing*."

His voice is too masculine, almost condescending, and very unlike the way he usually talks to me. "You're scaring me," I say.

"Nothing to be scared of," he says in the same odd tone of voice. "Nothing I can't handle." There's practically a sneer on his face, and everything about his body language comes off as dismissive and filled with false confidence.

"Why don't we head back to Southport?" I suggest, needing to get him out of here to figure out what's really going on. "We could hit the beach and then nap and try to relax. You don't need to go into the office to deal with whatever this is?"

He jumps up like the wobbly figurine in a jack-in-the-box. "You're right," he says, pushing in his chair. "Let's get back to Southport and make a day of it. Let's *seize the day*."

"We haven't paid the check," I say, but he's already striding toward the counter.

"What's going on with him?" Millie asks as soon as he's out of earshot.

"I have no idea," I say, grabbing my purse, watching Tom at the counter fumbling for his credit card. Millie stands up now, too, and she's about to leave behind the tote bag with her doll. "For God's sake, Millie," I snap as she walks toward her father. "We came all this way for this doll, and you're about to just leave her here."

Millie's eyes widen, and for a second she looks like she might cry.

"I'm sorry," I say.

"Your *tone*," she says, mimicking what I sometimes say to her.

"I'm sorry, sweetie, I am." I pull her close and kiss the top of her blond head. "Forgive me."

She extracts herself from my hug and says "C'mon, Liza" to the doll, and it's so off-putting, both her talking to the doll like a real person and calling it Liza, that I have to make an effort not to let distaste show on my face. It feels juvenile, and like she's making a show of it.

I pick up my tote bag, slinging it over my shoulder as a loud *thwack* reverberates through the diner. I turn toward the sound, and suddenly I don't see Tom standing at the counter. I scan the restaurant, and then I see a few members of the staff rushing toward a spot on the floor that holds the crumpled body of my husband.

TWENTY-NINE

Anna. Waring Ridge, New York.

I close the door behind me and start sobbing. Every ounce of the hard shell I put on for Tom Carter comes crashing down, and I'm bawling my eyes out, the hardest I've cried since Sam died. I sit down on the floor and feel the checkerboard tiles cold against my sweaty palms.

What have I done?

The truth is that I had started to feel real feelings for Tom. I knew Georgia was married to him, and I'd loosely followed his career. (Because mostly, I followed Georgia, and sometimes Max, though he barely posted anything.) It's a little scary how closely you can follow someone's life without them even knowing. I knew when Georgia was on vacation; I knew when she was at one of Millie's tennis matches; and I knew that on Sundays, especially in warm weather, the three of them would likely be having brunch at Bubby's. Georgia always captioned those photos something cute and unclever, like *Back at Bubby's!* or *Sundays + family = pancakes at Bubby's!* She always posted innocuous stuff. She wasn't one of those women who shared their insecurities and vulnerabilities on Instagram; she didn't even post anything mildly political. It was all happy photos and brief captions. I couldn't stop checking her account because of the frequency with which she posted, but it was like eating sugary cereal—I was never really satisfied. And then last year, even before Sam died, I got this outlandish idea that I could take the train up to Waring Ridge and go to Bubby's, and that if I did it often enough, I would surely see Georgia and her family and be able to watch them from another table without being recognized. I never told Sam what I was thinking, because he would have freaked out and told me not to do it. Sam was a feeler and a thinker, and I was a feeler and a doer. His bipolar disorder didn't have an impulsivity component. It was a major difference between us; I was always more impulsive than he was, even as a child. When Sam was in a manic state, he was mostly elated and talking about all different kinds of creative ideas—which for him were usually things he could build with his hands. But there were only certain times when his mood was balanced enough that he could actually execute the ideas. If he came down too far, he could barely get out of bed, let alone make happen the projects he'd just been talking about the week before.

It always amazed Sam and me that Georgia and Max never tried to reach out to us at any point. It was one of the constant conversations we had with each other, sometimes out of the blue; we'd be hanging around my kitchen drinking coffee or beer, and one of us would say, "It's like that family just erased us after Mom died." Because that's how it felt. My dad was tight lipped about the fallout, so I suppose there's a chance Georgia and Max's dad tried to make amends, but I don't think so. And Georgia and Max, even in the age of today's internet when you can find anyone, never thought to find us. Weren't they curious how we were doing? How we'd survived losing our mother on a bloodied stone patio outside their home?

I never thought I'd see Georgia's family this early in my Waring Ridge stay. I always imagined it would be more dramatic, that maybe Georgia would find me out first by some small slip of the tongue, like the one I made about the diving board, a diving board that was no longer there, one I couldn't have seen in any pictures online.

I was there that day over twenty years ago when Max split his head open on the diving board. That diving board felt like sandpaper beneath our feet, and one day, when Sam and I were around four and Max was ten and Georgia fourteen, Max told us all to watch him do a *reverse*. None of us had any idea what that word meant except Georgia. Obviously, my mother would have stopped Max from trying that gravity-defying dive if she'd known what it was. But I could tell Georgia knew exactly what Max was about to attempt, because she stood there on the edge of the pool with her arms crossed over the front of her bathing suit, a slim hip cocked to the side, just waiting for him to try the dive and fail. She was like that, an ethereal ice queen laughing at the misguided attempts of the rest of us, and that day she stood there watching with a smug smile on her face as her little brother took off along the board like it was a runway and he was a plane. When his body flew off the end of the board, he tried to reverse into a backflip, his body tilting enthusiastically backward until a *crack* sounded when his head hit the edge of the diving board. His limp body splashed into the water like a rag doll, and bright red blood spotted the pool in blooming swirls. Sam and I stood paralyzed with fear as my mom jumped in after Max. And with her arm crossed over Max's chest as she dragged him to the side of the pool, my mom screamed to Georgia to call an ambulance. Georgia's mouth made a tiny O, and then she sprinted toward the house.

That diving board incident was seared into my memory, but I'd forgotten Georgia and Max's dad had the diving board taken out. And I'd blurted it on the phone call with Georgia before I could think better of it.

I guess there's always been a part of me, ever since I came up with this plan, that knew I could be discovered. When Georgia told me that her brother was staying on the property, I briefly worried Max would recognize me right away, but when I look at myself now I can barely see a trace of what I looked like back then.

I think about Tom and wonder what he's saying to Georgia. Is he telling her everything? Or is he lying to her, just like he has since the day we met and sparks lit the air between us? He never lied to me about being married. He knew I knew. But he certainly lied to Georgia, which makes him a liar, just like me.

I recline against the couch that's so clearly Tom's domain, his property. I lift my phone and turn the camera around on myself, trying to angle it for the best shot. And then I decide to do one better.

I tear up the curving staircase, no longer afraid of this house. In Georgia's closet I find a nightie. I get naked and slip it on, the silk cool against my body. It's black with yellow ribbon weaving over the top in a pattern so specific that there's no way Tom won't recognize it as Georgia's. I get into their bed and I lie on my back, resting a hand between my head and the pillow. With the camera flipped I can see myself as others would see me right now: cheeks stained with mascara, my green eyes brighter than ever from crying, beautiful and deadly. I snap the photo and load it onto Instagram, which I know for sure that Tom will check. I imagine how he'll feel seeing me in his bed in his wife's clothing, and it gives me such perverse pleasure I almost start laughing.

I caption it *#gotcha* and press post.

I'm in charge here. I can't forget that.

THIRTY

Georgia. Waring Ridge, New York.

I race through the diner with Millie at my heels. Tom's lying on his back, completely still. "Tom!" I cry, kneeling down beside him along with what feels like half the staff. Someone's checking his pulse as I bend forward and wrap my arms around him. He's so incredibly warm. "Tom!" I shout, shaking his shoulders, and his eyes finally flutter open and find Millie.

"Mills?" he asks, and then he looks at her like there's a follow-up question he can't remember.

"Are you all right?" I ask. "What happened?"

His eyes finally find mine. His pupils are too wide.

I turn to the college-age girl working the register. "Did you see how he fell? Did he hit his head?" I run my hands through his hair to feel for a bump or any bleeding, but there's nothing.

"I don't think so," she says, her face pale. Millie cries softly beside me, holding Tom's hand. "He sorta seemed dizzy and weird, and then he fainted forward into the hostess stand, and then he kinda slumped onto the ground. His head definitely didn't hit first."

Tom tries to sit up. I go to help him, but one of the cooks has emerged from the kitchen with a first aid kit and says, "Buddy, you're just gonna lie here for a few minutes, okay? And then we'll get you all on your way. No rush after you've passed out, yeah? We don't need you falling again."

Tom's suddenly alert enough to seem mortified. He passes a hand over his eyes.

"We should go get you checked out," I say.

"No, we shouldn't," says Tom. "I was hot, I felt faint, I passed out."

"It's not really that hot in here, buddy," says the cook, to which Tom replies, "I was just outside, where it's boiling."

"Something could be wrong," I say.

"Trust me, Georgia, it's nothing," Tom says. "We just need to get home."

THIRTY-ONE

Anna. Waring Ridge, New York.

That evening, I'm curled up in a ball in Georgia's bed when there's a hard knock on the door.

I trek down the stairs, still wearing Georgia's nightie. I fling open the door and see a man who looks familiar, and then my brain pieces together that it's the same man I saw outside in the brush last night, spying on me.

"Hi," the man says, and if he notices that I'm wearing lingerie, he's adept at not showing it. "I'm Ethan, I live just down the road in the barn."

It's hilarious that he calls his multimillion dollar home a barn, but that's kind of the vibe in Waring Ridge. So be it, I guess.

"Cool house," I say.

"Thanks," the man says with a genuine smile, like he's just so proud of the home his multimillions have bought him.

"I saw you last night in the brush outside my window," I snap. "Watching me."

His eyebrows go up, and he takes a small step back. "You might have seen me outside," he says quickly, "because my property line is right there." He gestures to the side of Georgia's house.

"Or maybe you have a thing for spying on people."

"I can assure you I don't," he says.

"Can I help you with something?" I ask, suddenly annoyed that he's even here, feeling so bored and dark that I'm considering trying to just fall asleep for the night once he leaves.

"Actually, I'm here to offer *you* help," he says. "There's a storm coming in tomorrow with high winds, and you'll likely lose power. Your house doesn't have a generator, but ours does. So if you need anything, I just want to let you know my wife and I are home and willing to help. I'll text Max, too, so he knows you're both welcome."

"I might feel more psyched about that if you weren't a Peeping Tom," I say.

Ethan's eyes widen. I lean out the doorframe a little and see that Max's red truck is back. And then I shut the door in Ethan's face.

I take off through the house and exit through the screen porch. I fly across the green-black grass, praying the bats aren't out yet. It's that time of night when nocturnal animals wake up and prepare to hunt and feast, and I feel wild out here, surrounded by nothing but woods and memories. I rap my knuckles hard against the door of the cottage, and Max answers my knock in Adidas shorts and a gray T-shirt. I light up at the sight of him.

"Hey, what's up?" he asks, his lip curled in a smile that tells me he's glad I came.

"You wanna go check out the cliffs?" I ask.

Max shifts his weight, giving me a once-over like there's no way I'm dressed for any kind of cliffs. To start with, I'm barefoot, my gray toenail polish looking nearly black beneath the darkening sky. "C'mon," I say. "I saw the cliffs on the map, and I want to check them out. You aren't afraid of heights, are you?"

"I'm not," he says, stalling. "I just haven't been back there in a really long time. Since I was a kid."

I look over my shoulder at the gate. "It's not locked," I say. "And I don't want to go by myself and get eaten by a bear, you know what I mean? And I think you'd scare off a bear, on account of you being so big and strong."

Max laughs, but he still doesn't say yes.

"Do you have a blanket we could bring?" I ask.

He bites his lower lip, looking suddenly like the child I once knew. "Yeah, I do," he says slowly, like he's considering it.

I smile. "Then what are we waiting for?"

His eyes are saucers. "Okay," he says. "I'll go with you. But you haven't been drinking or anything, right? We aren't going toward the edge in the dark. It's too dangerous back there."

But you and Georgia went out there when nobody was watching you . . .

My dad used to say that even when Georgia's mom was alive, her drinking took so much of my mother's attention that Max and Georgia got away with murder.

Maybe it was my mom's fault, too.

Maybe it was everyone's fault. All of it.

I brush off the thought and back down the porch steps. Max disappears inside his cottage and then emerges with a wool blanket the color of oatmeal.

We start together in silence toward the gate. "What the heck are you wearing?" Max asks, his voice breaking through the quiet, echoing the closer we get to the cliffs.

"Lingerie," I say.

"Do you need a sweatshirt?" he asks.

"Do you not like lingerie?" I ask.

He laughs, but it's a nervous one, and adrenaline charges the air between us like something electrical.

We slip through the gate. "Why isn't it locked?" I ask.

"Because Georgia's kid, Millie, is such a city kid, and so risk averse, that she'd never come out here by herself and do something this outdoorsy and risky."

"What's she like?" I ask as we edge beneath the cover of trees.

"Millie?" He shrugs. "A little aloof, actually. When I moved up here I thought I'd have a relationship with her, because she's my niece and everything, and I thought it would be nice to have the extra time together. But she always seems so distracted. And sometimes she leaves the room all together when I arrive. So it's not like I've made much progress."

"And Georgia? What's she like?"

Max pushes aside brush so we can pass. "Georgia's great," he says. "I love my sister. And she's a good mom. Worries a lot, but I think that's most moms."

"Did yours?" I ask.

"Nope," Max said. "Not in the typical way. I think the other emotions were so overwhelming that she never really made it all the way down the line to worry."

"What about your nanny?" I need to be careful. But I'm so desperate to hear him say anything about my mom and us, even a kernel of something I don't know, a perspective I didn't have back then. "Did she have her own kids?"

"Yeah."

"Did she worry about them?"

Max shrugs. "Not really. I don't think it was in her nature. With her own kids it always looked so easy, and so effortless. She was a mom to them in a way that felt way more normal compared to what Georgia and I had with our mom."

A zing of longing fires through me. To have it back—to have my mom with me now. To have her still mothering and caring for Sam when he needed her in his darkest moments. I'm not saying her death caused his bipolar disorder, but if she were alive, maybe it would have been enough to keep *him* alive. Because I clearly wasn't enough. Or at least that's what it feels like to me. I didn't stop Sam from doing what he did, that's the truth of it, and I don't know how I'm ever supposed to recover from that.

Max and I are quiet for a few moments, twigs crunching beneath our feet as we walk toward the cliffs. And then Max says, "My family drove Eliza to worry, I guess. Not her own kids. Because my mom drank herself to death and then Georgia set off on that same path. Georgia would be dead without Eliza's worry and care and intervention. It still amazes me that my sister survived after she killed Eliza."

I freeze. "What do you mean, *killed* her?" I ask, barely managing to get the words out. I have to work to make myself start walking again so Max won't suspect how upset he's made me.

Max focuses on his feet passing over the earth, and his entire being seems to sink as he travels over the ground, like he's shrinking in response to what he's said. "I don't mean *killed her*, not really," he says slowly. "I just mean that Georgia's drugs are why Eliza went onto the roof in the first place. She died trying to get them. Georgia already blames herself, and I don't usually blame her, because it wasn't her intention—it was only a horrible accident. Maybe I'm just in a mood."

Maybe he is. I don't dare say anything more, I'm too scared I'll give myself away.

Max is quiet as we step carefully toward the cliffs. At this point on the property, the cliffs drop two hundred feet to a ravine. On the other side of the ravine, they swing upward at an angle so that you can see a beautiful, solid rocky cliff face to the north. A full moon hangs high in the ever-darkening sky. "It's gorgeous out here," I say.

"It is," Max says as we creep closer to the edge. There's a grassy spot about ten feet away from where it all drops off, and Max whips the blanket high into the air and lets it fall. Maybe he thinks if he plants a spot this far away from the edge, then I'll sit down and behave myself. But I've never been the kind of person who can resist danger.

I creep closer without him.

"Anna," he says, but the wind has picked up, and it nearly carries away his voice. Maybe that creepy neighbor Ethan was right about an incoming storm.

I inch closer to the cliffs, the hair on the back of my neck standing on edge.

"That's close enough," Max says. "Come back."

A few more feet and I'm almost there. A bird cries out in the branches high above my head. The grass is still silky beneath my bare feet, which feels like a trick. If you were walking out here on this plush carpet, you'd never know the terrain was about to turn treacherous. That's exactly what it was like growing up. We had everything, and then it was gone. My dad was the only one who'd seen the warning signs, the writing on the wall. Sam and I could only see a dreamy cottage in the countryside with two parents who loved us. We were too young to be anything other than foolish.

I'm at the cliff's edge, and Max's voice has faded behind me, and for a moment I just stare down into the abyss. It's mind-blowingly cavernous, there's only one small ledge about fifty feet down, and then another one hundred fifty feet to a rocky bottom. I'm dizzy with vertigo peering into it, and the dizziness is the only thing that makes me take a step back, and then there's a strong, warm hand on my bare shoulder.

"Anna," Max says, a slight shake in his voice. "I'm serious. It's too dangerous to be this close. Please."

I stare into his deep brown eyes, and right then I want nothing more than to tell him who I really am.

"Max," I say, and I almost do it, it's right there on the tip of my tongue. I can feel the cliff's edge, too close, too dangerous, and I open my mouth to speak the words: *It's me, Anna, Sam's twin, Eliza's daughter, the girl from your childhood . . .*

But nothing comes out. And then, instead of telling him the truth, I kiss him. My mouth is suddenly on his, and at first, he's surprised, but then he's returning the kiss, truly kissing me, every ounce of him awake and alive and suddenly very much in charge. His hands are on the small of my back, pulling me against him. My hands are on his face, in his hair, and the night is so dark back here that I can barely see the blanket a few feet away, but I know that's where we need to go, so I tug him there, and then we're tumbling down together. An animal cries out, but nothing matters except the feeling of Max's hand on my bare skin, and his mouth on mine.

As Max takes everything further, I turn my head to see the Waring Ridge house lit up against the sky, and I revel in the feeling of being more tethered to my past than I ever could have imagined.

THIRTY-TWO

Georgia. Southport, Connecticut.

That night, Millie and I are snuggled up on the full-size bed in her room. We crashed there with books after spending hours at the beach by ourselves. Tom's been shut inside the downstairs office all day, and every time I tried to check on him, he grumbled that he still had to deal with his work emergency. After the incident at Bubby's, I insisted on driving us from Waring Ridge back to Southport, and Tom continually assured me he was fine and didn't need to see his doctor. But he also told me that the sun was too bright in the car and that he needed to close his eyes. He's obviously not okay.

Millie and I had oatmeal for dinner, too exhausted to go out again, and now Millie's drifting off to sleep with a well-loved library copy of *Shatter Me* in her small hands. I tuck a soft blanket over her and curl up along her spine, my arm slung over her torso. Her body is so warm against mine. Her blond head rests against her doll, and I think about how much I used to love that doll when I was a child, and how quickly it went from a beloved plaything to something much darker. Imagine going from tea party companion to drug mule? I must be exhausted and half-sunstroked to be thinking of the tragedies of my life from the doll's perspective, but it's hard not to imagine the scene on the roof from the ever-seeing eyes of the doll: Eliza coming through the window and onto the roof to sweep it into her arms, and then losing her balance and slipping. It's what I've been told must have happened.

An uneasy feeling comes over me. I check the clock: it's only eight thirty, but Millie's fast asleep. I slip from her bed, eager to talk to Tom without her listening ears picking up everything.

My palm is light on the banister as I descend the staircase. I open the door to the downstairs office without knocking and see Tom sitting in front of his open laptop, his body slumped forward and his head in his hands.

"Tom, please," I say. "What happened this morning? Can't you at least tell me something?"

Tom looks up, his blue eyes angrier than I've seen them in a long time. Whatever happened at work must have been personal, because none of this matches the way Tom normally reacts to a work obstacle.

"Tom, please," I say again when he gives me nothing.

"I made a mistake with someone we hired," he finally says. "And now this person is causing me trouble. I really can't say much more than that, Georgia. It's confidential."

His eyes are pleading, but I'm not sure what he's asking. I step into the office with its cool-gray wooden tones and stacked books. A chrome desk sits by the window facing the front yard. During the daylight, the white picket fence and rose bushes are visible through the window, but now I just see darkness and moonlight splashed across the yard.

I move closer to Tom, and I don't fight him when he pulls me into his lap. I'm straddling him, feeling him react beneath me to the presence of my body against his. I put a hand to the side of his face. "I'm sorry," I whisper.

"You're not the one who should be apologizing," he says, his hands on my hips. "*I'm* sorry." His fingers dig in so hard it starts to hurt. "Is Millie sleeping?" he asks.

I nod.

"Lock the door," he says.

I do it because I want what he's asking for. I want us back on track. I want this awful period of our marriage to be *over*, to be something we look back upon like a hazy nightmare.

"Shut the shades," Tom says, his voice softer now, and I do that, too. Then I pull my pajamas off and stand there naked before him. I can feel longing deep in my stomach, a wish for something so much more than just sex. I want him back. All of him. I don't know what has happened this past year, I really don't, but I know it's my doing.

"I've done something terrible to us, and I want to fix it," I say, trying to put a voice to my feelings for once, to make him stop guessing.

He stands up, towering over me. "So have I," he says, closing the inches between us. "The problems between us are my fault, too, Georgia, trust me." He puts a hand on the side of my face and then kisses me so deeply I lose my breath. "And I'm going to make it up to you," he says, his voice cracking with emotion. Anger? Guilt? Regret? I have no idea what's going on with him, and then he pushes me back against the wall and his hand goes between my legs. We kiss, so immersed in each other that I feel completely thrown. And then Tom lifts me up and we're having sex, and it starts like something wild but then slows to resemble the kind of lovemaking that we did all through our twenties. It should bring me to my knees to have the sensuality and tenderness back, but instead it scares me a little. I have the sickening feeling that I'm missing something, like there's a piece to the puzzle of my marriage just outside my peripheral vision.

"Tom," I say when he finishes. "I love you."

"I love you, too, Georgie."

"Are we okay?" I ask, searching his eyes in the dark.

"Maybe not," he says. "But we will be."

THIRTY-THREE

Anna. Waring Ridge, New York.

Max and I are lying on our backs gazing up at the stars visible through a light cover of trees. There's a stillness in the air, as though the fury of what we just did has exhausted the night around us. My body feels wrung out and refilled with purpose. There's a sinking melancholy I've felt ever since losing Sam, maybe even since losing my mom. And certainly, this property has haunted me ever since my mom fell, but seeing it through adult eyes is a little bit like a balm on old wounds. The pain isn't gone. But it's like the melancholy has moved over just an inch to make way for something new, even if I'm not exactly sure what that is.

Max's fingers find mine. "That was a surprise," he says softly, both of us still looking up into the sky.

"Not really," I say.

He doesn't say anything, but a part of him must know it's true. There was a way we saw each other that first day he came to meet me at the house, a very specific way our eyes met. And even if he didn't recognize me, a part of him must have recognized *something* in me, the way a soul recognizes another they're destined to be with in a larger way. Not forever or anything like that. I'm not talking about love at first sight, only the energy that passes between two people who are drawn to each other for an intangible purpose. I could tell he felt it too.

I didn't have that the first time I met Tom Carter. There was attraction, sure, but it was clouded by my ulterior motives. And then whatever was there grew, slowly at first, then snowballing into a full-blown love affair. Tom talked about Georgia, of course. The first time he came to my apartment, when it was clear what was going to happen, he said, "I know you know I have a wife. You must know, through work chatter?"

I nodded.

"I know what we're doing is wrong," he said. "But I want to do it, and I just want to make absolutely sure that you didn't invite me here with any other understanding."

No one had ever been so straightforward with me, even under the murkiest circumstances. And as we went on sleeping together over the next few weeks, he kept bringing things up about Georgia and the strain his marriage was under in Waring Ridge, until I had to tell him to shut up. At first, I loved hearing about Georgia. I loved hearing Tom tell me how much he hated living outside the city, but how Georgia was taking to it like white on rice, like she'd been born to live in that house. I loved hearing about the neighbors who wouldn't cut down some ash tree Tom was obsessed with. I loved hearing how Tom felt like a fish out of water at the school events with the other dads who were mostly in finance, with Connecticut upbringings and boarding school pedigrees. I especially loved when Tom took a turn and decided his new house in Waring Ridge was haunted by the ghost of Georgia's mom and my mom. *My wife's mother died in our bathroom, and her nanny fell from the roof right outside our bedroom!* he once told me after sex, with total indignation. He said there were nights he swore he heard the cries of both women, but Georgia had assured him it was only coyotes. There were times I was sure he was nearly losing it with how often he talked about the supernatural. *You hear my mother in that house?* I wanted to ask him, but of course I couldn't, not without terrifying him and giving away my entire plan. I toyed with the idea of asking him if there was a weekend I could sneak up to the house when Georgia was away, but I worried it was too forward and that I'd scare him off by even thinking about it. But suddenly I wanted to revisit that house with all my being, because if it was really haunted, then I wanted to see or hear my mom, too.

I haven't seen her here in this house, and I haven't heard her. But if I try really hard, I think I can feel her on this property, and certainly when I visited the cottage and all my memories came flooding back. Even being with Max and remembering the way she took care of him has healed a small part of me, just remembering how loving she was, how hardworking. So maybe I don't believe in the supernatural, but I do believe in memories and a place holding the energy of the people who once lived there.

"What is it, do you think?" I ask Max now, our fingers laced together. "That draws people into each other's orbits?"

Max shrugs beside me. "I dunno. I haven't figured any of that out yet."

"Do you have a girlfriend?" I ask.

His head whips toward me. "I would never have done what I just did with you if I had a girlfriend. What's the point of having a girlfriend you cheat on?"

I laugh. "Plenty of people do not agree with you."

"Well, I feel strongly about it. I'm not settling down until it's the person to settle down for. It's weird seeing Tom and Georgia up close. It looks downright boring and halfway miserable."

"So you're a romantic," I say.

"I actually *am*," he says. "I'm looking for *the one*, I'm not even kidding you. I think my mom was that for my dad. I mean, they fought, and my mom caused everyone all kinds of stress with her alcoholism, but my dad was singularly in love with her."

"And was she in love with him?"

"I think so, but she was harder to read. It's impossible for me to understand what it was that made her so miserable she had to drink."

"I don't think it goes like that," I say.

"Yeah?"

"Yeah. I think your mom could have been in love with your dad, in love with you and Georgia, and still want to drink herself into oblivion."

"You're probably right, but it's hard to truly believe that when you're the child of an alcoholic."

"I'm sorry," I say.

"Me too," he says.

We're quiet for a moment, and then I just go for it. "And Eliza? Your nanny? Was she *singularly in love* with her husband?" I ask, using his wording. I need to hear it from him. It's so hard for me to remember my parents together, I was so little.

"I think she was," he says, still looking up into the night sky, resting the crook of his arm over his head. "But I rarely saw them together. They lived in that little cottage, you know. But we didn't see the dad a lot."

"The dad?" I ask.

"Yeah. I guess I thought of him as *the dad*. He and Eliza were married, and they had twins. Anna and Sam."

My heart floods with emotion to hear him use our names together.

"What happened to them?" I ask, my blood picking up speed inside my veins. I can't believe I'm doing this.

"I don't know," Max says, his voice careful, guarded. "My dad never spoke about them. I had a lot of problems with my dad, and one of them was that he just wouldn't talk about any of it after it happened. Not my mom's death, nor Eliza's."

"But didn't you ever look them up?" I blurt. I can't seem to stop myself. It's what Sam and I always wanted to know, and here's my chance to ask it for both of us.

Max turns onto his side. He looks into my eyes, his hand softly grazing my cheek. He shakes his head and says, "Things got bad after Eliza died. I turned thirteen that fall and got into all kinds of shit. And

I couldn't really bear to think about the kids. I loved them, you know? They were just kids. Nice kids, too, unlike Georgia and me."

I make myself stop asking questions. I can't safely push this any further. I gently pull him to me, feeling his soft, full lips against mine. I'm aware of the cliffs' edge near, and the moon shining against the cliff face to the north, making the rocks glow. Max kisses me back, and then his lips travel to my neck. I turn my head and feel the warmth of him against my body. From this angle, I can see a single light on in the cottage. Everything around me feels dangerous tonight, and nothing about me feels *nice* anymore.

"We should swim," Max whispers into my ear.

"Right now?" I ask.

"Yeah," Max says. "Unless you're busy."

I laugh. "I don't think that's a good idea," I say. "I saw something dead in there. Something bloated and furry floating in the water." I'm not sure why I'm lying. But I suddenly feel scared of the dark corners of this property, the water that looks black beneath the night sky.

"Really? Gross," says Max, kissing along my collarbone.

"That neighbor Ethan came by today," I say to change the subject.

Max's hands trail my body, turning me toward him. "That guy is overly nice," he says, and I enjoy every second of it, the way we're kissing and talking like old lovers, instead of new ones. "It weirds me out."

"Me too," I say. "And I saw him yesterday in the brush. He says it's because that's his property line, but I swear to God he was staring through the window and spying on me."

Max lets out a chuckle, like it's pathetic instead of scary. "Fucking Ethan," he says. "What a creep."

THIRTY-FOUR

Georgia. Southport, Connecticut.

At three a.m. I wake to screaming. Tom and I are still in the downstairs office—we must have fallen asleep there—and his arms are like tentacles pinning me to the sea floor. It takes all my might to fling them off and free myself from his grip. I sprint from the room and up the stairs.

"Millie! I'm coming!"

I can hear Tom pounding the steps behind me. Millie's screaming intensifies until the entire house feels like it's shaking. I fling open the door to her bedroom and see her standing straight up in the middle of her bed, clutching her doll to her chest, and screaming bloody murder.

"Millie," I say, moving toward her, climbing onto the bed and wrapping my arms around her, both of us standing among the tangled blankets.

Tom closes in on us. He gently tugs Millie from a standing position down onto the bed and into his arms. "Shhhhh, baby, you're okay."

I kneel beside her, kissing her face. "I'm so sorry, sweetie," I say, "I thought we'd get a break from these dreams in Southport." My eyes drop to the doll beside Millie. We just got her back, and now here we are again with the nightmares.

"What was it, Mills?" Tom asks. "Do you remember?"

Sometimes when Millie has nightmares, she's still half-asleep. But this time, when she speaks, her words and meaning are clear as a bell.

"Mom," she says, turning to me. "I saw that girl. *Anna.* The one who's renting our house."

"You saw her in your dream?"

"Yes. We were at our house. Anna was there and so was Ethan, I mean, Mr. Campbell. And the three of you were arguing, and then . . ." Her voice trails off, and before starting again, she lets out a choked sob that sears me. "And then Mr. Campbell . . . he tried to kill you."

I turn to Tom, and he looks like he might be sick.

"It was just a dream," I say, but I can already feel goose bumps on my skin. Millie's crying now, her head in her hands. "There've been so many changes, Millie," I try, rubbing circles on her shoulder. "We're out of our house, Dad collapsed in the restaurant, and it must have been so scary for you to see that, to not know at first if he was okay. But it *is* going to be okay. We're going to have a good month here, it's just what we all need. And you can sleep in our room the entire rest of the month, all right, my love?"

Tom catches my glance over Millie's head, and I shrug. What else are we going to do?

Millie nods, not looking at us. "The dreams are just so scary when I'm in them," she says. "It's like they're really happening, like I'm watching all of this unfold. Every time."

"I get it, sweetheart. Maybe when we leave the house . . . and the doll behind . . ."

"Why would we ever leave Liza behind?" she asks.

I swallow. "Why did you name her that, Millie?"

She still won't look at me. "I don't know," she says, staring down at the doll's glassy face. "I guess because I keep dreaming of your nanny, Eliza, and the doll reminds me of her."

I shiver. I'm suddenly desperate for it to be morning, for the doll to be just a doll, for the nightmares to stop. "So many tragedies happened in our house, Millie," I say carefully. "Maybe it was wrong of me to want to move you there. You're obviously sensitive, and maybe you're picking up on things, and anyway that doll was around for all the things that happened there, and I know I sound ridiculous, but maybe we really do need a clean break from it all."

"That's what I've been saying," says Tom.

"I know," I snap. "I don't need you to tell me you told me so."

Millie glances from me to Tom. "Don't fight," she says. "And I'm not giving up the doll, so don't even try to take her away from me."

"I won't," I say quickly, even though I'm fantasizing about throwing the thing into a burning fireplace. "I'm sorry, Millie." And then I take Tom's hand to make a good show of it and bring it to my lips for a kiss. He's hiding something from me. I felt sure of it last night as we were falling asleep in each other's arms, and I can feel it now, a secret heavy in the ocean air between us.

"Come on, sweetie, we all need to sleep," I say, tugging Millie gently from the bed and leading her and Tom down the dark hall.

THIRTY-FIVE

Anna. Waring Ridge, New York.

The next morning the sun is hidden behind thick gray clouds, and I'm in Georgia's office, peering onto the front lawn, where four massive hawks circle something dead in the grass. My mood is sour, despite how good it felt to be with Max last night. *Why* did it feel that good? I honestly have no idea, or at least, it defies my ability with words to give it a proper explanation. And I'm not sure I want to dig deeper into it, because after he figures out who I am and what I've done with his sister's husband, and how I've infiltrated his childhood home under false pretenses, he'll never want to see or touch me again. Which I guess I can add to my little list of tragedies.

Last night, Max and I talked for hours—not any more directly about my mom or his—mostly about my photography, his film work, our friends, money, apartments, travel, food, and a bunch of things that feel easy to talk about with someone else who lives in your city. Turns out we have a lot of crossover and things in common, some creative people we both know, bars we like, neighborhoods we rented in. I was a little surprised we hadn't run into each other before at the bars near the one where I bartended, because Max said he went out in that neighborhood all the time, but the city is like that: it can feel like a small world or a vast ocean depending on whether you want to find someone or be found.

Around midnight, when we started to feel like we were freezing to death by the cliffs, we went to Max's cottage and drank tea, and then Max walked me back to Georgia's house around two a.m. I spent the next few hours searching every corner of Georgia's house for my mom's journal, but I turned up nothing. And then at daybreak an idea hit: What if Georgia slipped my mom's journal into a suitcase and took it with her to Southport? Maybe she didn't want me snooping through her things. I'd feel the same way if I were renting my house to a stranger, and I'd either hide my journal in an impossible hiding spot or take it with me. If the journal had anything incendiary about Georgia, why wouldn't she do the same?

In Georgia's office, I fire up her desktop computer. She doesn't keep it locked, which is a joke, and then I easily figure out her new address in Southport, because her search history shows she searched it dozens of times: *5655 Shore Drive Lane, Southport, Connecticut 06890.* On the map it's obvious that it's walkable to town.

I book an Uber. I'll have them drop me in downtown Southport, and then I'll figure it out from there.

Hi, Georgia, I imagine myself saying when she swings open the door to her extravagant beach house. *Remember me?*

THIRTY-SIX

Georgia. Southport, Connecticut.

Late the next morning, Tom, Millie, and I are under sun umbrellas at the beach eating chocolates. Millie leans back on her elbows, her green-and-white towel plush beneath her, candy wrappers everywhere. Tom walked into town this morning to a market called Spic & Span and picked up her favorites. I can feel both of us hovering over that razor-sharp edge of desperation, wanting Millie to be okay after last night, wanting this problem to be fixed. A few months ago, we did a few sessions with a really good children's therapist one town over. But then summer hit and Millie's tennis schedule got busy, and I know how bad that sounds that I would start missing her therapy appointments so she could play tennis . . .

Obviously we need to start going back.

The Southport sea is very pretty, all deep blues and calm waters. I'm desperate to be happy here, to start anew, but it doesn't even seem possible after yesterday. I watch Tom as he frantically scrolls an iPad, his hands moving too quickly, pausing every so often to stab a finger at the screen.

"Look at this one," he says to Millie and me, and then thrusts the iPad toward us. It's hard to get a good look with the sun's glare, but I squint and make out a photo of a living room.

"It's a tiny two-bedroom in SoHo," he says, his voice urgent. "But it's doable, we could easily rent there for a year while we sort out what to do with the Waring Ridge house."

All morning, his words have poured from his mouth too quickly, like rainwater tearing down the city streets during a storm. "I think you need to chill on the caffeine," I say.

"What?" he asks. I can't make out his eyes through his sunglasses.

"You seem really amped up," I say.

"I told you I had shit going on at work," Tom says.

Millie watches Tom carefully, taking a bite of a chewy caramel chocolate.

"You basically collapsed in front of our eyes yesterday," I say. "I'm just asking that you try to slow down today. Even enjoy this vacation, rather than search online for new apartments." I gesture to the water. "It's beautiful here."

Tom shoves the iPad into the beach bag and sits back on his elbows, irritated. I reach for his hand and give it a squeeze. "I want you to feel better," I say.

"And that's going to take some time," he says.

"For all of us," I say.

"For all of us," he says.

THIRTY-SEVEN

Anna. Southport, Connecticut.

I have the Uber drop me off a few houses down from Georgia and Tom's beach house. Southport is bright and sunny compared to the current weather in Waring Ridge; maybe the storm is going to miss them entirely. I hop out of the Uber and realize the street is more populated than I was hoping for. The houses are pretty close together, and I'm worried I'll look too conspicuous creeping over the sidewalk and trying to scope out Tom and Georgia's house. But maybe this kind of activity—joggers, a couple walking their golden retriever, a family pushing a stroller with a beach bag looped over the side—is exactly what I need to blend in.

The neighborhood is straight out of a movie: clapboard beach houses on the water with meticulously white picket fences. Behind the houses, the sun bounces off the water in a hard yellow ball that sears my vision. Between each house you can make out a strip of sand grass and then half a football field of sandy beach before the sea. I keep walking along the sidewalk, cursing myself for not wearing a disguise or at least a hat as I trod closer to a mailbox with a golden sticker marking *5655*. What am I going to say if Georgia and Tom see me through the front window? My heart pounds as I edge toward the house. When it's upon me, I turn to the left and can't believe my luck: through the alley between the houses, I see that Georgia, Tom, and Millie are out at the beach, sitting about forty yards away beneath an umbrella, all three of them staring off into the ocean like a postcard.

I take a sharp left through their front gate, walking with purpose so the neighbors don't think anything's weird about me being there. I climb two steps onto a front porch and try the front door, my palms sweating against the warm metal doorknob, but it's locked. I need to try the back of the house and hope they don't see me.

I retreat down the front porch steps and wind along the side of the house. My heart pounds to see the three of them out there on the beach and to be this exposed. If they turn back and see me, I have no idea what I'll do. Run? Tom's leaning on his elbows, staring at the water. Georgia is turned slightly toward him, and it looks like she's holding his hand, so obviously he hasn't told her about us yet. Or is this just what rich married people do? Maybe she knew he was having an affair this year, and the only piece of the puzzle she's missing is that it was with me? Millie's brushing sand off her legs, and I decide to just make a break for it. I tuck my head and sprint the rest of the way along the house to the back, where there's a screen door. Bingo. I open it and flinch at the loud *creak* it makes.

I practically throw myself into the kitchen and out of their sight. My heart is thumping wildly, skipping beats. I peer out the window to the beach, because if they heard the door and they're coming to check the house, I need to hide. But they're all still sitting there staring at the ocean, enjoying the view like nothing could ever possibly go wrong in their saccharine existence.

I race through the kitchen and scamper up the stairs. The house is simple and lovely, decorated like a Pottery Barn catalog. I head to the bedroom at the top of the stairs and start flinging open drawers. Georgia has neatly unpacked everything, but unlike in Waring Ridge, where I can take my time looking through all her stuff, here I feel frantic. And once I move something, it's hard to get it back into place the way Georgia had it, because she has folding skills like a Banana Republic merchandiser, and I don't. I've gone through all the drawers, and then I'm working on a side table when I hear a hard knock on the front door.

I freeze. Nothing happens, until a few moments later when the screen door makes the exact same *creak* it did when I opened it.

"Hello?" a voice calls from downstairs. "Is someone here?"

The voice is warbly—it doesn't sound like Georgia.

I'm clutching a notepad in midair, my fingers sweaty. On the notepad, Georgia wrote down a few notes, mostly groceries and a few mundane to-do items. I slowly lower it back down into the top drawer of the bedside table and slide it shut. I try to breathe, to just relax for a second. I don't hear anyone moving downstairs, and I still have time to hide in a closet if they come upstairs. I don't move my feet for fear of making a noise, but I turn my head to look out the window onto the beach. Tom, Georgia, and Millie are still out there. Who in the world is inside their house?

"Hello?" the voice calls again, elongating the second syllable like a question. "Anyone home?"

After what feels like an eternity, I hear the door shut again. I stay frozen in place, listening. The window is open, and I can see Georgia and Tom still sitting beneath the umbrella, and Georgia's resting her head on Tom's shoulder. They both watch Millie splashing in the surf. A moment later I see a figure emerge onto the beach, walking unsteadily toward Tom, Georgia, and Millie. It's a woman who looks to be in her sixties or seventies, and she seems to be injured in some way based on the way she's walking. She calls to Tom and Georgia, and Georgia turns first. I can't make out Georgia's face well enough to discern if she recognizes the woman. Maybe she's someone Georgia invited? Why else would she enter the house?

A text comes through on my phone. It's Max.

Hey. You coming back soon?

I ignore the text and shove the phone back inside my pocket, my fingers trembling.

THIRTY-EIGHT

Georgia. Southport, Connecticut.

"Hello, hello!" says an elderly woman walking toward us on the beach.

"Hi," I say, pushing to a stand, unsteady on the sand. Tom stays sitting. In some ways, Tom is refreshingly unsnobbish: he has no interest in talking to the rich banker dads he's met in town, and he's completely uninterested in wealth, only in career achievements, particularly creative ones, whether or not they lead to great financial reward. But the snottiest thing about him is the way he sizes up someone and decides whether he wants or needs to put the extra effort in to charm them. He's taken one look at this woman and decided he can't be bothered to stand up.

"I'm Harriet, from next door," the woman says, extending an arm. I shake her hand. And then my phone rings, and I see it's Max. I silence it.

"Oh, hi," I say. "I'm Georgia, and this is Tom, and our daughter, Millie." I gesture toward the surf, and Millie waves obligingly.

"I live right next door in that one," Harriet says, pointing to the light blue house next to ours.

"It's very pretty," I say.

Tom says nothing. He's still sitting on the towel, gazing up at Harriet like he's waiting for her to say something interesting. "Lived there forty-one years," she says proudly. "Just after I got married to Bill, the love of my life, God rest his soul."

"Oh, I'm sorry," I say.

"Me too," says the woman. "Not everyone is lucky to have a marriage like we did."

"I'm sure that's true," I say.

"Indeed," she says. "Anyway, I won't bother you anymore other than to say I'd love to have you all over for dinner tonight."

Oh, dear. Kind as the invitation is, this is potentially the last thing we all need. I'm about to tell her we could do another night, but she looks so hopeful standing there, and she's probably lonely. And really, what can it hurt? "Sure," I say. "What can we bring?"

"Georgia," says Tom from his spot on the towel. He practically snarls it.

Harriet ignores him. "Just yourselves. I'll pick up corn from the market, fresh tomatoes. You're not vegetarians, are you? Or one of those people who don't eat bread or milk?"

"We eat everything," I say.

"All right, then, it's set. How about seven thirty, is that too late for you all? I've got an SEI meeting tonight, that's Southport Environmental Initiative, and we'll be discussing some invasive species we've seen planted by residents in Southport, if you can believe that, and sometimes these conversations really get emotional and take a long time, and . . ."

"Isn't there a storm coming tonight?" Tom asks.

"Yes, that's right, let's exchange numbers just in case you need me," she says.

I'm standing there clutching my phone, so it's not like I can say no. I avoid Tom's glance as we enter each other's phone numbers.

"All right, then," says Harriet. "I'll leave you to this beautiful day." A salty breeze pushes my hair in front of my face. I tuck it behind my ears and force myself to smile at Harriet, as if my husband, daughter, and I are just a typical family enjoying their vacation, not one that seems to be imploding.

"It was nice to meet you," I say as pleasantly as I can.

"Likewise," says Harriet, and then she makes her way slowly back over the sand toward her house.

"Come on, Georgia," Tom snaps when she's out of ear shot.

"What was I supposed to say?"

"You could have said *no,* that's what you could have said."

"And how rude would that have been?"

"It's okay to say a thing that's best for our family. That's not rudeness."

"It's just dinner!" I say.

"It's not what we need right now," Tom says, and it's not like I can disagree with him when I was just thinking the same thing. "She might take this as an invitation to invade our entire trip. And I'm really over people invading my space these days."

"And what's that supposed to mean?" I ask.

"Nothing," Tom says, shaking his head.

I glance over at Millie wading into the surf. At the shoreline, seagulls surround something dead or forgotten and start savagely pecking at it, taking huge gulps of whatever it is.

"Let's go back inside," I say. "I've had enough of the heat."

THIRTY-NINE

Anna. Southport, Connecticut.

I can't find the journal anywhere inside Georgia and Tom's rental. Unless Georgia hid the journal in some bizarre hiding place . . . But it's certainly not anywhere among her clothes and the things she's unpacked.

From a quick glance out the window, I can tell Georgia and Tom are arguing about something. The older woman is making her way down the beach away from them, and then Georgia beckons Millie out of the surf. I need to get out of here before they come back to the house.

I leave the bedroom and hightail it down the stairs, racing through the lower level to the back, where the kitchen is. My mood feels erratic: I'm terrified of getting discovered inside the house and frustrated that I haven't found the journal here or in Waring Ridge, and that I haven't done much of anything except make a mess of things. When I get to the kitchen, before I really know what I'm doing, I pick up a water glass, raise it above my head, and with the force of God, I smash it down onto the floor. It shatters into a glittering snowflake pattern, and I just stare at it, mesmerized, and then I start to cry.

What am I even doing here? How desperate is this—how desperate am *I*?

Isn't that the truth of it? Without my mom and now Sam, it's a perpetual state of loneliness and desperation, and how am I supposed to live the rest of my life this way? It doesn't seem to matter whether I'm surrounded by Bee and my friends, or seducing Max, or plotting the demise of Tom and Georgia Carter. I'm still *me*, a person without her mom and her brother. The tears blur my vision as I sidestep the glass on the kitchen floor. I push through the screen door, and when I step into the side yard I give a quick glance toward the beach. Millie is only twenty-five yards away from me, hurrying toward the house with her arms wrapped over her soaked bathing suit, looking freezing. Tom and Georgia are behind her, shoving beach towels into a bag.

I stop dead. There's nowhere for me to hide.

Millie glances up, and we lock eyes.

FORTY

Georgia. Southport, Connecticut.

Tom lifts the beach bag and angrily shoves his feet into sandy flip-flops. He can't get them on right away, and the way he's frustratedly trying to arrange his feet reminds me of a toddler.

"Tom, please," I say, annoyed now. "It's just one dinner. Can we at least try to enjoy the rest of this day together?"

He gets his flip-flops on and seems to calm down a little. He looks out to the sea, and then, unexpectedly, he puts a warm, sun-kissed arm around my shoulders and squeezes me against his bare chest. "I'm sorry," he says. "I'm not sure I've ever felt this bad. Not for a long time. With what happened at work. With trying to make things right with you, Millie, and me. I feel this crushing pain in my chest, like I'm going to freaking die, Georgia."

He takes his sunglasses off and wipes beneath his eyes.

"Are you crying?" I ask.

"No," he says quickly, returning the sunglasses to his face. "I got sunscreen in my eye or something."

"We're going to be okay," I say, not sure how true that really could ever be. I need it to be true, but it feels so far away.

Tom kisses the top of my head. "I'm sorry, Georgia," he says again, like he means it for so many more things than just getting mad about a dinner with our new Southport neighbor.

"Tom, is there anything you need to tell me?" I ask carefully, my heart inching into my throat. I study his face for clues that everything is exactly as bad as I'm scared it is, but he doesn't even flinch.

"Mom!"

I look toward the house to see Millie racing back in our direction. She's soaking wet, and I reach into the bag to grab her green-striped beach towel.

"Dad!" she cries, and then she's upon us, out of breath from sprinting. "I just saw that woman."

"Harriet?" I ask.

"No!" says Millie. "The woman who's renting our house."

"Our house in Waring Ridge?" asks Tom.

"Anna?" I ask.

Millie nods. "Anna," she says.

"What are you talking about?" Tom demands, his voice shrill. "Where did you see her?"

Millie gestures broadly toward our rental. "She was on the side of the house, toward the back."

"Are you absolutely sure it was her?" I ask.

"Where is she now, Millie?" Tom asks, his entire body coiled like he's ready for a fight.

"Tom," I say. "Relax."

He ignores me. "Did she talk to you, Millie? Did she say anything?" he asks.

Millie shakes her head. "No. She just ran away along the side of the house. And I'm absolutely sure it was her, Mom."

"What the *hell*?" I ask, turning to Tom. "Should I call her? Ask if something's wrong? Maybe she's been trying to get in touch with us about something at the house?"

I open my phone, but there's nothing.

Tom looks completely enraged.

"There could be a good reason," I say, "it could be that the cell service wasn't working here, and she's been trying to call."

"And she just somehow knew our address in Southport?" he hurls.

"I'm sure I wrote it down somewhere in the house." Really, though, what could possibly be going on? "I'm calling Max," I say, but when I press his number, it goes straight to voicemail. I dial Maya next, but she doesn't pick up, so I call Ethan.

"Hey," he answers. "How's Southport?"

"Oh, it's great," I lie. "Weird question for you. Millie swears she just saw Anna, the young woman renting our house back home, here in Southport. Is anything amiss over there? I just want to make sure she's not looking for me?"

"I don't think anything's amiss, per se," Ethan says, "but I think your tenant might be a little off. I went over there yesterday to tell her we could help if she loses power in the storm, and she accused me of being a Peeping Tom and shut the door in my face."

"Oh," I say. "Jeez. Sorry."

Tom's texting on his phone, looking furious.

"No worries," says Ethan. "Maybe she just wanted to see Southport. It's beautiful there."

"It is," I say. "But we saw her at our rental, which is kind of weird."

"What?" Ethan asks.

"Millie saw her," I say again. "Outside in the back."

Tom makes a furious circular motion with his hands, like I should wrap up the call with Ethan immediately.

"I should go," I say to Ethan. There's a family with towels and a beach umbrella that has just emerged from their house on the stretch of beach next to ours. The last thing we need is another conversation. "Can you call me if anything seems odd?" I ask Ethan.

"Yikes. Yeah, sure," he says. "I really hope it's some kind of misunderstanding."

"Yeah, me too," I say. "It probably is."

We get off the phone, and then all three of us head silently along the beach toward our rental. Clouds are rolling in now, hinting at what might be coming tonight. At the house, we step through the screen door into the kitchen and see glass shattered across the tiled floor.

"What the *fuck*?" Tom says.

"Millie, wait outside, sweetie," I say, panic rising in my throat. "Or try the front door and head up to your room. Let Dad and me clean up the glass, okay?" Is it possible that we left a glass out and it fell off the counter? Or does this mean Anna came inside?

"I don't want to go upstairs by myself," Millie whines.

"Should we call the police?" I ask.

"What? No, *no*," Tom says. "I don't think anyone's inside this house right now."

"Do you think Anna came inside and broke the glass?"

"I don't think so," Tom says. "And if she did, she's gone now."

"How can you possibly know that for sure?" I'm trying to keep my voice calm for Millie's sake, but I can't. "What the fuck, Tom?"

Tom gets a broom out from a side closet and starts to sweep. The shake in his hands only scares me more.

I pick up my phone and call Max again, but it goes straight to voicemail. So I text him: Something weird is going on, and I might be wrong, but Millie swore she saw Anna just outside our Southport rental. Makes no sense. But then we came inside and there's glass shattered on the floor. I have no idea what's going on. Please just be careful, ok? Call me.

I move to start to help Tom sweep up the glass, but my phone buzzes, and I pick up.

"Max," I say into the phone.

"You can't be serious," he says. "You think she came there?"

I can't put my finger on it, but he doesn't sound as surprised or confused as I thought he'd be. And the way he says *she* sounds so familiar, so colloquial. Like he and Anna are in cahoots in some way.

I take a beat, but in the silence I doubt myself too much to accuse him of anything untoward. "Millie thinks she saw her," I say.

"Let me talk to her," Max says.

"To Anna?"

"Yes. To Anna," he says. And then he disconnects our call. I stare down at my phone and a chill passes over my skin. I lean into the kitchen island, trying to regain my balance. There's a spinning feeling that sometimes descends upon me; it's something that's happened ever since I was a little girl and could sense that my mother's drinking was edging out of control. It used to feel like a cyclone inside of me that I tried to tamp down but couldn't, a feeling that came when I knew deep down that things might not be okay. My pills quieted it, patted it on the head and put it to bed, just for a little while until they wore off, and then the feeling was back, worse than ever.

I have the feeling again now, and I can feel it growing in size, fueled by an absolute certainty that I'm missing something so big it's about to decimate my entire world.

I set the phone down on the counter.

There's nothing left to use anymore to numb the feeling. At least, not for me. I close my eyes and stand there until the spinning feeling becomes nearly intolerable, until I feel like I'm about to be swallowed up by a cyclone.

But nothing like that happens.

I open my eyes, and it's still just me and my family in our overpriced vacation rental, about to face whatever it is that threatens to break us.

FORTY-ONE

Anna. Waring Ridge, New York.

I take an Uber back to Waring Ridge, reading and rereading the text Tom sent.

Stay away from my family. Come close to them again, and you'll be sorry.

It's the most emotion he's ever shown me over text, and I guess I should be flattered. Our other correspondence was always so flat, Tom writing just a few words to coordinate what time we'd meet. We always met at my apartment. Tom knew too many people in the city to take me out to restaurants and bars, and there was too great a chance we'd get sloppy and someone would see us together and know. As our time together marched on, I found myself wanting to be the person Tom took out in New York. And that's when I really started to worry.

When the driver pulls onto Georgia's street, I pray that Max is gone so I can search his cottage. But when we wind up Georgia's driveway, I can see he's waiting for me on the front steps of the main house. And he doesn't look happy.

I get out of the Uber. Max and I stare at each other while the driver reverses and disappears onto the road. It's late afternoon and the sky looks angry, the slate-gray clouds swollen with rain. The wind makes Georgia's hydrangeas quiver. The pale green underbellies of the leaves show themselves, turning skyward, and I remember how my dad had taught Sam and me that seeing them was a telltale sign of an impending storm.

"What's up, Max?" I ask.

"What's up with *you*?" he retorts. He's wearing an awkward smile, much less open and friendly than I've seen him look before. Maybe because we messed around last night. I really hope he's not going to be weird now; I liked him as he was.

"Um, nothing, I guess," I say, shrugging a shoulder. "Do you want to go inside? It's getting chilly."

He nods, not really looking at me. I unlock the front door and we head into the living room and settle next to each other on a plush white couch. He takes a blanket from the back of the couch and gently rests it over my bare legs. "You look cold," he says.

"I am. Thanks."

"What'd you do today?" he asks, leaning awkwardly back against the cushions. There's a pale upright piano on the side of the room, and it makes me remember the choppy sonatas that used to filter through the house when Max practiced.

"Not much," I say. "This and that."

"Yeah?"

"Yeah. Waring Ridge has lots to offer," I say with a smirk.

"So you stayed in Waring Ridge all day?" he asks, raising an eyebrow.

My heart beats a little faster. Maybe Millie told Georgia she saw me, and Georgia called Max right away. It's what I would do. I'd warn Sam the second I sniffed something batshit like this.

"Yes, Max. I stayed in Waring Ridge all day." I stare at him, daring him to call me out.

He doesn't. He crosses his arms over his chest, all guarded and not at all how he was last night.

Remember what we did beside the cliffs? I want to ask him.

"So is it a lot like where you grew up?" he asks. "Waring Ridge, I mean. Where did you grow up, by the way? We talked about so many things, and I forgot to ask you."

My heart beats a little faster. "In Kingston," I say quickly, because one of my dad's brothers lived there, and we used to visit. "It's only like an hour and a half northwest of here."

"I know where Kingston is."

"Oh. Well, yeah. It was nice there. We lived in a ranch," I say, thinking of my uncle's house and the way his three kids each had their own rooms with beanbag chairs and small wooden desks. My brother and I thought it was luxurious. We loved going there, even though our cousins grew a little mean as they got older.

"Good art scene in Kingston," Max says. "Did it inspire your photography, growing up somewhere like that?"

"Nope," I say, my heart pounding. I'm pretty sure all of this means that not only does he know I went to Southport today and spied on Georgia, Tom, and Millie, but that he's also figured out exactly who I am. Why else would he be asking these kinds of questions about my childhood?

Still, I keep the lie going with a truth. I say, "What inspired my photography was a desire to preserve something. I lost my mom before I started taking pictures. So then, when I was nine and got my first camera, I started photographing everything important to me. And even now, even with my brother dead, it's a comfort to have thousands of photos of him for my dad and me to look back upon."

Max's brown eyes are filled with something I can't discern, a combination of love and fear I've never seen before. "I'm sorry about your twin," he says, his voice gentle, his eyes hard.

I shudder. I never told him Sam was my twin.

FORTY-TWO

Georgia. Southport, Connecticut.

By evening we've gotten Millie settled upstairs with her headphones on, drawing God knows what. Maybe Eliza again, or some other ghost from my past. But she can't hear us, can't pick up on the tension in our voices as we get the house ready for the storm. The sky has made its intentions clear in the last half hour or so, but Tom is so distracted I can't get him to focus on the things that need to be done. "Do we have enough water?" I ask.

"I already told you I loaded bottles into the closet," Tom snaps.

"You don't think Harriet still wants us for dinner in this storm, right?" I ask.

"I'm sure she does."

"Did you close the window in our bedroom?" I ask, and Tom doesn't bother answering me. He's practically manic, sweeping through the house, checking things that probably don't need checking. Neither of us seems to be able to look at the other since the Anna thing. It just doesn't make any sense. I wanted to call her, but Tom said I shouldn't, and then he said that if she does anything like that again, we'll call the police. He said we can't even be completely sure that Millie saw Anna, that it could have been a look-alike, and that then we'd really be embarrassing ourselves by calling our tenant and accusing her of stalking us and possibly entering our Southport rental and breaking a glass. And when he said it like that, I couldn't really argue. But if he's wrong, if it was her, then what the fuck is happening in my own house right now? What kind of person did I rent my house to?

I double-check the kitchen cabinets for the lentil soup I always travel with in case of a storm. It seems like overkill, until you lose power and have to survive on potato chips. "We really need to get a generator back home," I say, aware that I'm just filling the air with nervous chatter, but unable to stop. "Though, I guess not, if we're planning to actually move back to the city . . ."

Tom's riffling through a drawer in the kitchen, looking for batteries for a flashlight. And then the doorbell rings.

"Now what?" he snaps.

I wind through the front hall and open the door to see Max.

"Hey!" I say. "What are you doing here?"

"Can I come in?"

"Of course, come in; we're just getting ready for the storm. And you should probably just stay the night . . ."

We make our way into the kitchen. Tom looks up and says, "Hey, Max." He's gruff and rushed, completely unfriendly.

"You guys okay?" Max asks.

"We're fine," says Tom.

"Where's Millie?" he asks.

"She's upstairs. Go say hi if you want." There's a shake in my voice, and I can't tell if Max picks up on it. I'm so tired of trying to act like everything's normal when everything's only been getting worse.

"Can we sit down?" Max asks, gesturing to the stools around the kitchen island. "Somewhere out of Millie's earshot?"

My blood starts to pump faster. "What is it? What's wrong?"

Tom folds his arms over his chest, leaning back against the kitchen counter.

"Sit, Georgia," Max says, pulling out a stool.

I do. A shiver runs over my skin, and I remind myself that my daughter is safe and sound upstairs.

Max stands at the head of the island, facing Tom and me. I try to grab Tom's glance, but he stares straight ahead at Max.

Max clears his throat, then leans forward with his palms on the kitchen island. "Something has come to my attention," he says formally, nothing like how he usually talks. "I've been spending time with Anna at the house. Actually, um, unfortunately maybe, we got a little close."

"What the fuck does that mean?" asks Tom.

"It means things got physical, Tom," Max says rudely.

Tom's mouth actually drops. "Are you fucking kidding me?"

"That's not why I'm here," Max says.

"Oh, please, then, do inform us why you're here," Tom says, his face suddenly flushing with circular blooms of blood beneath the skin.

"You're an asshole," says Max. "You know that?"

"Max, please, you're scaring me," I say.

Max turns to me and says, "Last night, Anna and I were hanging out back by the cliffs. And we were talking about lots of different things. But she was asking me a lot of stuff about our childhood, Georgia. Stuff about Eliza, stuff about Mom. But mostly about Eliza. Something didn't sit right with me, and then I did some digging on her Instagram. Her real name is Anna Byrne, and I found Sam Byrne, the account that she mostly communicated with through comments, and then, of course, photos of them together, her twin." He swallows, his eyes red. "Georgia, they're Anna and Sam, Eliza's twins. She's Eliza's *daughter*."

The ground seems to open beneath me, and my entire body starts shaking uncontrollably. Max comes to my side, his hand on my back, rubbing furious circles over my skin.

"I wasn't even sure what to do with the information," Max says. "Last night and this morning I thought I would try to deal with her myself to protect you from it. I thought maybe she just wanted some closure, or something like that, because that's the feeling I got from her the night before with everything she was asking. I didn't want to tell you right away and stress you out and ruin your vacation, and I thought maybe I could handle her, like, talk to her first about who she really was and what exactly she was trying to do. But then when you told me she came to Southport, and that she maybe even broke in or was spying on you guys or something . . ."

My head goes into my hands, and I start to cry. I try to breathe, but my lungs feel like they're closing. I can't seem to lift my head from my hands.

How can this be happening?

How did I not recognize Eliza's *child*, the little girl I used to hold when she was a baby, the toddler I sometimes ignored but often played with? And why is Anna doing this *now*, after all these years? The thought of her planning this, of deliberately stalking my home, the thought of her there now, all of it makes me sick. I sob into my palms, and an eternity seems to pass, but I can't stop crying. Maybe a part of me is waiting for Tom to come over, to put his arms around me, to tell me that everything is going to be okay. But he doesn't. I finally look up to see him standing there with his face pale, his eyes wild. He swallows, and then staggers toward me.

"Georgia," he says. "I've made a terrible mistake."

FORTY-THREE

Anna. Waring Ridge, New York.

Upstairs in Georgia's bedroom, I'm furiously packing my things. What else can I possibly do?

The sky is dark now, the storm whistling outside the window.

I can't stay here. They'll come for me, I know they will. Max left right after our conversation, I'm sure to go tell Georgia everything he knows.

Sam. My mom. Me.

And as soon as Tom figures it all out, he won't let me stay here, no matter what. It was one thing when I was just the jilted mistress; but the woman who stalked him so that she could intentionally become the jilted mistress? That's another kind of story.

I can deal with them all later, I can drive up one day and have some big confrontation, but I can't linger in this house until they descend upon me. I won't be the same sitting duck I was as a child, just waiting around for something bad to happen. For Georgia to do something bad to me yet again.

I shove shirts, shorts, and toiletries into my bag. Rain has started outside my window, and I take a moment to press my face against the glass.

The cottage. A single light blazes from Max's window.

I've waited for the cottage to be empty, and now it is. And I can't leave this place without at least trying to find Georgia's hiding spot for my mother's journal, at least giving it one more shot. I grab a sweatshirt and hurry down the stairs and out onto the lawn. The air is too hot and heavy. A stinging bug lands on my neck and punctures my skin, and when I try to slap it away I see blood on my fingers.

Lightning fires up the sky as I make my way toward the last place I saw my mother alive.

FORTY-FOUR

Georgia. Southport, Connecticut.

My eyes are all over Tom. Max's hand is frozen on my back, no longer rubbing circles.

"What kind of mistake, Tom?" I ask.

Tom is currently trying to grip the kitchen island, as though he can't stay standing without its support. "I slept with her, Georgia."

"What?" The word escapes my mouth like a shot. "With Anna?"

Tom nods. "With Anna," he says.

Nothing feels real. The kitchen starts to swim before my eyes—the silver toaster seems to melt like butter, and the counters sway. *"What are you talking about?"* I hear myself say, the words burning my tongue. "You mean the other day? When you went to get Millie's doll?"

"No," Tom says, his eyes rimmed with red, his dark curls stuck up at odd angles. "I've been having an affair with her for several months."

The blood has drained from my legs. I can't feel them anymore in the chair, and it gives me the odd sensation of floating above the stool. I shake my head. Time seems to slow as my brain tries to put it together. *"How could you?"* I finally manage to say, but the words are lost in the sudden commotion: Max lunges at Tom, his hands reaching for his neck.

"You lying piece of shit! That's my *sister*. Your *wife*. Does that mean nothing to you?"

Tom fends him off, both of them scuffling but not landing anything hard. I watch them like it's a television show, like it isn't really happening to me. Tom has an elbow on Max's chest, and he's out of breath when he says, "We have bigger fucking fish to fry right now, Max. Like what kind of pathological person is staying in our house and what she wants to do to us."

It works—Max quits. He takes a step back, breathing hard. Tom turns to me. "I've already called our lawyer, Georgia. I did it as soon as we met Anna in town and I realized what she'd done. Our entire life is inside that house. Our computers, passports, financial information, banking codes, *everything*. And we have no idea what she's planning. She found *me*, Georgia," he pants. "And if she's Eliza's daughter, then finding me must have been very much on purpose. She applied for a job at *Culture*, and she approached me at a party. It's all my fault, the affair is my fault, Georgia, and I know that, and I am so sorry, but I'm telling you, she found me on purpose, for some fucking reason, to start this all up with me. There's no way it was a coincidence. She had some sort of plan, and now she's *living in our fucking house!*"

I look at Tom, truly seeing him for the first time in what feels like a while. His flaws, his lies, his desperation and unhappiness, the waning of his feelings for me and for our life together. I didn't want to see it, of course, but it's all right there on his face, and it's been there for months. And there's no way it was just the Waring Ridge house that's to blame—a house doesn't cause someone to have an affair. Tom had an affair because he wanted to. Because he'd lost interest in me, or our life together, or some other reason that doesn't really matter. We were over in his mind, and he didn't have the guts to tell me.

"You gaslighting son of a bitch," I say into the dead air of the kitchen. Max is back by my side, still panting from the fight with Tom. "You've lied to me for months. And you kept lying to me even after you realized your fucking mistress was living in our house, and then you *still* didn't tell me the truth when she came to Southport and broke into the house where your wife and *daughter* are staying! She could have hurt us, Tom. Do you realize how unforgivable it is that you've waited until right now, when you've realized the situation is out of your control, and that your mistress is someone from my past, to fess up to what you've done? You're the pathological one, Tom. You and Anna deserve each other, really."

"Georgia," Tom says, like he can't believe it.

I turn to Max. "Anna must have done this to get back at us somehow," I say. "But why now?"

Max blinks, letting it sink in. Maybe today, before he knew that Tom had been carrying on with Anna behind my back, Max might have had a more generous interpretation of the situation: like maybe Anna Byrne had some reason to lie to all of us, to spend the month in the house where she lost her mother. But not now that we know she sought out Tom. Now he knows better.

"Her twin died this year," Max says softly.

I flinch, thinking of Sam dead. He was cherubic, all dimples and soft flesh. He was a sweet child and loving—I saw that back then, even in my drug-addled spiral.

"He killed himself," says Tom.

I look at my husband. That he knows all of this from Anna's perspective feels like a knife in my gut. "Did you talk about it together?" I asked. "Lying together in bed after sex? Did she open up while you were naked, tangled among the sheets?"

He looks bewildered, like for once he's at a loss for words. I turn to Max. "That's awful about Sam," I say, "and it makes it even more likely that she did this to seek revenge, to get back at *me*. I caused Eliza's death, Max." As I hear the words in the air between us, I have a feeling of a little scratching inside my brain, as though something buried is trying to dig its way into the light. "You never blame me," I say to Max, "but I was the reason Eliza went onto the roof. She knew I kept my stash of pills hidden in my doll, and she went to get it so she could find out what I was on and try to get me help. She wrote it in her journal, which I still have. Sometimes I even torture myself by reading it." I turn to Tom and let out a sick little laugh. "I always think of these as my deep dark secrets. But it looks like you were the one keeping secrets. Isn't that ironic?"

"I'm so sorry," Tom says, coming toward me.

"Stay away from me," I say. And it's easier to say than I would have thought, because if I am anything, I am my mother's daughter, and while we both may look pretty and small from the outside, we are not that way on the inside. Inside, my mother and I are fire and fury.

I stand on shaking legs and walk into the foyer with Max and Tom following me, a plan already taking shape.

FORTY-FIVE

Anna. Waring Ridge, New York.

The door to Max's cottage is unlocked, and I let myself in. Everything inside this place feels like a memory. My dad was usually in motion, because he said he'd fall asleep if he sat too long in one place, but there was a recliner where he sometimes took a catnap before he worked the night shift. He only worked three night shifts per week once we were born, because four or five nights was too exhausting. But on the nights that he catnapped before work, he'd read the paper in that recliner until his eyes grew heavy. I'd color right beside his feet, periodically checking in to see whether he was sleeping. His breath would hitch as he drifted off into sleep, and I felt such fondness to see him that way, the strong father I knew giving in to quiet rest.

I move into Max's bedroom as rain pounds the roof. I remember this sound, too, the sharp pelting like bullets against the metal roof. The cottage wasn't built like a fortress the way Georgia's house was. It was built modestly, and it was perfect for us, but in a storm, it felt like it was under attack.

There's not much in Max's drawers: a few scattered receipts, six of the same soft gray T-shirt I always see him wearing, and a notebook that I open. I flip through the pages, most of them filled with story ideas, probably for TV and film projects he's working on. *A woman with a dark past,* one of Max's notes reads. *Something she can't tell anyone, something that can't be undone, something she can never atone for and certainly cannot forget.* I flip to the following page, but that's all he has written. I move back to the living room and start opening drawers of an old armoire that was ours when we lived here. The drawers are filled with clutter, and I recognize an old metal airplane as one of Sam's. My eyes fill with tears, but I keep going until I get to the bottom drawer, where a stack of pictures stops me in my tracks. The very top photo shows my mom holding me outside our cottage on the lawn. My hands shake wildly as I flip through the photos, none of which I've ever seen before. Most of them feature my parents, Sam, Max, and me. There's one of my dad pitching a ball to Sam, and Max hovering on a makeshift first base. I don't remember this baseball game ever happening, but there I am, bent at the knees on second base, holding my mitt like I'm ready to scoop up a ground ball, like I actually know what I'm doing. Did my parents take these photos?

I flip the photo over and see handwriting that isn't my mother's: *September 18th baseball game Anna, Max, Sam, Mr. Byrne.* We're too old in these photos for them to have been taken by Georgia's mother; she would have already been dead a few years. And Georgia is likely the only person who would have called my dad Mr. Byrne.

I keep flipping, tears hot on my cheeks. Did Georgia take all these photos?

There's one of me sitting outside on a large rock we used to pretend was a ship, eating a muffin. Sam's next to me, his tiny lips stained with blueberries. His palm rests over my free hand, and he's looking off to the side, but I'm smiling directly at the camera, appearing truly happy. There's one of us in the library in town playing with the plastic veterinary toys I still remember; Sam has a stethoscope around his neck, nursing a stuffed dog back to health with a plastic bottle.

These photos must be Georgia's, she's the only one not in the pictures. And it's not just the photos that leave me gutted, it's the captions Georgia wrote on the back of each photo.

Eliza takes Sam, Anna, Max, and me to the park on Chestnut Street. We have a picnic around noon with cucumber sandwiches, because Anna read about them in a book. Rain started around four, we headed home and put on a film.

Georgia would have been somewhere around fifteen or sixteen when she wrote these captions. It was right when she was struggling the most, but I remember her trying to use words like *film* instead of *movie* to sound more sophisticated.

There's one of us all gathered around the kitchen table in the main house, Max arching forward to blow out candles on a cake, Sam trying to stick his fingers in the icing. On the back Georgia scrawled *March 16th, 2002, Max turns ten!* There's a photo taken in town at the home shop, the same one where yesterday I ran into Georgia, Tom, and Millie. In this shot, Georgia has caught my mom studying a glossy cookbook, a lock of red hair falling over her face. On the back, Georgia wrote, *Eliza finds a new cookbook, she can never say no to Ina Garten or to Sam!* And then she scrawled a smiley face and a heart next to what she wrote, so that you could tell she meant it with fondness. In fact, all the captions Georgia wrote seem to have come from a great place of love and fondness, and it gives me pause. Did I underestimate how much Georgia loved my family? I knew she loved my mom. But these photos show a life together that I can barely remember. Was I just too young to understand what was really happening? Did I get it all wrong?

My heart surges with emotion. I brush away tears, trying to sort it out, and then the power goes off inside the cottage. I'm suddenly sitting in blackness with my thoughts.

Georgia always came off as aloof with us, as though we were too little, and like she didn't want to be part of the trio that Max, Sam, and I often made. And then of course there were the times she was high, and we weren't allowed to be around her. Both emotionally and physically, to me she always seemed like a princess shut away inside a castle. But these tiny glimpses into who she was sometimes when she was with us, or at least who she wanted to be when she'd printed the photos and captioned them so nostalgically . . . it makes me feel like we were more important to her than I ever wanted to believe.

My eyes are still blurry with tears, but they've adjusted to the darkness. I shove the photos back into the drawer.

I need to get out of here. I know it in every bone of my body. I've gone too far, and I need to leave Waring Ridge right now, before it's too late. I open my phone to call an Uber, but I can't get any service without Wi-Fi. There's an old text from Bee. Missing you! And NYC misses you, too. It's not the same without you.

I'm not sure if I'm ever going to be able to tell her, or anyone else, what I've done. I open the flashlight on my phone and let myself out of the cottage. I curve left around the side of the porch. Right beneath the window of Sam's and my old bedroom I drop to my knees in the dirt and start digging with my hands, feeling the cold, wet earth against my fingertips. When I'm satisfied with the size of the hole, I remove a tiny wooden figurine from my pocket. Sam had made it for me when he was in high school, about the time when his talent with sculpture and woodworking was becoming evident. It's only a few inches tall, carved into the shape of a compact, muscular man with a lopsided hat. I set it into the ground and say a silent prayer, and then cover it with dirt and line stones around it like a tiny grave.

"I miss you, Sam," I say into the night.

FORTY-SIX

Georgia. Southport, Connecticut.

My heart sinks when I see Millie sitting on the stairs.

"Oh, Millie," I say, putting my hand through the space in the rails to hold hers.

"I heard you and Dad," she says, tears spilling over her cheeks. Tom's behind me, and so is Max, but she only looks at me. "I heard everything."

I climb up the staircase and sit beside her. I'm not sure what she heard—but it seems, from her sobbing, that she knows the worst of it. I begin to cry angry tears at the sight of how wretched she looks—furious with Tom, with Anna, and with myself for letting her hear what we've said.

Max disappears back into the kitchen to give us privacy, and then Tom sits on the step beside Millie and the three of us are all alone, an island of grief.

"I'm so sorry, Millie," Tom says. He tries to put an arm around her, but she shrinks back, pressing her body against me.

I stroke our daughter's hair and hold her against my chest. We're both trembling, and then I can't help asking Tom the one question I really need the answer to. "How could any moment you ever spent with Anna ever be worth this moment right now?"

He turns away.

My car keys are sitting on the table beside the stairs. I press my lips against Millie's head and whisper, "I'll be right back. I love you, Millie. Wait up for me, okay? I'll sleep in your bed tonight, and we'll talk through everything."

She squeezes my hand, her eyes questioning.

Without telling Tom what I'm doing, I stand and move quickly down the stairs, grab the keys from the table, and open the front door.

Outside the house, beneath an angry gray sky, the rain is slick on my bare arms as I sprint toward my car. I hear the front door open and the sound of Tom calling my name, but then I'm inside and starting the engine. Through the windshield I see the neighbor, Harriet, starting toward our house again beneath an umbrella, her head down, eyes focused on the wet grass beneath her feet. I check the time and realize that we completely forgot about dinner at her house, and I'm grateful for the extra minutes she'll buy me when she tries to talk Tom into coming over for dinner with Millie and Max.

I reverse quickly down the driveway and speed down the street past the quaint clapboard houses. Another right turn and the ocean's in view, the waves choppier with the weather rolling in. I stop at a light, my fingers gripping the wheel. I need the light to change *now*—I need time alone with Anna. Max, Tom, and Millie will eventually follow me when they realize the only place I could possibly be going is Waring Ridge, but first they'll have to deal with Harriet. And I'm relying on being at least a few minutes ahead of them by taking back roads, plus Tom and Max will have a huge argument about who's going to stay behind with Millie. Tom will win, but not before Max makes his case about why he should be the one to face Anna with me.

The light changes and I gun the engine, thunder punctuating my mood. I speed down the winding road along the sea and think about Anna, about who she was when she was little. She only lived with us until she was six, but I remember her vividly. She was shy and wild eyed, just like Sam. She was an observer, and often nervous to speak, but when she did, her words were kind and perceptive. She and Sam adored Max. He was only six when they were born, and I was ten, and when they were babies, we doted on them. I loved taking care of them alongside Eliza, fetching things like diapers and squeaky baby toys, patting Anna's back and shushing Sam to sleep like Eliza had taught me. Sometimes Eliza would let me give one of them a bottle, usually Anna, because she took a bottle easier than Sam. Giving the bottle was the moment I lived for the most, the way Anna would quiet down and lock eyes with me as she drank the milk. My mom adored them, too, but if anything, the presence of the twins only increased her drinking, maybe because Eliza was suddenly so occupied, so in love with her children. Even though Anna and Sam's dad was home in the cottage most days taking care of them, it was natural that Eliza would want to take us there all the time to see her own babies. My mother couldn't handle these new, all-consuming loves of Eliza's life. Before Eliza had Anna and Sam, my mother was often the focus of Eliza's attention. Eliza was the glue holding my mom together, and maybe it shouldn't have come as a surprise when my mom drank herself to death right before the twins' second birthday.

I was using by the time Sam and Anna were four and I was fourteen. The Dilaudid was the only thing that could relieve the sadness. I still tagged along with Eliza, Sam, and Anna when there was nothing better to do with my friends, but by then my mind was already addled.

After Eliza died, I knew what I'd done to Sam and Anna by being the cause of their mom's death. I already blamed myself for destroying everyone, including myself, and no amount of therapy could convince me I was forgivable. Once, a few years ago and against the advice of my therapist, I'd googled both Anna and Sam to see if they were okay, and Sam's page showcased him doing all kinds of construction projects, some utilitarian, some highly artistic, and all of them impressive. Anna's page held only photographs, no selfies, and the photographs were extraordinary. I only let myself look for a few minutes, just to make sure they were both alive and functioning. And then I slammed my computer shut and tried to forget them.

But now here she is, Anna. Sleeping in my house and sleeping with my husband.

I pull into my driveway, relieved to see my beautiful home on top of the hill, even though I know who waits inside.

FORTY-SEVEN

Anna. Waring Ridge, New York.

The power is out at Georgia's house, too, of course, and I'm frantically trying to pack my clothes using only my phone's flashlight. I still can't get an Uber or call a taxi with the Wi-Fi down, and I'm increasingly claustrophobic as the storm rages outside.

The doorbell rings, and my hand freezes over my suitcase. Is it *them*? Have they come for me?

I've locked all the doors. I suppose I could just not answer the door, but if it's Georgia, Tom, and Max, they have the keys anyway.

I hurry down the stairs as fast as I can in the dark, but right at the bottom of the steps I slip and crash into a side table, knocking a vase of fresh flowers to the ground. It breaks, and now there's water everywhere. I sidestep a slab of the vase, and then I peer through the peephole. It's Georgia, her face soaked with rain.

I collapse back against the door. I have to do this—I have to face Georgia and what I've done.

I turn the knob and swing open the door. Rain slashes the air and the porch lights aren't working, and I can barely make out Georgia's features.

"Hi, Anna," she says, eerily calm. "Can I come in?"

Her face is a blank canvas, and I have no idea what she knows. Maybe she found out about Tom and is planning to murder me.

"Sure," I say, moving aside, allowing her to step into the foyer. And then I slam the door, just to make a point. She flinches, the first sign of weakness she's shown me, and I know there won't be many more. Georgia always looked slim and delicate as a teenager, and even now as a woman and a mother. But beneath that delicate frame is a constitution of steel. Plenty of people would be dead if they put the amount of drugs into their bodies that Georgia did.

She stands very still in the foyer, first looking around in the blackness, like she's waiting for her eyes to adjust so she can be sure her things are the way she left them.

Finally she turns to me and stares directly into my eyes. Neither of us moves for a moment; neither of us pretends like this is the kind of conversation we should move into the living room to have.

"I know who you are," Georgia finally says, her voice quiet but unwavering.

My heart pounds. "Oh?" I ask. I'm not sure I've ever felt this morbidly curious: Does she mean she knows I'm her husband's mistress, or her nanny's daughter? Or both?

"Anna Byrne," says Georgia. "Eliza's daughter, Sam's sister. And here's the kicker, which I do have to applaud you for: you're also my husband's lover."

I should feel pride at my plan playing out the way it did. It's what I intended, after all. But all I feel is crushing sadness. "That's me," I say, trying to make my voice sound haughty, even though it's not how I feel. "Guilty as charged."

Georgia's soaked to the bone. A normal person would be shivering, but like I said: Georgia's not normal. "So, you blame me, then, yeah?" she asks. "For your mom dying?"

I swallow. I expected her to come here and rail at me for sleeping with her husband, to make it all seem like my fault when it's equally his. But as usual, I've gravely underestimated her.

"Well, yeah," I say. "I do blame you for my mom's death. Because it's your fault."

"The doll?" she asks. Her body is so still, like a statue in the shadows.

"The doll," I say, shifting my weight, unsure how she can stay so tranquil during this kind of conversation. "And so much more," I make myself say. "Your general sense of entitlement and power over my lowly mother working for you."

"You'd call your mother *lowly*?"

"Not to me she wasn't," I say, but now I just feel foolish, because I was the one who used the word.

"Nor to me," Georgia says. "But I think you know that. If you're smart enough to have figured out how to do all of this . . ." She pauses to gesture around the house like a tour guide. "Then I bet you know how much I loved your mom."

I cross my arms over my chest. "Loving her doesn't change what you did. You hid drugs in a doll and made my mom go get it."

"You're *almost* right, Anna," Georgia says, a frightening, implacable edge to her voice. "I hid drugs in a doll because I was in horrible pain over losing my own mother and could barely survive without using pills, which was partly genetic and chemical, and partly due to my mother's death, and partly having access to extremely addictive opioids, and also my own fault for not saying no. I never asked your mom to get the doll—it was the last thing I would have wanted. Your mom went onto the roof to get the doll because she had a whole plan to find the drugs and then take them to an addiction center to determine exactly what they were so she and my dad would know what I was using. I know all of this because, after she died, I read about her intentions in a journal she used to keep."

My pulse picks up. "The journal? You have it?"

"I do," Georgia says. "And it belongs to you, really, and I'm sorry that I never found you and gave it to you, but I was scared out of my mind to face you. You blame me for your mother's death? Join the club. So do I."

Tears prick my eyes, and I try to blink them back. "Can I have it, please?"

"Yes, you can," Georgia says, and I hate her for it. The way she still holds so much power over my life, like a gatekeeper. "And then you're leaving, Anna. You slept with my husband and lived in my house, and now it's *over*. You accomplished exactly what you seem to have wanted to accomplish: you scared my family and ruined my marriage."

She draws a breath. Neither of us says anything.

Finally, voice softer, Georgia asks, "Are you happy now, Anna?"

"No," I say truthfully. But the answer is more complicated than that. I regret sleeping with Tom, and I've regretted it since the second I laid eyes on Millie, the second I realized that I hurt another child just like I was hurt when I was little. If what Georgia says is true, that I ruined her marriage, then that also means I deeply messed up Millie's life, and I'm not really sure how I'm ever going to forgive myself for that.

I don't regret coming to this house. There are memories and secrets here, and I have a feeling this house isn't done with me yet. It's like a creeping sense of something to come, something this house still needs me to understand about my family and my past. "Follow me and I'll get you the journal, and then you're gone," Georgia says, moving quickly across the foyer.

"Watch out! It's wet there—" I say, but I'm too late. Georgia can't see the water in the dark, and all of a sudden her feet are out from under her, and then her head hits the ground with a sickening *smack*.

"Oh *no*, oh my God," I say, crouching down beside her. It's hard to see, but there's a pool of liquid shadowing the back of her head. "Georgia?" I put my hands to the side of her skull and into her hair to feel for blood. It's there, soaking the right half of her head. It's not the water from the vase, it's too warm and sticky; it's definitely Georgia's blood. I rip off my sweatshirt and use it to press hard against the wound to try to stop the bleeding. There's no cell service for me to call for help, and I can't leave Georgia here bleeding to death to get help. My hands shake against Georgia's body, and then I hear a car crunching over the gravel and voices shouting.

FORTY-EIGHT

Georgia. Waring Ridge, New York.

I'm dreaming. And though I can still vaguely hear a woman screaming and the rain pounding the side of the house from the world outside that I know is my real world, I don't ever want to go back to that world, the one where my marriage is crumbling, the one where my childhood was lost to drugs and the deaths of the women I loved.

I want to stay inside this dreamworld, where Eliza and I are on the roof together and she's still alive. The sun is shining, and in this world I'm still young and any life can be mine for the taking. If only I make a different choice.

Yes, that's what I'll do: I'll make a different choice. I'll say no. I won't use drugs, and I won't hurt Eliza. I'll be good.

I can't tell if I'm inside a dream or a memory, but all of a sudden whatever it is starts to spin out of control. I feel myself crossing the roof to where Eliza is bent over, getting my doll from the chimney where I used to hide her. I don't want to see the doll, but I can't seem to make myself stop moving toward Eliza.

"What are you doing?" I snap at Eliza. Is that really my voice? The cruelty there feels like a slap. I know I love Eliza. Why would I ever be speaking this way?

Inside the dream, I have the precise feeling of being high. I used to dream about it all the time when I was in rehab detoxing: the hard snap, the feeling of fire in my veins. I'm not *regular Georgia* in this dream on the roof. I'm *high Georgia*. And high Georgia is a beast, a tornado changing course, a hunter in the forest decked with the kind of equipment no ordinary animal can withstand.

"Get away from my doll," I snarl at Eliza.

She turns. Her light eyes are wide, her shiny red hair wild in the wind. She says, "Georgia, please. Go back inside."

I can see that she's terrified. She knows I'm high, and she knows that means I could do anything right now: sing a song or sail off the roof.

"*Get away from my doll,* Eliza," I hurl again, feeling utterly invincible, like the daylight is mine for the taking.

She doesn't listen. She gently scoops the doll into her arms like a football, just like how she used to hold Sam and Anna when they were newborns. But of course, I don't care about any of that right now, not her tenderness nor her unconditional love for her children and for me. I care about my drugs. The high is growing out of control and into a manic, furious state as I stalk toward Eliza and my doll. The wind is heavy like water in my hair, trying to drag me back. I reach out my arms to try to snatch back my doll, but my movements are too jagged—I can't coordinate anything when I'm on these damned pills. But, *oh, how I love them.*

I can feel my mouth curl into a sneer as Eliza twists out of my reach. *"Go inside, Georgia,"* she says again, her voice desperate, pleading.

I lunge at her. My arms are on the doll, trying to wrench it free. We shuffle a few steps together, and then Eliza yanks the doll away from me, and the doll's dress catches and rips, splitting open the pocket and sending pills scattering over the roof like confetti. I start screaming and get down on my hands and knees, frantically trying to gather the pills. Eliza stands there, out of breath, watching me crawl across the roof, desperately picking up my little treasures one by one.

"No, Georgia, don't," she says. But she's so smart, too smart for her own good. She knows I won't stop until every last pill is rescued, so she moves ahead and tries to pick up the ones closest to the roof's edge so I won't have to do it in my drugged-out state. "We're going to figure this out," she tells me. "We're going to get you help."

The problem is, that's my biggest fear. So I stand on warm, gooey legs that feel the full force of whatever I just took, and I say, "Don't you get it? I don't *want* help."

"Georgia, no!" I hear a voice say behind us. I turn to see Max at the bedroom window, looking out at Eliza and me. I don't care. I need my doll; I need the drugs. I lunge at Eliza, giving my doll one final yank toward me, as my other hand gives Eliza a hard shove.

FORTY-NINE

Anna. Waring Ridge, New York.

I'm nearly catatonic with fear, murmuring over and over to Georgia to please wake up, and then I lift my head to see Tom, Max, and Millie standing in the doorway. I open my mouth to speak, but then Tom is flying at me. "Get off of her! What have you *done*?" he screams.

"Mom!" Millie sobs. Max pushes past her and holds back Tom.

"Please," I plead, my voice shrill. "I swear I didn't hurt her. She fell and hit her head."

Tom is trying to get at me, but Max is saying something to him that I can't make out. *"What did you do, Anna?"* Tom snarls, fighting against Max's grip.

"She *slipped*," I say. "I swear to God, she slipped in the water right there where the vase broke."

Tom turns to look, but it's hard to make out water or anything at all, it's just so dark in here. "Call an ambulance," he says to Max. I can almost see Millie's face in the shadows, her arms covering her body as she whimpers. To Tom I say, "Don't take her from me, please. I'm holding a wound I can't even see." I'm crying again, me and Millie both. Millie sinks to her knees beside her mom, and Tom switches on the flashlight on his phone, shining it over Georgia's eerily beautiful face. There's blood lining her hair, and some on my hands and on the sweatshirt, but it's less than I would have thought. Georgia's face is pale, but it's hard to tell if that's just the harsh light of the phone.

"Mom," Millie says, gently patting Georgia's leg. "Please, please, wake up."

The lights flicker once, and then come to life. The light is so surprising, so searing, that we're all blinking at each other. I must have left nearly all the lights on earlier, and now we're flooded in an operating room of blood and brightness. There's water everywhere, and the vase has broken into two clean pieces. Maybe in the light it's clear that I'm not trying to hurt Georgia, because Tom lowers himself beside me and tries to determine what kind of shape his wife is in. He checks her pulse and her breathing, while Max seems to finally get through to someone on the phone, looking like he's going to be sick as he steps out onto the porch, exhaling a torrent of details for the 911 operator.

Georgia's eyes flutter open. Tears prick the edges.

"Georgia, honey," Tom says. "You're going to be okay, we're all right here with you." His voice is so gentle it startles me. I've never heard him talk like that. It makes me realize what a fool I've been to think he had real, true feelings for me. I only saw one small part of him: the part of a discontented husband engaging in an extramarital affair. I didn't even come close to knowing the layers of him that Georgia does. And now Tom and I had ruined whatever it was they had. And I'm not close enough to them to know whether what they had was worth fighting for, but it probably was.

Millie says, "Mama, I'm here, too. Just relax."

But Georgia looks the opposite of relaxed. Her eyes dart between us, and she jolts up a few inches and tries to turn onto her side, but she can't. Her head is out of my hands now, and the bleeding seems to have stopped. I guide Tom's hands to cradle her head and shoulders, knowing it's the last time I'll ever touch him, and I scooch back a bit, away from this family so that they can take care of her. Max comes back inside, phone in his hand.

"An ambulance is on its way," he says. He kneels at Georgia's side and takes her hand. Now that he's here, Georgia's eyes have stopped darting around. She stares only at her brother.

"Max," she says. "I did it, didn't I?"

Tom and Millie stare into her face, but she only has eyes for Max. "I killed Eliza," she says. "I pushed her off the roof, didn't I? It was me. And you saw the whole thing."

FIFTY

Georgia. Waring Ridge, New York.

My brother's eyes are wide and wild. He's kneeling beside me, squeezing my hand so hard I feel like the tiny bones in my fingers could break.

"Georgia," he says.

"I know what I did, Max," I say, seeing him, only him. I have a vague understanding that other people are here in the room with me, important people. But right now, I can only focus on Max, because he's the only one who was there, the one who saw me do what I think I did, what I must have done. "I remember it now. At least, I think I do. I saw images when I fell, and I need you to tell me that what I just saw was real, and not a dream brought on by this house." I stare into his eyes like I haven't done since we were children. People stop doing that, don't they? Even lovers stop staring into each other's eyes as the years pass. Certainly, siblings do. It's only Millie who still holds my gaze this way, and maybe one day that will fall away, too. "I was going to get my doll," I say slowly. "I was high out of my mind. The doll's dress ripped, the pills spilled, and I was down on all fours trying to pick them up. Eliza wouldn't give me my doll back, and I was desperate for my drugs. I yanked back the doll and shoved Eliza off the roof."

I cover my eyes with my hands, but only to wipe away my tears. And then I lock eyes on my brother again, needing to face what it is I know I've done. Max is broken with emotion, and I don't even need him to confirm what I've said—I see it all over him—but I ask, anyway. "It's the truth, isn't it? I killed Eliza. And you were there, Max, at the window. You saw it. You saw everything."

His gaze leaves mine for the first time. I follow his stare to see Anna, standing now, her back pressed against the wall, her face as white as a phantom.

"Is it true?" she asks him, her voice barely audible. Her green eyes are on fire, her entire body coiled like a spring.

Max looks at Anna, and then back at me. He shudders as though the words are painful leaving his body. "It's true," he says.

FIFTY-ONE

Anna. Waring Ridge, New York.

White pinpricks swim through my vision as I stare at Georgia and Max on the ground, Georgia crying softly. "I'm sorry, Anna. I'm so sorry," she keeps saying.

I can feel cold air inside my mouth, and I have the sensation of choking on oxygen, suddenly all of it coming in too quickly. I start to sway, but then Max is there beside me. His face is blurry, but I can make out the whites of his eyes. "Hang tight, Anna," he says. "I've got you."

A chill travels over my skin. It's not right—something is so very wrong here. My brain can't put it together—I'm missing something. I can see a blur of my mother. A ghost, maybe. A delusion? I try to hang on to reality—Georgia killed my mother. I feel like I'm about to pass out, and then I hear my mother's voice . . .

Breathe, Anna. Focus on your surroundings, on the here and now. Look. Listen. Stay in the moment. See what's really there.

She sounds more insistent than ever. Max's arm is under mine now, holding me up, and all I can hear is the echo of his voice. *Hang tight, Anna. I've got you.*

I blink, and a piece of the puzzle starts to make itself clear, but before it can click into place, I close my eyes and start screaming.

FIFTY-TWO

Georgia. Waring Ridge, New York.

Paramedics swarm into our home. Somehow Ethan and Maya are here now, staring at the bloody mess of us, trying to help Max calm down Anna. Tom is with Millie, holding her tightly against him as she sobs. And that leaves Maya to take care of me, and confused as I am right now, there's one thing I do know: Maya and my other friends in Waring Ridge are the ones who are going to piece us all back together. Not Tom.

I want to go to Millie, to hold her, and I want to make sure Anna is okay. But I'm too shocked, too confused and overwhelmed, to do anything except let Maya comfort me.

I close my eyes. *I killed Eliza.* It feels like a nightmare from which I can't awaken.

"Georgia, please," I hear Maya say over the sound of Anna wailing. "Look at me. I need to know you're okay."

I open my eyes. "Something is really wrong, Maya, I . . ."

The paramedics descend upon us, loading me onto a stretcher. "We'll talk later, Georgia, we'll figure it all out," Maya's saying, but then out the door and into the storm we go.

FIFTY-THREE

Anna. Waring Ridge, New York.

At the hospital, hours later, I wait alone. Max, Georgia, and Millie are in Georgia's room, of course. Even Maya and Ethan were ushered inside, but not me. I'm hanging out in the ER waiting room like an uninvited guest, along with a demon truth set free upon me.

I imagine them sewing up Georgia's gash in one of these rooms, and tears start again. My limbs haven't stopped trembling, and my entire body is exhausted, as though crying and trembling for hours has been the same as running a marathon. All I want to do is sleep, but I can't bring myself to leave the ER before Georgia gets out, and anyway, where am I even supposed to go? I don't know why I came with them all in the first place, but it was such a flurry of activity when they were getting Georgia onto the stretcher, and I couldn't stop screaming, so I guess no one wanted to leave me alone. Max practically shoved me into his pickup, and then we were following the ambulance to the ER.

The scary thing is just how badly I want to tell Sam that Georgia killed our mom. But I can't. And I haven't called my dad yet, because it's something I'll need to tell him in person. I can only imagine how he'll feel hearing the story unfold, both what Georgia did all those years ago, and what I did to Georgia, Tom, Millie, and Max here in Waring Ridge.

Finally the door to the waiting room swings open and out comes Georgia. She's in her street clothes, a canvas tote over her shoulder. I think of her being ushered from the house on a stretcher, and I can only imagine what the news in sleepy Waring Ridge will have to offer tomorrow for its inhabitants.

"Where are the others?" I ask meekly.

"They're bringing the car around," she says, her voice steady, considering. We stare at each other. I can't imagine anyone in the waiting room would be able to discern the havoc we've wreaked on each other's lives. Georgia walks very slowly over to the chair where I'm sitting. I take in the sight of the bandage on the side of her head. "Can I talk to you?" she asks. "Can I sit?"

I gesture to the empty chair beside me, and she sits gingerly, like her legs hurt. "I'm going to tell the police everything," she says. "What I did to your mom. I need to tell someone, I mean officially tell someone, like report it."

"It won't change it," I say, my voice hard.

"I know that," she says. Her eyes are soft and bloodshot, but she's still *her*: the gatekeeper of the Waring Ridge house, the beautiful and imposing teenage figure from my childhood. "Are you going to be okay?" she asks, her voice kinder than I've ever heard it.

"I don't know. Are you?" I ask.

She shrugs. "I'm not sure," she says. "I don't know how I'm ever going to get past what I did to your mother. I *killed* someone, someone I loved. A *mother*, your mother." She leans a little closer, and I can feel how uncomfortable we both are with our proximity to each other. There's a hot fizz in the air between us, so much history hanging in the balance of our stories streaked with tragedy. "I'm so sorry, Anna, you have no idea how sorry I am. I will never, ever forgive myself, and I would never expect you to forgive me."

"I don't," I say. "At least, not yet."

She swallows. "I understand, I do," she says.

"I'm sorry I slept with Tom," I say. "*I* pursued *him*, not the other way around. If that makes you feel any better."

Georgia shrugs. "But it takes two to tango, doesn't it?" She looks toward the front desk of the ER, where a man is scanning licenses, and then back at me. "Tom and I won't make it through this," she says.

"I'm sorry," I say again.

"I'm not telling you so you can apologize," she says carefully. "I'm saying it out loud so that I can get used to saying the words." She clears her throat and begins again. "Anna, I need you to leave Waring Ridge. I know you'll need to pack your things. You can even sleep at the house tonight if you don't feel well enough to travel. It's the middle of the night already, anyway. But I need you to leave in the morning. Max says he's going to wait and drive you wherever you want to go."

"I can't sleep in that house," I say.

"I understand," says Georgia. "Like I said, Max will bring you wherever you want to go. He's waiting for you now outside the hospital. But tomorrow, at some point, I need to get back to my house with my daughter. Tom can finish out the stay in the Southport rental until we figure out what to do."

I nod. "At some point I'm going to head to my dad's house. I'll need to tell him everything, including what happened to my mom, what you did to her. I'm sure you understand."

Georgia shudders. And it takes her a few moments to gather herself, but she finally says, "Tell anyone you want to tell. What I did isn't a secret anymore. You don't need to protect me."

I nod. I wasn't planning to.

"So, it's goodbye, then," Georgia says.

"It's goodbye," I say. "For now."

She blinks, considers me. "I'm sorry," she says.

"I'm sorry, too," I say. "I really am."

She stretches a hand forward like she might take mine, but then she changes her mind. She reaches into her canvas tote bag and retrieves my mother's journal. I freeze at the sight of it, recognizing the purple dahlia right away.

"This belongs to you," she says. "I had Tom go back to the house and retrieve it."

I don't bother asking her where her diabolical hiding spot in the Waring Ridge house was, and why I couldn't find it. I guess it's water under the bridge now, like everything else. Georgia passes it into my hands, careful not to touch me. And then she stands up and brushes her hands over her legs. "You'll never know how sorry I am," she says softly as she backs away. Then she turns and hurries out of the ER, leaving me alone with the journal.

FIFTY-FOUR

Georgia. Waring Ridge, New York.

Tears burn my eyes as I head outside the hospital, where Millie, Max, and Tom are waiting for me on a bench beneath an awning. The rain has slowed for now, leaving warm night air that smells like the world has been washed clean.

"Mama," Millie says, jumping up and throwing her arms around me.

"Hi, sweetheart," I say, kissing the top of her head. She's already been allowed to see me in the room where I was getting a few stitches, but being separated for the five minutes I went to find Anna has her crying again. I hold her against me, terrified of what will happen when I tell the world that I killed someone. I try to brush away the fear—but it's right there, edging up against me. *What will happen to Millie and me?* Charges pressed? A trial? Will they take me away?

"Is Anna okay?" Millie asks.

"She is. And she's so happy to have her mom's journal." I turn to Tom. "Thanks for getting it for me."

I'm speaking politely to him for Millie's benefit. I have a feeling there will be a lot of this type of conversation, me forcing myself to be cordial to Tom in Millie's presence. I wonder how long it will take for the rage to subside, for every civil word not to feel like it's being pried from my mouth.

Max glares darkly at Tom. His leg is going even faster than usual, his knee bouncing up and down with the force of God. He turns to me. "So now what, Georgia? Do I seriously have to wait for her? Can't she take a cab?"

I raise my eyebrow. "I thought you and Anna were friends."

"We were friends before she slept with your husband and stalked you," Max spits.

"Max!" I say, glancing at Millie.

"I already know," Millie says. She's aged in the last few hours, and it breaks my heart. And all of it is Tom's fault.

Or is that not true? I shoved a woman off a roof. Didn't I set everything in motion?

I sit next to Max. Everything suddenly feels too heavy to carry, and I drop my head into my hands.

"I'm sorry, Georgia," Max says.

"No. *I'm* sorry." I pick up my head and look at him. "I'm sorry that you saw me do what I did to Eliza all those years ago, that you felt like you had to cover it up and keep it a secret. It must have nearly killed you."

Millie's blinking hard, staring from Max to me. I can tell she's trying to be strong, and I'm sure I should shield her from all of this, but it's already out in the open. She may as well see me grieve it, rather than shut it away.

But then she surprises me. She lifts her chin, and to Max she says, "Why didn't you ever tell the police what you saw my mom do?"

I can't stop staring at her—she seems so much tougher than she usually does, as though her fragile shell has hardened in the face of what she now knows about her family.

Max looks away. "I'd already lost my mom." He swallows, then turns back to look at Tom and Millie. "Neither one of you will ever understand what that feels like. You'll never know what it's like to lose your mom when you're a kid." He seems to consider what he's saying, and then turns to me. "Well, I mean, hopefully Millie will never know that."

"Hopefully not," I say. "But you and I did."

"Exactly," says Max. He turns back to Millie and Tom. "And I knew if I told the police about Georgia and everything that happened, that she'd be sent away and then she'd be gone, too. And I would have no one, except my dad, and I wouldn't have survived that."

He's being gentle about it because Millie's the one who asked the question. I have a feeling that if Tom ever presses him on it, which Tom *would* do, then Max will slug him.

Millie looks down into her hands. "I'm sorry, Uncle Max," she says, but she can't seem to meet his eyes. I can only pray that what's happened to our family won't break her the way my family's tragedy broke me.

FIFTY-FIVE

Anna. Waring Ridge, New York.

I make my way outside the hospital and see Max waiting for me on a bench with a sour expression on his face. I hold the journal tightly against my side.

"Hi," I say softly, feeling sick as I walk toward him. I knew he was going to hate me after he realized what I'd done, but it still makes me feel awful to see how he feels written all over him.

He stands when he sees me. He says nothing, not even hello.

"I'm sure you hate me," I say. "I'd hate me, too."

"I don't think *hate* is the right word," says Max.

I shrug. "Maybe something like that, though."

"Maybe," agrees Max.

"You don't need to drive me to the house. I'm capable of getting an Uber. But thank you, I appreciate it."

"It's Georgia's instructions," Max says. "And I'm not about to let my sister down with all she's going through."

His voice is so hard it makes me want to cry. I let go of a breath and try to steady myself as he takes in the sight of the journal.

"Your mom's diary?" Max asks.

I nod.

"Is that what you were rifling through my cottage for?" he asks. "I know you broke in and went through my stuff."

"And are you seriously going to give me a hard time after what I just found out your sister did to my mom? Something you *knew* about, and told no one?"

"You stalked my sister and slept with her husband."

"There's a pecking order to tragedy, Max. And if Georgia doesn't seem to be judging me, then maybe neither should you. No matter how much I deserve it."

Max shrugs. "Whatever. Let's get you back to the house so you can pack your shit and leave us alone and never, ever come back."

"Trust me, that's what I want, too."

"I don't trust you," Max says as we head through the light rain toward the parking lot.

I tuck my mom's journal beneath my sweatshirt so it doesn't get wet. We get into Max's truck and drive in silence back to Georgia's house, Max's headlights illuminating the slick road beneath us. There's so much we could say to each other—but I don't think either of us knows where to start.

It's nearly two in the morning when we get back, hours since Georgia hit her head. In the foyer, we turn on all the lights. The blood and water have been cleaned from the checkerboard tiles, and I wonder if Ethan and his wife did it. Our shoes are drenched, and we leave them by the front door. My mom's journal is still tucked beneath my sweatshirt, and it feels like it's burning a hole into my skin.

"I'm going upstairs to pack," I say to Max.

"I'll wait down here," he says, looking anywhere but at me. "Just let me know when you're ready and I'll bring your suitcases down." And then he walks into Georgia's living room without saying anything else, slumps onto the sofa, and takes out his phone.

I start the climb up the steps slowly, my entire body throbbing with exhaustion. At the top of the staircase, as soon as I'm out of Max's sight, I sit down and take a rest on the landing. At first I think I'm just wiped out from everything that happened tonight—but then I realize that I feel the same way I felt the first day I came here, overwhelmed by the prospect of getting so close to the roof where my mom fell. Through the doorway to Georgia's room, I can see my suitcase halfway packed from hours ago when I was trying to get everything ready in the dark. And when I turn my gaze to look through the slats between the ebony spokes of the railing, I can see the checkerboard floors and our soaked sneakers.

I try to breathe there for a moment, taking in the upstairs and downstairs from my vantage point. And then I hear an alert sound from Max's phone, maybe a text from Georgia or Tom.

I wipe a tear from my face. I hold my mom's journal in my hands and stare at the cover. I wanted to wait until I was back in the city to start reading it, but I don't think I can. I've waited nearly twenty years to hear her voice again.

I open to the first page. It's dated the Christmas we got her the journal. And she's scrawled across it: *Will you just look at this beautiful journal! From my Anna and my Sam. How lucky am I to be the mother to these two incredibly loving children?*

I flip to the next page and it's a to-do list for the week of January first. From the contents on the list, it seems like she was already back at work, because most of the items involve things she had to do for Georgia and Max, like *New pair of soccer cleats Max. Georgia dentist Jan 4 2:15. Bread mix.*

I flip to the next page and see a drawing of an angel with a charcoal halo and feathery wings. It ignites a memory inside of me. I'd completely forgotten how I'd loved drawing angels after hearing about them in church and from my mom. And next to the drawing, my mom wrote: *Anna draws an angel with me. Here we are, tucked into bed drawing on what feels like a perfect night. Anna is four years old and so artistic already!*

Downstairs, Max's phone rings, and I can hear him say, "She's packing now, Georgia. You're going to be able to come back tomorrow. Okay? Just hang tight."

Listen.

It's my mother's voice. I hear it like I always do, but now I feel more connected to it than ever because her journal, her words, her thoughts and feelings, are right in my hands.

Listen.

Max's phone call goes quiet. But I hear the phrasing of the words he said to Georgia echo through my mind.

Hang tight.

It's exactly what Max said tonight at the house when I was slipping, about to pass out, right when Georgia had just admitted to killing my mom. *Hang tight, Anna, I've got you.*

My mind sharpens, and something clicks into place.

Hang tight, Anna, is also what the commenter on TikTok wrote when he told me he was coming to find me at the Lower East Side bar.

My heartbeat quickens, and my hands immediately warm against the journal. Could it *be*? My thoughts start to race. It would make sense, wouldn't it? If Max had been following me online, just like I'd been following Georgia. But to take it to the next step—to follow me that closely to the point where he was always commenting right away—and to comment such weird things about coming to find me?

It's deadly quiet downstairs. My breathing quickens, and I stand gingerly on shaking legs. My muscles don't feel like the blood is moving into them the way it should be, and I swear my hands are tingly, too, and then all of a sudden, I drop the journal and a small folded piece of paper slips from the pages and falls onto the steps. It's a lined sheet of bright white loose-leaf paper, different from the pale-yellow pages in my mom's journal. My name is printed on the front.

I bend down to pick it up, unfolding the creases to see a letter signed by Millie.

Anna, I hope you see this note. I'm in my mom's room in the ER with my mom, my dad, and my uncle Max, and this letter is about something I need to tell you, and I tried to tell my mom this, but she says that it's only a dream, and that we can't trust our dreams, we need to trust our memories. Like her memory and my uncle Max's memory of the night your mom died.

But I can't seem to explain to anyone that my dreams never feel like dreams. They feel real, like your mom is with me, telling me what happened to her.

I always see your mom in my dreams, ever since we came to this new house in Waring Ridge last year. And in my dreams, your mom is always out on the roof with my mom. Usually they're arguing, sometimes saying nonsense dream stuff I can't always understand. Sometimes in the dream I feel like I'm the one out on the roof with your mom, but other times I can see my mom clearly, that she's the one out on the roof with Eliza. But no matter what, the dream always ends the same. My uncle Max comes through the bedroom window onto the roof and pushes your mom off of it.

I don't know what else to tell you. I never even knew who the woman in my dreams was until we got to Southport and my mom caught me drawing your mom. And then she told me the image I'd made was of Eliza, and that's when I knew she was the woman I'd been dreaming about. Sorry if this is weird for me to stash this letter in your mom's journal, but I don't think I'm going to get a chance to talk to you, and I'm afraid my uncle Max will be with us anyway.

I have to go now. I'm really sorry about your mom.

Millie.

My blood is like fire in my veins.

My mother. Max.

Could Millie be right? That it was never Georgia, that Max is lying about what he saw? That he was the one who actually did it?

It's not like I don't believe in the chance of Millie's dreams being real, or that by dreaming, she's somehow picking up on some truth the house carries within its bones. Who am I to say that's not possible? And who am I to say my mother's ghost doesn't haunt this house? Just because I haven't felt her here, doesn't mean it isn't true. Maybe Millie, a child, is picking up on something that the rest of us can't.

I descend the stairs toward Max, my heart nearly breaking through my chest wall. Each step feels like I'm drowning. When I get to the bottom, I walk slowly toward where he's sitting on the couch, his features drawn together, still staring at his phone.

When he finally looks up at me and asks, "What now?" there's not a single trace of the old Max in his voice.

"Did you kill my mother?" I ask.

Max's eyebrows shoot up, and then he laughs. "Come on, Anna. You heard my sister say she did it." An overhead light bathes the top of Max's head, and shadows etch his face.

"I heard your sister repeat what she thinks she remembers. You're not answering my question." The words sit so very still in the dead of night, but Max doesn't seem to be bothered by it.

"Why would Georgia lie?" he asks.

"I'm not saying she lied, I—"

"And by the way," he interrupts, the words haughty. "When my sister tries to turn herself in for the murder of your mother, which she'll no doubt try to do, because she's a good person like that, it'll be too late. No one will believe her. I certainly won't say I saw it happen."

I'm still standing, but the muscles in my legs are trembling so much I'm worried I'll need to sit down, and the last thing I want is to get closer to him. "So you'll just let everyone think my mother fell off the roof of her own accord, like you've always done? That's the lie you've been peddling for years, isn't it? You didn't think my mother, or any of us, deserved the truth about her death?"

"You don't deserve anything," he says.

I can feel my mouth drop. "You can't really believe that," I say.

He shrugs. "I loved your mom. But she was trying to get Georgia sent away to some kind of psychiatric hospital, never to return to me."

"You mean *rehab*? The place people go to get better?"

He lets out a sound that's halfway between a laugh and a sob. "It didn't work like that for my mom. Rehab never fixed her, because she didn't want help. And neither did Georgia. All those rehabs do is tell you that you need to go for longer, you need to try harder. And I wasn't going to survive without Georgia, that's the thing none of you realize."

"So you killed my mother?"

"I didn't say that. You heard my sister say she did it."

"Yeah," I say. "But I don't believe that anymore. I think there's quite a few secrets you've been keeping from me, Max." It feels good to say all of it—I feel stronger now, standing there, rooted to the floor. But then Max jumps up and snatches Millie's note from my hands.

"Hey!" I say, but he's already reading it, his lips curling into the oddest smirk.

"Is this why you think I killed your mom?" he asks, laughing as he looks down at the letter. "Is this your evidence? So *what*, Anna? Do you think anyone's going to listen to the rantings of a twelve-year-old having bad dreams?"

"Who *are* you, Max? Was it all an act? Your friendliness when I got here, the conversations we had? What we did by the cliffs?"

"Who am *I*?" Max asks, looking like he might attack me. "I'm the guy whose sister you fucked with."

"The same sister you're letting take the blame for my mother's death?"

Max shakes Millie's letter in his hands, practically crumpling it with the force of his fist. "You can't possibly be taking this letter seriously, Anna. Millie's bad dreams?" He squeezes the letter into a ball and throws it at me like we're kids again. "Go ahead and show this to the world. See if I care."

"I think I'll do one better," I say, reaching into my pocket for my phone. "I think I'll show them *this*."

I open up TikTok and click on one of my videos. I scroll until I find the comment I'm looking for: *Hang tight,* commented by the same user who's been writing creepy things on my page for months. I know I'm taking a chance here, but I also know I'll be able to tell right away by Max's face if I'm right.

"I know this is you, Max," I say, trying to sound surer than I really am. I turn my phone toward him. "I know you've been following me. I know it was all an act, you pretending like you didn't know me when I showed up here. You knew I was Eliza's daughter the second I arrived. Because you've been following me for a long time."

Max's brow furrows, and he smirks so darkly it makes me shiver. His eyes look bottomless as they narrow on me. "So the fuck what?"

I shift my weight, try to get my bearings. "We know my mother was pushed, Max. Georgia remembers you both up there fighting with her. You can't take that back now—it's out there in the world. And Georgia won't take it back, because unlike you and me, she's at least trying to live a moral life now, no matter who she once was. All I need to do is cast doubts on your story with Millie's dreams, and then, I'll cinch it by showing Georgia—or the whole world when I blast it onto my social media—that it was *you* . . . this very comment that you wrote yourself . . ." I tap the comment on my phone to make it bigger, my hands shaking as I turn the phone toward Max and show him the comment he wrote beneath a video I'd posted about that photo of the woman drinking sangria in front of the dogfight in *Culture* magazine.

From the same username, the comment reads: *People do bad things, Anna. But if no one sees a tree fall in the woods, did it really happen? You could say the same thing for me. No one saw me do what I did so many years ago. Sometimes I can even convince myself it never really happened.*

A vein on his temple pulses as he reads it; his hairline goes slick with sweat; and I feel a sick satisfaction to see him this way—to know that I've uncovered the truth of what he's done. "You pushed my mother off a roof and then you stalked me . . . ," I say, my heart pounding. He's still staring down at the comment he's written. "At the time," I manage to say, "I just thought that it was one of a hundred super weird comments I've gotten on my TikTok over the years. But combined with everything else, I'm pretty sure when I show Georgia this, she's going to know exactly what you did. I don't need to convince the police. I just need to convince *Georgia*. Because then you'll have to admit it, and the truth of my mom's death will finally be set free."

Max's face contorts into anger, his whole being tightening, and I know that I'm right. That Millie's right. That Georgia's wrong. She didn't kill my mom. Max did.

But he's not saying anything. So I say, "Pretty sure we could trace that username to you, am I right, Max?"

He's so very quiet. He's just staring at me. But then with one wild motion, he lifts his arm and smashes my phone out of my hand. It crashes onto the floor, and I can hear the screen crack.

"Max! What the—"

His hands are on my shoulders, his thumbs too close to my neck, his fingers starting to press so deeply into my skin that I cry out in pain. "Stop it," I manage to eke out. "I can't breathe!"

"You little bitch," he says, his eyes two dark holes boring into mine. It makes me flash back to when we were little and Georgia was using, the way her pupils would be tiny black pinpricks amid the wide expanse of her icy blue irises.

"Max . . . please . . ."

But he won't let me go. I knee him as hard as I can, and it seems to land exactly where I wanted it to because he lets go of me and stumbles back.

"Don't touch me again," I say, panting, the words barely coming out. "Are you trying to fucking kill me, too, Max?"

There's a body length between us filled with loathing. Max is writhing in pain and barely standing, but he still looks up and holds my gaze. "Don't you get it?" he asks. "I'm not going to be the person who killed my nanny. Do you understand that? My life isn't Netflix. I'm not going to be the talk of the town or the *joke*—the kid who was always messed up, even before his mom died, and then lost his shit and killed someone. My life has sucked enough, Anna, don't you see that?"

"So now what? You want me to just shut up and not tell anyone the truth?"

He shakes his head, suddenly looking so very sad, like a little boy again. "No, Anna. I know there's no way you could keep the truth about your mom to yourself." He straightens, and I can tell the pain of me kicking him is starting to fade. Watching him get his strength back scares me more than anything else. I know I should run, but he'll just catch me—and then what? Overpower me in a struggle?

I need to try to calm him down—if I can do that, maybe he'll remember that I'm someone he once cared about, someone who's part of his tragic past through no choice of her own. That's what I'm thinking even as he takes a step toward me, closing the space between us. I inch back toward the front door. "Please, Max. Just please, let me go home. I won't bother you and Georgia again. I promise."

But even as I say the words, I know no one in their right mind would believe me. Max shakes his head and says, "I know that's not true. I know *you*, Anna—I know exactly who you are. And now that you know who I am, I'm going to have to kill you. It's the only way, don't you see?"

My limbs weaken as Max taps a finger against his cheek like he's pretending to think hard about something.

"But what should my story be?" he asks, the words trickling from his mouth eerily. "Maybe you slipped in the shower and cracked your head open . . . or maybe you fell off the cliffs when we went out to the woods to be romantic again for one last time before you left . . . or maybe . . . oh, I think this might be it—you tiptoed to the edge of the roof to relive your mother's last moments and then you fell to your death." His pace is faster now, and he's almost breathless as he goes on. "That would be so poetic, especially when, after your death, everyone finds out the way you stalked Tom and Georgia and came to live in their house under false pretenses. And then *you'll* look like the total psycho out of a Netflix drama instead of me."

He smiles like a satisfied cat, and my stomach drops, a cutting feeling of fear sweeping through me.

"What do you say, Anna? Should we take a little trip to the roof?"

FIFTY-SIX

Georgia. Waring Ridge, New York.

Millie and I are waiting in the back seat of our car while Tom stands outside at the ticket vending machine, trying to pay for the hospital parking. For some reason it won't take his credit card, and I can see through the car window how frustrated he's getting.

Millie's watching him like an animal through glass at the zoo. "Dad looks like he's about to cry," she says, choking up. It might be her empathy that gets us all through this.

"I don't think so, Millie," I say carefully. "He doesn't cry very often, even when he's sad."

Her silver-blue nail polish catches the fluorescent lighting in the parking garage as she taps an index finger against the leather interior. "I just don't understand *why*," she says, still watching Tom at the machine. "Does Dad love Anna?"

I tighten, but she doesn't see it. I try to breathe, to settle into the knowledge that I've always been honest with her and I can't stop now. "I don't know, Millie," I say. "But even if I don't know why Dad did this, I do know that he never, ever would have wanted to hurt you, and I can't even imagine the pain he's in knowing the pain he caused you."

"And you, too," Millie says. "He wouldn't want to hurt you, either."

"I know, sweetie. That's part of what makes the whole thing so sad. Because he did hurt us."

A single tear falls down Millie's cheek. I want to wring Tom's neck for putting it there, but I also know that she and I will survive this. "I'll always be here for you and so will Dad," I tell her. "And as awful as this is, it's going to get better. Not right away. But at some point. I promise you, Millie."

She folds into my arms and lets me hold her while she cries.

Tom finally returns, opening the car door and swearing under his breath. He turns on the ignition and doesn't say anything to us as he pulls out of the parking garage and heads east toward Southport.

"Guys?" Millie asks, nervous. She buries her head into my sweater, her voice muffled. "I wrote Anna a note," she says. Tom hits the brakes too hard at a red light, and we lurch forward. Millie's voice is shaking. "About what Max did in my dreams, what I told you he did, Mom. I'm sorry. I know neither of you probably wanted me to do that, but I wanted her to know."

Tom turns around to look at us. "What did Max do in your dreams, Millie?"

FIFTY-SEVEN

Anna. Waring Ridge, New York.

Max drags me up the stairs as I scream and kick and try to land punches, but none of it seems to matter, because he's so much stronger than I am. He's got me beneath the arms, yanking me step by step until we're on the landing at the top of the stairs. I switch tactics and try to let my body go limp like a rag doll so I'll be harder to drag, but it doesn't work—Max is still covering ground, lugging my body into Georgia's room, where he throws me onto the ground and kicks me as hard as he can in my stomach. It makes my vision go black. I can't breathe. I'm alert enough to know he's knocked the wind out of me, but I still can't move. I try to get to my hands and knees but it's impossible—I can't get a breath in. My lungs feel like they're inside of a vise.

I hear the window open with a *creak*, and then Max is back, lifting me beneath the arms, dragging me onto the bench beneath the window, the roof in view now, glistening with rain. "Stop it, Max!" I try to scream, my breathing still hitching in my chest, my voice barely audible. Something jagged scratches inside of me, like a rib out of place knifing one of my lungs. I try to save my breath—if I can scream loudly enough on the roof, there's a chance someone could hear us.

I let my body go limp again as Max drags me through the window. My skin rips against the metal ledge, and I can feel every one of my vertebrae scrape against it. The second Max gets me onto the roof I suck in a huge breath, and then tighten every abdominal muscle I have and force out the loudest scream I can muster. The sound rips from my chest and the momentum gets going until I'm screaming like a banshee. Max drops me, and my head hits the roof.

"Shut up, Anna," he says, covering my mouth with his hand. I bite into his fingers so hard I can feel the bone. Something warm fills my mouth like water, and I know it's his blood and not mine. I clench his hand in my mouth until I can't any longer and then I turn to my side and vomit.

"Fucking shit!" Max screams as he holds his hand against his stomach. The blood darkens his gray T-shirt.

"You can't kill me," I rasp. "Everyone will know it's you."

"They *won't*," he says, panting. "They'll think it was you—when they find out what you did, that you're obviously extremely damaged, they'll think you fell off the roof or jumped off on purpose."

"Maybe I *am* damaged," I say. "Maybe your family and this house made me that way." I push myself up on my arms so that I'm almost sitting. "Or maybe there's no such thing as damaged. Maybe there's just *human*. And either way, I don't deserve your shit."

A light goes on in Ethan's house. I can see it from here. A single light in a dark, dark house. *Please, Ethan. Come find me.*

"Don't you understand, Max?" I ask, my words breathy, each one painful. I'm stalling. I don't even know how to finish my sentence. But Max is a storyteller at heart—from the films he works on to the stories he tells himself to sleep at night, and maybe I can stall him now if he doesn't think he knows the ending quite yet.

He cocks his head to the side. "And what don't you think I understand, Anna?" he asks.

I consider him carefully. He reminds me of one of the subjects I like to shoot: *vulnerable, in pain, and beautiful, even with his tragic flaws.* I almost wish I had my camera. But instead, all I have are my words, the ones I've always doubted ever since I was a little girl when I was motherless and adrift. "We were children here," I finally say, and I swear to God I see a figure far away, directly behind Max and out of his sight line—a man, running across his yard, coming to help me. *Ethan.* Please, God, let it be Ethan. "You and me," I say, my gaze holding Max's. "We were kids together. Our mothers raised us on this property. I know they died, I know they left us, and we were lost then, and we're lost now. But doesn't it count for anything? What we went through together?"

Max sniffs. He looks down at his bloody hand and then up at me again. "You're right, Anna, that I knew it was you when you showed up here." He shakes his head, looking forlorn, as though he's deeply disappointed in me and what I've done, and says, "At first, I was fucking thrilled about it. Why wouldn't I be? I'd been keeping tabs on you and Sam for years. Curious about you both, about who you'd become after I killed your mom." The way he utters the words, so matter-of-factly, takes the breath out of me. And hearing Sam's name from his mouth makes me want to be sick. "You showed up on the doorstep like a present." He smiles like a wolf, and I try not to let on how scared I am, but my limbs are shaking, and I know he sees it. "And it was fun pretending to be Georgia's harmless little brother who had no idea who the houseguest was." He lights up suddenly, snapping his fingers. "Hey, maybe I should be an actor instead of trying to make it in TV production," he says, and then he lets out a little laugh. Watching him enjoy this is so unnerving I almost start screaming. "You thought you were pulling one over on me," he goes on, "but you were very wrong. So don't insult me by acting like we're on the same team. You've been stalking my sister and sleeping with her husband for months, and now you want to tell everyone that I killed your mother. And that's not going to happen."

I can barely move I'm so scared. But I can see Ethan behind Max now—I'm sure it's him, and he's sprinting. I just need to keep him talking—he can't kill me if Ethan is here.

"How could you let Georgia think she killed my mom?" I ask. "Do you really want her bearing horrible guilt for something she didn't do?"

"Of course I don't," Max says, emotion twisting his face. He loves Georgia, that part is obvious. "But Georgia was high out of her mind," he says. "At least she has an excuse. Can you imagine the world knowing that a completely sober and in-his-right-mind twelve-year-old pushed his nanny off a roof?"

Tears come to my eyes to hear him say it. "But you weren't in your right mind, not really," I say, struggling to get the words over the knot lodged in my throat. "You were destroyed with grief over your own mom, and terrified that my mom was going to send your sister away."

Max shakes his head. "No one will see it like that. You know they won't."

"Then I won't tell anyone—I promise, I won't."

It's not true, and Max knows it.

"You're lying," he says softly.

"Hello?" calls a booming voice.

Max whirls around to scan the scene—but Ethan is out of sight now. He must be on the patio right below the roof.

"Are you guys okay up there?" he asks, voice rising.

I open my mouth to cry out for help, but Max jumps toward me and clamps his bloody hand over my mouth. *"Shut up, Anna,"* he says. "I mean it this time."

"Hello?" Ethan calls.

Max pulls me up by the arms and guides me by an elbow across the roof toward Georgia's bedroom window. I pretend to follow, but then I squirm free and scream, "Ethan! Help me! I'm up here!"

Max rips an arm over my chest and pulls me across the roof, me kicking as hard as I can, trying to strike and landing nothing. Too quickly we're next to the open window, and Max gives me one huge push and shoves my whole body through the window so hard that I clear the bench and land on the bedroom carpet. "You pathological fucking liar," Max says as he climbs through the window and steps onto Georgia's floor. "I knew I couldn't trust you! All your bullshit about growing up together, none of it means anything to you." He shuts and locks the window behind him. "You're a cold, scheming bitch who infiltrated my family, and now I'm going to fucking kill you," he says. He limps toward me and descends onto my body like a heavy blanket, suffocating me with his form and fury.

His hands are on my neck—pressing tighter—and I can hear Ethan trying the back door, but everything's locked per Georgia's instructions, and there's no way he's going to be able to get inside. And no one has Georgia's keys. Not even Max. She told me that first day on our phone call, and at the time I thought she was paranoid, but maybe she was trying to make me feel safe.

Breath drains from my lungs. I can't believe Max is going to kill me here, so close to the spot where he killed my mother.

I can feel myself going somewhere else, slipping and sliding, when I hear footsteps pound the floor downstairs. Did Ethan get inside?

Voices call my name—I can hear them. Tom? Georgia?

"Anna!"

Max's hands throttle my windpipe and I can't cry out—I can't tell them where we are.

Their voices become smaller, like they're no longer in the foyer. They must be checking the back of the house. They have it all wrong.

I'm fading away, I can feel myself slipping into something warm and thick, somewhere dreamlike. From inside this place I hear small footsteps and the sharp *crack* of what sounds like glass breaking.

I turn my head the tiniest bit, using every ounce of strength I have to open my eyes, feeling the lids scrape my eyes like sandpaper.

Everything hurts.

I blink and see Millie standing there with the fractured face of her porcelain doll, one of its eyes still intact, staring at me. In her small hands, Millie holds the jagged porcelain piece containing the rest of the doll's face. And then she crosses the floor, and with one swoop she plunges the porcelain piece of the doll's face into Max's body.

Max's eyes widen above me. He takes his hands off my neck, and I gasp for breath. With one shaking arm Max rips the jagged porcelain from where it's punctured his torso, and warm blood gushes over me as he falls to the ground.

I turn to face Millie. "Millie," I say, panting, barely able to get the words out of my mouth.

Footsteps pound the stairs. Tom enters the room with Georgia right behind him, both of them crying out for Millie. And then Georgia sees Max and starts screaming. She bends to the floor to cover Max's wound, and Tom reaches into his pocket and dials 911.

I turn to my side, my gaze finding Millie's again. "You saved me," I whisper to her, unsure if she can hear me with all the commotion.

She looks down at the mangled porcelain face of her doll. "Maybe it wasn't all me," she says, starting to cry. "I think your mom has been talking to me, communicating with me all this time. I've felt her here—I've seen her in my dreams, and I think she's in this house now, watching over us, watching over *you*."

My heart pounds as I stare at Millie, waiting for her to say more.

Millie cradles the broken doll in her arms like a baby. Her eyes are bleary with tears, but there's a ghost of a smile on her lips. She looks once again at the doll's shattered face, and then back at me.

"I think your mom wanted you to finally know the truth, Anna," she says, her blue eyes coming back into focus, meeting mine.

"Thank you," I whisper to her as Tom crouches on the rug beside me. He doesn't touch me. He barely looks at me. He only says, "An ambulance is on its way," and then goes to his daughter. My body feels like its glued to the floor—my limbs feel too heavy, like they can't possibly be mine. I turn away from Tom and Millie and see Georgia crying softly beside Max, her hands pressed against his stomach. His eyes are closed, but I can see his rib cage moving up and down as he breathes.

I close my eyes and think about my mother, her soft voice, the feel of her arms around me. I try to summon her—like Millie's been able to. I think of my father and of Sam, and of how much she loved us. There's nothing for a few moments, but right when I think there's no chance of it happening, I swear I smell my mother's vanilla scent. It's just for a breath—a moment really, like a secret whispered in my ear—and then it's gone.

EPILOGUE. ONE YEAR LATER.

Anna. New York City, New York.

I'm photographing an actor for the interior of *Vogue*. He's tall and languid, dripping with sensuality and power, and he makes me think of Tom Carter.

I haven't thought about Tom in a day or two. Sometimes I'll even go a few days without thinking about Tom, Georgia, or Millie, but then one of them pops into my head, uninvited though not entirely unwelcome. Of all of them, I'm sure it's Tom who still hasn't forgiven me, and I don't blame him. He lost his job at *Culture* after everything leaked. It didn't leak through me, but I guess these things have a way of getting out, and maybe we weren't as careful as we thought we were. He's recently started working again at a well-respected online magazine, and when I've checked in to see his work there, it's still impressive, the same boundary-pushing photography and content he was known for at *Culture*. I hope he's happy, and though I'm sorry that he (and especially Millie) got caught in my crossfire and my mistakes, I do know that he bears responsibility for what he chose to do with me.

Georgia and I are in touch. Sometimes phone calls, mostly texts. And we've met in person a handful of times since what happened last year in Waring Ridge, both of us desperate to talk things over, to try to find some closure, to understand what happened when we were children in that house, and what happened again last summer. And to understand Max and his role in it, which I can tell for Georgia is the hardest part.

For so many years I blamed Georgia and decided that she and her family were the enemy, and the truth, that Max killed my mother, is even more painful than I could have imagined. At first, I was furious that Max never told the police what he did, that he got away with it. But he's certainly paying for it now. He lived with the secret his entire life, and it nearly destroyed him. Same for Georgia, seeing what she saw—even under the influence and having blocked it from her memory—nearly destroyed her, too.

Sometimes I'm glad I didn't learn the truth of how my mom fell until now, because to have known the truth as a child might have haunted me even more. Maybe, like Sam, I wouldn't have survived.

Max isn't getting away with anything anymore. I pressed attempted murder charges against him for what he did to me in Waring Ridge, and he's in custody with a trial set to begin later this year. I don't really know how I'm going to get through the trial, and I'll be forced to spend a whole lot of time inside a courtroom with Tom, Georgia, Max, and Millie as we all recount what happened. Maybe our families were always meant to be intertwined, dark as our fates together have been.

I lift my camera and focus in on the actor's face. His hazel eyes hold the camera, and I wonder what he sees and what he's thinking. All of us with our different lenses, even Georgia and me, and the way we both saw Tom: a classic case of the same man viewed through different lenses. Everything is and will always be a unique experience for each viewer, and maybe that's why I'm so determined to show the world the view through my lens. Or maybe I'm just waxing poetic.

I wait, lost in my thoughts, while the actor rearranges himself in a chair. He's sitting at a long wooden table set with paintbrushes, a pitcher of water, fruit, and drawing paper. The set is meant to evoke the vibe of the artists' colony where the actor spent three years painting after getting his acting MFA, trying to forget the world; then he drove to LA one morning and hit it big.

Anything can happen, I guess.

The early-August sun blazes into the room where we're shooting. This time last year, I was in Waring Ridge. It feels hard to believe, like a dream, even though I know it wasn't, even though I know that the consequences of what I did to Tom, Georgia, and Millie are very real.

The house changed me as a child, and it changed me again last summer. It gave me closure on my mother's death, not only to know how she truly died, but to spend time in the place where she'd raised Sam and me. In some ways, I was able to say goodbye to both my mother and my brother there. And though mourning Sam is still beyond painful, there's more peace after being in Waring Ridge, even after what happened. The house brought back welcome memories of all of us that I'd forgotten, and then there are the physical memories, the photographs I'd never have if I hadn't gone back to the house, the ones I found in the bottom drawer at the cottage, hundreds of scenes of my mom, my dad, Sam, and me, all taken with Georgia's camera. I'd started taking photographs when I was nine to remember my life with my dad and my brother. I'd had no idea hundreds of photos existed that included my mother, and I have Georgia to thank for that. A month after what happened in Waring Ridge, Georgia sent the box down to my apartment. No note, but her name and return address on the top left of the box.

And then, of course, there's my mom's journal. When I read it in its entirety, I didn't find standard journal entries. Sure, there were a few notes, doctor's appointments for herself or for Sam and me. And then there were the notes that Georgia saw, notes with numbers of addiction doctors and rehab places, and the most condemning note of all, the one where my mom jotted down: *Confiscate the pills, bring them to the rehab so we'll know what Georgia's on and we can go from there.*

That, of course, was what Georgia didn't want the police or anyone else to see.

On the day she fell, my mom had made a plan to confiscate the pills and then meet with Georgia's dad at eight when he got home from work. Apparently, that's what the cryptic note the police found in her pocket meant. Reading my mom's journal made it glaringly clear that Georgia's dad and my mom had become confidants, both on a singular mission together to help Georgia get clean. Especially after they lost the woman they loved so deeply to her addiction—Georgia's mother—Georgia's dad and my mom seemed determined not to let it happen again. And in that regard, they succeeded.

But the journal was much more than these sparse notes about Georgia and Max sprinkled throughout. It was filled with hundreds of letters dated and addressed to Sam and me. Sometimes they were short notes, like: *My sweet Anna and Sam, I see you playing outside on the lawn with Dad! Do you have any idea how much I love you?* And sometimes they were long missives about all the ways she loved us, and the devoted and deep way she loved our dad, too. My dad wept when I showed him the things my mom wrote about him.

Usually, the letters were addressed to both Sam and me, but sometimes my mom broke off and wrote a letter to just one of us, especially if she had a story about something we'd done that was funny or poignant. She once wrote about how I needed less physical touch than Sam—no surprise there—and that Sam loved to hug me for a full minute at a time, which I tolerated because I loved him, but after too long I'd start to squirm, and that's when he'd bury his face in my neck and give me kisses and tell me he loved me and that he wanted to hug me forever. And apparently once, when I was three, I'd said to him, "But I have things to do," which my mom found hilarious. The way she wrote about us was so moving, with love flooding every page. And she wrote about Georgia and Max, not just how much she loved them, too, but how much they loved Sam and me. Too much of what I remember were the years when I was five and six and Georgia was starting to use. But my mom often referenced the years before, when Georgia delighted in taking care of Sam and me as babies and toddlers. She wrote that Sam demanded my mother's arms, but I often loved being held and rocked to sleep by Georgia in an oversized rocker in the main house. And Max played with us, just as I remembered, and reading those portions of the journals was the hardest, trying to reconcile the Max I'd remembered from my childhood with what he eventually did to my mother and then to me. On the nights when I can't get past it, when I can't really fathom the horror of what happened, I try to remember how young he was when he did what he did, and how traumatized he'd been by his own mother's death, finding her alone and dead on a bathroom floor, and by the thought of losing his sister. He was a child who made a grave mistake. It still doesn't absolve him for what he did to me in Waring Ridge. And it still nearly kills me to think of how my mother must have felt seeing him charging toward her, a child she'd loved and raised, a child who lost control and pushed her to her death.

There hasn't been a day since Georgia gave me the journal that I haven't read from it, and I don't think there ever will be. Sometimes, when I work or go out with Bee, I can almost forget Georgia and her family. These days I mostly spend my time freelancing for different magazines and hanging out in Brooklyn and Manhattan with my friends, maybe trying to prove to myself that I'm a normal twenty-something with a New York City life, rather than a broken child of the house in Waring Ridge. Some days, it works. Missing Sam and my mom will always feel visceral. But my dad and I talk more than ever—the truth took him a long time to process, too—and when I need to feel grounded, I pick up the phone and call him, or head out on the weekend for a visit.

Some days I even feel hopeful. Those are the days when I can feel my brother and my mother the most, the days when I know that no matter who I become, I will always be a sister and a daughter first, and nothing and no one can ever take that away from me.

Georgia. Waring Ridge, New York.

I'm sitting at the pool outside our house, watching Millie swim in the still blue water. She submerges herself, then pops up with her face to the sun and runs her hands over her soaked hair. From this angle, out at the pool, I can see the ledge of the roof from where Max pushed Eliza. For so many reasons, I'll never leave this house, but one of those reasons is that every day it forces me to face what my family did to Eliza. And every day for the past year, I have. If my house is haunted, it's haunted with the good and the bad, the love and the pain, and the truth of what happened here: the way we all loved each other and the darkness of my drug use and what Max eventually did to Eliza. And living here, every day, is my only path to coming to terms with it.

Therapy helps. I see a therapist weekly who specializes in PTSD to process what I saw Max do to Eliza all those years ago. Sometimes I wonder what Max's life and my life would have been like if these newer trauma therapies were available to us when we were just scared kids who had lost their mom—and, in Max's case, had found her dead body in a bathroom. I wonder at the things that could have been different.

The therapist is the one who explained why the combination of the drugs and the trauma made it pretty easy for my brain to block out what I'd seen Max do. Max was never able to block it out and forget, and he's lived with it ever since. I imagine I'd feel sorrier for him if not for what he tried to do to Anna. He made a horrible, fatal mistake as a child. But rather than come clean and admit what he'd done, he tried to kill Anna, and I still can't comprehend it. I don't think I'll ever be able to. And it's not up to me to decide his fate. All I can do is testify, visit him in prison, and try to work toward some type of forgiveness. I love him, and he's my brother, and I'm the only person he has left who's never going to abandon him. It's as simple and as complicated as that.

Millie is in therapy twice a week. At first we started her with a child psychologist to process what she did to Max. And she was able to come to terms with what she did, partly because Max recovered, but mostly because Millie understands that she most likely saved Anna's life.

That night one year ago when I was hospitalized after I slipped and fell, Millie told me what her dreams had been about: that in them she'd seen scenes of Max killing Eliza on the roof. I told Millie they were just dreams, but when she told Tom in the car as we were leaving the hospital, Tom put enough stock in what she was saying to go back to our house to check on Anna instead of heading to Southport. Maybe because he always believed the house was haunted, he didn't seem to think it was much of a stretch to believe in the possibility that Millie's dreams were haunted by the ghost of Eliza. I remember his words that night in the car as he switched directions and took off toward our house. *Your brother is off, Georgia. Maybe we shouldn't have left him alone with Anna.* And when I scoffed at Tom, as though my precious brother couldn't possibly be capable of doing anything wrong, he snarled, *I'm not the only one who senses it, Georgia. Even your beloved Ethan and Maya think something's wrong with Max.* Months later, when I was ready to talk about it, I confronted Ethan. He was sheepish, but he admitted to feeling wary of my brother as the weeks of Max living in the cottage wore on. Ethan said that there was something about him—a quicksilver flash of darkness and anger that Max quickly and expertly hid—that reminded him of his own violent father. And then Ethan admitted to constantly checking on Anna to make sure she was okay all alone in our house, which ended up freaking her out. I suppose all of us can sometimes be spot on in our instincts about people, and then other times be devastatingly wrong.

That night everything went down, Tom, Millie, and I let ourselves in the front door and Tom and I headed to the back of the house, where we heard pounding on the back door. We opened it to find Ethan and then we realized Millie wasn't with us. She'd gone directly up to my bedroom, which is where she saw the scene unfolding with Max. And judging by the wounds on Anna's neck and based on her workup at the hospital, it might have only taken another minute for Max to have killed her if Millie hadn't intervened.

Millie doesn't talk much with Tom and me about that night, but she promises me she talks about it with her psychologist, and I have to believe her. She tells us it feels hazy when she thinks back on that time: the nightmares, and the way she was sure Eliza was haunting the house and entering her dreams. She says she never wanted to admit it, but that she was sure the woman in her dreams was somehow using the doll to communicate with her; and that the first night in Southport without the doll, when she didn't have a nightmare, she felt sure of it. I asked her why she wanted Tom to go back and get the doll—I couldn't understand why she'd want the doll if she thought it was causing her nightmares. And Millie said, *Because as soon as I realized the woman in my nightmares was Eliza, I understood that she was trying to tell me something, that she maybe even needed me for some important reason. I wasn't sure what that was until I saw Uncle Max trying to kill her daughter. And then I knew what she was trying to tell me, and I knew what I needed to do.*

It chilled me for weeks. And not only because I still can't believe what my brother was trying to do to Anna, but also because the supernatural feels so true when described in Millie's voice. And although I never feel anything more than Eliza's memory in my house, sometimes I wonder if she isn't still here, watching over all of us, mourning her son's untimely death and her own, but maybe reunited with him somehow. After what happened last year, I believe in the possibility of anything. When we got home to our house in Waring Ridge, I found plenty of photographs of Eliza in Max's cottage and a few scattered in one of my drawers. Maybe Millie saw them once or twice, and the image of Eliza stuck itself somewhere inside her subconscious, and maybe that's why she was able to draw Eliza's image. Or maybe the supernatural is all around us and Millie was just able to tap into it—maybe none of us will really know how it all works until we're gone, too. Somehow, the possibility of ghosts and otherworldly visitors makes me love the house more than ever before. To think of my mom and Eliza there, too, fills me with a kind of comfort I can't entirely explain.

Tom and I see a couples therapist every other week. And now I know that a house wasn't responsible for the demise of my marriage. I did that, and mostly, Tom did it for the both of us. Tom and I are separated, but seeing the therapist helps us coparent Millie. Tom doesn't see Anna anymore, of course. He won't even say her name. Maybe the difference between Tom and me, and the reason that I was able to forgive Anna, is that I'd spent years loving her as a child. That makes it much easier to forgive someone, to understand, to make allowances. And after what Max and I did to her mother, how could I not? I can only hope that somewhere, somehow, Eliza has forgiven me. For me, keeping tabs on Anna and making sure she's okay is like a silent prayer offered up to Eliza. I guess I plan to always do it.

Tom only knew Anna as an adult, as a woman with ulterior motives who destroyed a life he was desperately trying to hold on to. Whenever I try to bring her up in therapy Tom goes red faced and silent. It was one of the many reasons I knew he and I wouldn't make it through. Tom was falling out of love with me before Anna—we've gotten that far in therapy. And maybe without Anna, we somehow would have been able to get what we had back. But that tiny crack, his dissatisfaction with me and our life in Waring Ridge, made it too easy for Anna to slip inside and shatter the rest.

Something changed inside of me when my brain set free the memory of Max pushing Eliza off the roof. Yes, I was high, and I was sixteen. But I still saw my brother kill someone I loved. It's a darkness I'll always have to live with, a feeling so big that sometimes it nearly pulls me to the bottom. But letting go of the effort it took to repress the memory and facing the part I'd played in what happened to Eliza that night set free a part of me I hadn't been able to access since I was sixteen. Suddenly, I could write again. Pages and pages, every day. Besides Millie, it was the only thing that saved me. I wrote about what happened on the roof, admitting everything that led up to it, and what I saw. I shared my writing with anyone who wanted to read it, and now our town is aware of exactly what I did that night I was high, the fight I'd caused, and then what Max eventually did to Eliza, killing her. No one looks at me the same anymore. I don't care, and if I get even a little close to caring about what everyone thinks, I think about my mom, and the way she held her head high and marched us through town, even with her demons. My mother never made me feel like I had to be perfect, and thank God for that, because I'm not. I wrote and published stories about what happened during my childhood and the way my mother's addiction and my own spiraled. Over the winter I wrote the first draft of a manuscript and found an agent, who sold the novel, which comes out next spring. I'm in the process of editing it now.

Millie hops out of the pool and comes to sit next to me on a lounge chair. She commutes to the city on the weekends to stay with Tom, and she's gotten used to school out here; she's starting to enjoy it, even, making new friends on her school tennis team and going to parties. We plan to continue the therapy for years to come. My nightmares have stopped, and so have Millie's. I'm even able to remember some of the better times with my mom and Eliza more clearly. Millie still writes, but she's stopped writing poetry about Eliza ever since the night she saved Anna's life. Whether that's because some pearl of truth was set free, or because we threw the doll over the cliffs the next day, I'll never know.

"I love you, Millie," I say.

Her light eyebrows go up, and a small smile lands on her beautiful face. She takes my hand and holds it in hers, and after a lifetime spent needing so many different things, it's a wonder to think that *this*, my daughter's hand in mine and this kind of love, is the one thing I was truly after.

ACKNOWLEDGMENTS

I am very grateful to all the readers who spent their time in these pages. Having readers of my books continues to feel like a pinch-me moment. Thank you very much.

Thank you to Carmen Johnson and Faith Ross Black, whose editing and keen attention to details and themes made this book much stronger than it ever could have been without them. I'm very grateful for your hard work, and for your dedication to getting this story where it needed to go. Thank you to everyone at Amazon Publishing who treats my books with such care, skill, enthusiasm, and professionalism.

My agent, Dan Mandel, has been guiding my career for the past fifteen years. He is the kindest, wisest, and most talented agent I could ever ask for. Thank you, Dan, for your friendship and unparalleled career guidance.

Thank you to Mary Pender at UTA who has skillfully represented my books. Thank you to Susie Fox at Management 360 for believing in me as a writer and storyteller and making me feel like the future is bright and limitless.

Thank you to Zibby Owens, a force of literary nature, who has championed my books since the moment we met. I'm honored to call you my friend.

Thank you to a group of early readers who gave me thoughtful and helpful feedback: Artika Loganathan, Chrissie Irwin, Liv Peters, Nina Levine, Lauren Locke, Janelle Lika, Olivia Reighley, Jodi Kimmel, Ally

Reuben, Sherri Owles, Annie Manning, Janine O'Dowd, Antonia and Olivia Davis, Wendy Levey, Stacey Armand, and Rachel Patino. Thank you to Jeremy Randol for reading a final draft that I thought was as good as I could make it, and then giving me such insightful and incisive feedback that I happily went back to the drawing board. Thank you especially to Audrey Birnbaum; Erika Grevelding; my aunt, Joan Miller; my parents, Jack and Mary Sise; my godfather, Bill Sise; my sister-in-law, Ali Sise; my brother-in-law, Roby Bhattacharyya; and the most supportive sister and best friend in the world, Meghan Sise, who all read every word I write before it gets published and help me make it better. You have been my team for a long time now, and I am very grateful to you!

Thank you to the booksellers, librarians, reviewers, and the book bloggers and communities on social media who spread the word about my books and many others. Thank you to the teachers who teach my children so well, and thank you to the coaches who encourage them (and me), especially Olga, Bob, Seth, Dinah, Brad, and Scott. Thank you to the many incredible teachers from whom I've been lucky enough to learn, especially in high school and college during those formative years when I was trying to gain the skills to work creatively. Thank you to my family, who raised me to believe in hard work, kindness, and respect. Thank you to my very supportive mother-in-law and father-in-law, Carole and Ray Sweeney. Thank you to my brother, Jack, and to Lorena, Posie, Angela, Linda, and Bob. Thank you to Jamie, Caroline, Brinn, Claire, Tricia, Megan, Jessica, Kim, Jesse, Fran, and Isabel, and all my friends and family who support me. You know who you are!

Thank you especially to my husband, Brian, my best friend and true love after all these years together.

An endless thank-you belongs to the loves of my life: Luke, William, Isabel, and Eloise Sweeney. I'll love you to the stars and back forever.

ABOUT THE AUTHOR

Photo © 2022 Jennifer Mullowney

Katie Sise is a bestselling author of seven novels, including *The Break*, *Open House*, and *We Were Mothers*. Katie is a former TV host and jewelry designer, and lives outside New York City with her husband, four children, and a golden retriever who has finally calmed down. For more information, visit katiesise.com.